MW01148237

WE BLEED FOR EACH OTHER

Benjamin D. Copple

WESTBOW
PRESS®
A DIVISION OF THOMAS NELSON
& ZONDERVAN

WestBow Press books may be ordered through booksellers or by contacting:

WestBow Press
A Division of Thomas Nelson & Zondervan
1663 Liberty Drive
Bloomington, IN 47403
www.westbowpress.com
1 (866) 928-1240

ISBN: 978-1-9736-6151-1 (sc)
ISBN: 978-1-9736-6152-8 (hc)
ISBN: 978-1-9736-6150-4 (e)

Library of Congress Control Number: 2019907017

Print information available on the last page.

WestBow Press rev. date: 06/27/2019

*To my generation, the millennial
generation—let's get out and change the world.*

Contents

Introduction

The country known today as the Central African Republic (C.A.R.) was created in 1960 when the French government granted independence to one of its former colonies called Ubangi-Shari. This came about in large part due to the efforts of Barthélémy Boganda, the first native Central African to serve on the French National Assembly, who negotiated for the colony's independence. Boganda should have been the new country's first democratically elected president, but his plane mysteriously exploded just before the first elections. Several years of disastrous democratic rule ended when Col. Jean-Bedel Bokassa took control of the government. Initially ruling with some popular support, Bokassa grew more and more corrupt, eventually crowning himself Emperor in a ceremony that reportedly cost $22,000,000, all while his citizens starved. Bokassa was overthrown in 1979 but was succeeded by a line of dictators who abused and misused the land's resources and inhabitants. Civilian rule was established in 1993 but ended only a decade later in 2003 when General François Bozizé assumed command in a violent coup. Bozizé was aided by several Muslim tribes long fed up with being under-represented in the predominantly Christian nation. But, Bozizé never fulfilled the promises he made to the Muslim citizens to gain their help and instead ruled as a dictator for another decade.

Tired of the General's lies, the tribes that Bozizé spurned banded together into a group that became known as the Seleka. In 2013, they burned their way to the capital where they violently seized control, forcing Bozizé to flee the country. Unable to rule a nation effectively, the Seleka were pressured into disbanding by the United Nations, which sent a peace force to initiate a smooth transition to a democratic government. Elections took place, and today, an elected president and national assembly run the country. But instead of cooperating with the government they made possible, the ex-Seleka fighters returned to their homes, fortified them, and refused to submit to outside authority, eventually dominating most of the northern and central regions of the country. In response, a predominantly Christian coalition of rebels called the Anti-Balaka formed to oppose the predominantly Muslim Seleka. Today, the Anti-Balaka dominates the western region while the south-eastern corner remains uncontrolled. The Central African government does not yet have the infrastructure or strength to control the competing factions. Fighting between the Seleka and the Anti-Balaka is an almost daily occurrence. The native Central Africans have a name for the war and the violence that has taken place over the past five years: The Crisis.

As the physical center of the African continent, the C.A.R. is also at the center of many of the colossal problems that are often associated with Sub-Saharan Africa. It is a landlocked nation bordered by six countries through which many of the continent's worst problems bleed. On top of the years of human rights violations by successive governments and religious violence among its citizens, AIDS and human trafficking have also ravaged the Central African people. Despite efforts by the government, illegal exploitation such as poaching and diamond smuggling continue. The country hosts hundreds of thousands of internally displaced persons, and half a million refugees have already left its borders to escape the fighting and find safety elsewhere.

But despite the issues it faces, Central Africa is still a place of great natural beauty where almost six hundred species of butterfly flourish amongst gorgeous flowers, majestic elephants populate rolling hills of verdant rainforest, and the world's highest concentration of lowland gorillas live quietly in peaceful thickets. It is a land thick with natural resources such as timber (the country's number one export) and precious metals like gold and uranium. It may even have untapped oil deposits. Its greatest resource, however, is its people. With a population of over five million, an estimated 4.5 million live without electricity, thousands die of preventable diseases, and thousands more are trapped in forced labor. The Crisis continues to rage, yet still they live on, working, loving, and caring for each other, striving and hoping for the day when things will improve. And things are improving, slowly perhaps, maybe imperceptibly to the outside observer, but improving nonetheless, because of the perseverance and beauty of the Central African people.

The story you are about to read is fictional. The characters you will meet have never existed and are not meant to resemble any real people. But it is a story that could happen, perhaps even *should* happen. It is a story of love, passion, and selflessness. It is a story of adventure, valor, and tenacity. It's a story about people willing to bleed for each other and to sacrifice their lives to save the lives of others. It is a story of radical unity and radical peace. I hope it is a story that will radically turn your world upside down.

Silence

*T*he old lion crouches and waits. A boy, ebony skin darker than the dawning jungle around him, sits by the river and plays.

The old lion, stomach twisted in hunger, is motionless, his tired muscles taut like old ropes. The boy is relaxed, blissfully unaware of the silent jungle in which he sits.

The lion licks his lips. This will be his first meal in weeks. His once mighty flanks quiver from the stress they can no longer handle. Once lined with sinuous muscles, they now barely contain the ribs beneath them. His tawny hide, once beautiful and soft, is matted and frayed, like a rug worn thin by the trod of too many feet. His mane is full of creepers and twigs, a shadow of the glorious mantle that once crowned him as king. Once, he stood tall and strong upon the kopjes of the savannah, a noble beast of unsurpassed grandeur, a monarch of unchallenged glory. Now, in the depths of the jungle, far from the land of his birth, he slithers in the mud like a rat, a disgraced ruler with no more than a shred of his former dignity.

The boy sits in the dirt and plays with a stone, a young lifeform still in the morning of his power.

The old lion gathers what remains of his power beneath him and prepares to strike.

Suddenly, a cracking, thundering roar shatters the silence. The lion jerks in response—not much, but just enough to shift a leaf and snap a twig, a quiet sound drowned out by the distant fire. But the boy looks up. He is unaffected by the noise, yet the snapping of a twig draws his attention. Now he is looking at the lion, his deep brown eyes staring right back into the glowing yellow orbs of the beast.

The thundering stops, its echo bouncing between the hills. The lion does not know what machine-gun fire is, but he does recognize the sound and knows that it is always accompanied by the salty smell of hot blood. But now, he is only aware of the ruination of his hunt. The boy is still within his grasp, but something besides hunger grips the beast now. Perhaps it is the unknown nature of the rifle fire. Perhaps it is the boy's relentless stare. The beast's muscles begin to relax, and he lowers his massive haunches to the ground, settling into a leisurely sprawl.

To the lion, the sound of rifle fire means death, but it is distant and does not repeat. Now, as the silence of the jungle begins to settle once again, the boy drops his stone and scampers away.

The old lion watches him go. When he is gone, the king hoists his great body to his feet and approaches the spot where the boy stood. The boy's scent is hot upon the ground as well as upon the stone with which he played. The lion examines the stone with his nose, his tongue, and his teeth. It is rough and sharp, but also shiny. It is hard, too hard for the beast's great jaws to break. The lion returns the rock to the ground and, raising his great head, sniffs the air towards the west. As he holds his head high, the first ray of sunshine penetrates the gloom of the forest and strikes the stone at his feet, separating into a thousand scintillating splinters of light. The brief moment is radiant, but the lion does not see it.

Chapter 1
A Burning Desire

"Jenny, sweetheart, I just want to make sure you remember to call me when you get to JFK in New York, and when you land in Paris. Okay? And don't forget to call every day while you're gone, even if you don't get to charge your phone. That's why we bought you those three extra cell phone batteries, remember? You'll be seven hours ahead of us, so make sure you don't call too early or too late. If you call right before you go to bed, you should be able to reach me. And for goodness' sake, don't forget to charge your phone! You know how bad you are with remembering to charge it. Don't forget that you promised to save one of your extra batteries for emergencies only. Okay? And really wanting to listen to a song or uploading something to Instagram is *not* an emergency. And make sure… Jenny, are you listening to me?"

From her seat in the family's 2010 Chrysler mini-van, Jenny Clarkson repressed a sigh as her mother turned around in the front passenger seat and fixed her with an earnest stare. For the umpteenth time, Jenny swallowed a smart-aleck retort and answered with a simple, "Yes, Mother."

"Make sure you tell those missionaries to keep that special satellite phone working and in good condition," continued Rachelle Clarkson without missing a beat. "I want to be able to contact you at any time, okay? Oh Lord, three months is such a long time. I don't know how—Quiet!"

In the backseat of the van, Jenny's two brothers, Lucas and Eddie, ceased their bickering at the sound of their mother's command. The matriarch of the Clarkson family glared back at them, and they assumed expressions of angelic innocence. Their quarreling had been loud during the ride to the airport despite the early hour. They were only saved further discipline because their mother was too preoccupied with their older sister to give them much thought.

"Just make sure you call *me* at least once while you're gone," interjected Jenny's father from the driver's seat before his wife could get started again. Marcus Clarkson was a patient man, but sometimes he didn't have the patience to wait out his wife's loquacity.

Jenny had gone over these things with her parents a hundred times since she first told them that she had set her heart on going to the Central African Republic. But instead of reminding them of that fact, she replied with respect. "I will, Daddy. And, Mom, you know I'll hardly be able to spend a single minute not thinking about you."

Her words were well chosen. Her mother swallowed hard, fighting back tears for at least the tenth time so far that day. "Yes, I know," she replied, and turned back to look out the window.

Lucas and Eddie began to argue again. Jenny could ignore them, as only a sister could, but today was not a day she wanted to waste in frustration. Her mind was swimming with emotions—anxiety, excitement, melancholy, and nostalgia—and she needed to be able to think straight. She popped in her ear-buds and scrolled through her Spotify account until she came to a playlist titled "To Africa." She put weeks into creating this list and had only finished it the previous night. Like the rest of her generation, she was possessed by a strong cultural nostalgia for the eighties; her playlist reflected that nostalgia, along with the alternative rock days of the early 2000s, and several more current hits. It was an eclectic mix of travel songs, pop hits, melancholy ballads, and inspirational anthems, bound together by themes that were on her mind as she had packed. She started from the beginning with her favorite song and sat back to let it soak into her brain. As the muted acoustic guitar strums and

4

soft drum rhythms rose to an anthemic pitch, she felt the rest of the world fade away, and her thoughts began to soar.

This is Jenny Clarkson. She is a normal girl with a normal family and a normal life, but with an abnormal desire: she wants to change the world. Jenny didn't always have this desire. Once she was just an average American girl: white, middle-class, and satisfied. She was raised in comfort and security by loving parents who tried their hardest to provide for every one of her needs. Her parents raised her in church and were good examples of what strong, upstanding Christians should be. Jenny's best friends were other Christians, and her experiences have been such that she has tasted none the darker side of life. She has kept her nose clean and has displayed every trait a good Christian should. Yet she lacks one thing: she has not learned to serve. She does not know how to be a true disciple. She will learn soon enough.

Jenny's journey to this point has been long and agonizing, and, like those of many young girls, it started with a boy. She met Seth Jacobsen in seventh grade but didn't get to know him until her junior year of high school. She shared an English class with him where she learned that he too was a Christian. Up to that point in their acquaintance, she had seen nothing in him that suggested he was a Christian. He was a nice guy, outgoing and friendly, but there was nothing special about the way he lived that would have identified him as a follower of Jesus Christ. Had she thought hard enough, she would have realized that the same could be said of her.

But Jenny didn't think hard. Before long, she and Seth were spending a lot of time together. Their attraction was inevitable. She learned that, like her, he was raised in a middle-class, conservative Christian household and attended a church similar to hers in a neighboring city. He asked her to be his girlfriend on Valentine's Day (to which she said yes), and by the summer, they were inseparable. They spent their senior year hanging-out at each other's houses and churches, but in obedience to the wishes of their parents, they didn't start dating until after graduation. Once they did, they strove to keep their relationship as pure as possible. They didn't stay out too late, avoided compromising situations, and kept themselves accountable to their parents, pastors, and youth pastors. They prayed together in church, never missed church events to go on dates, and peppered their conversation with phrases like, "If God wills it," and "Jesus is my first love." If asked how they kept things so pure, they replied with something like, "It's easy when you put Jesus at the center of your relationship." They were the model Christian couple.

After high school, they both decided to be physician assistants, so they enrolled in the same university as biology majors and took the same classes together. They got part-time jobs at the local hospital as medical technicians, and both began to work in student ministry at their home churches. As the members of each church saw the two of them together more often, the "m-word" crept into their conversations. Though Seth and Jenny never talked openly about marriage, they began to act like they were married, or at least as if marriage was a forgone conclusion. They ate their meals together, sat together at church, took turns driving each other places, and even coordinated their schedules. People smiled and laughed at how cute they were. Neither of them meant to act in such a way, but neither could they imagine a future where they did not end up together. They were content in the lives they were living, and in the one they expected to share.

But God has a way of changing expectations. Looking back, Jenny couldn't pinpoint an exact time when Seth began to change. Perhaps it was the summer Bible camp they volunteered at over the summer, or one of the many sermons about discipleship that Seth heard his pastor preach. Maybe it was the years of mediocrity in his spiritual life that finally caught up to him. At any rate, sometime near the beginning of their third year of college, Seth grew restless. At first it was barely noticeable, just general irritation and less of a focus on school and Jenny, the things that usually occupied his time. But as the weeks and months passed, he became less and less interested in anatomy, medication, and dissection, and his grades began to suffer. He spent more time with his pastor and youth pastor, and at church. Months later, Jenny learned that he was also spending much of his time praying. She at first thought the disinterest in his life was because of her, so she made an extra effort to be the perfect girlfriend. But the more she tried to engage him, the less interested he seemed to grow. Their conversations took some strange turns. Instead of medical school, patient history, and house-hunting, they talked about human suffering, the Great Commission, and turning the world upside down. These topics weren't strange per se; they were just different. Jenny became more and more confused. She didn't yet realize that Seth had finally learned to think outside himself. He had seen the need to give his life for others, and until he could fulfill that mission, he would be trapped inside his own skin.

By the end of the semester, their relationship became strained for the first time. Seth wasn't upset with Jenny, nor was she upset with him, but they left unsaid things they needed to say. Jenny tried to talk to him about his behavior, but he saw nothing wrong with it. Things were particularly sensitive by the last week before finals. The early December weather hadn't frozen yet, but between Seth and Jenny things were icy. In an effort to show her dedication to him, Jenny attended midweek service at Seth's church in place of her own, something she never did. As fate (or God) would have it, that night Seth's pastor had invited Elias and Sharla Sharon, missionaries to the Central African Republic, to speak at the service. They had taken a sabbatical to raise funds for their work. As the Sharon's ascended the platform, Jenny settled in for the thirty-minute sales pitch followed by the inevitable request for funds. But instead she found herself listening to story after story, told in exquisite detail, of the many adventures the missionaries had experienced in their twenty-five years of service. The stories intrigued Jenny, but captivated Seth. He sat on the edge of his seat like a kid at a carnival, laughing at every joke, and clapping at the end of every story. The service ran long, and Jenny grew tired, but Seth's enthusiasm never flagged. She was hoping they would be able to slip out quickly to talk, but he hardly noticed her. As the service drew to a close, and she watched Seth run down to the front in response to Brother Sharon's invitation for prayer, she realized something was changing. When she saw Seth fall to his knees at Brother Sharon's feet and throw his hands in the air, she knew her life would never be the same.

Things changed immediately. Seth spent the next few days cloistered with the Sharon's in his pastor's office. When he emerged, he had decided he was going to the Central African Republic in the summer. Just like that. The next six months were full of planning, studying, and working as he struggled to get his affairs in order, learn the languages and culture of the C.A.R., and make enough money to finance his trip. He barely passed his finals and then dropped out of school entirely to work full-time and save money for his trip. For Jenny, the six months were full of worry and confusion. She still did not understand his sudden passion for missionary work, nor could she get more than a few minutes with him to talk about it. To his credit, Seth never tried to exclude Jenny from his preparations. In fact, he tried to make her a part of them in any way possible. He never talked about just himself going to Central Africa; it was always "us." Since they always did everything together, he assumed that Jenny would share his passion and would want to go with him. But his preparations so preoccupied him, he didn't notice she was growing more frustrated every day.

Finally, on a day in early May, less than a month before Seth was due to leave, the dam broke. They were having lunch at the college café for the first time in months, and he was talking incessantly about "their" trip when Jenny interrupted him. She told him she was not going to Africa, nor had she ever said she would. Her initial outburst left him speechless, so she seized her opportunity. She told him of the frustration she had experienced over being virtually ignored by him for the past six months. She told him how she couldn't leave the life they had built and forsake the future for which they had worked so hard. She told him he was making a poor decision to drop out of school and waste the hard work they had already done. She pleaded with him to stay with her, telling him that there were other ways for him to serve the kingdom of God. She poured her worries on him in a torrent of words which constituted the most passionate speech she had ever given in her life.

Seth sat quietly through her hurricane of feelings. But when she began say that she would try her hardest to please him, he interrupted and assured her his decisions had nothing to do with her. He told her that all he had ever wanted was a sweet, Christian life with her but now realized that there was more to being a Christian than just going to church. He told her again how he couldn't sleep at night because all he saw were the faces of the African people dying without the opportunity to know Jesus. As strong as her passion had been, his passion overwhelmed hers, and she saw that he had found something beyond her. Unfortunately, she saw it only as her replacement. She could not sway him, and, in the end, he left her in tears. She saw him only once more before he left, just a quick, awkward hug goodbye on the day before his flight, and then he was gone.

Now, two years later, Jenny is about to follow Seth into the wild world outside herself. She has come to understand what Seth grasped two years ago: life is worthless unless lived for others. Jenny has taken a long time to get to this place, and doubt has filled her journey. Her doubts remain, but they have been overshadowed by a desire that burns like a fire within her. She will not rest until the fire is fed.

Chapter 2
What Are You Afraid Of?

The rest of the car-ride passed swiftly for Jenny. Somewhere between an African folk rhythm and an eighties Christian pop song, her dad pulled off the freeway and onto the long drive leading into St. Louis Lambert International Airport. At 6:34 am in June, STL was already in full swing, and Marcus had to drive to the last row of lot E to find a spot. Jenny assured them they could drop her off at the terminal, but her mother insisted that the entire family accompany her as far as security would allow. At the ticket counter, Rachelle hovered over Jenny like a nervous helicopter while she checked in.

"So, St. Louis to New York…" the African-American woman behind the counter read as she printed Jenny's boarding passes.

"Then Paris…" That one she said with a smile and a wink at Jenny.

"And finally, the Central African Republic." There was no wink or smile as she read Jenny's final destination. She said it with a dry, even tone as if she were trying to keep from sounding surprised. She glanced at Jenny's waist-length blonde hair, pale complexion, and blue eyes.

Jenny would have felt self-conscious, but her mother didn't give her the chance.

"My daughter is going to work with the native Central African people for three months," Rachelle informed the woman. "It's a big commitment, but we are so proud of her for helping those less fortunate than the rest of us." The woman behind the counter smiled and congratulated her, but to Jenny, her mother's words sounded rehearsed and forced. She noticed with irritation that her mother said she would be gone for three months, even though she'd told her countless times she could be gone longer. She also noticed that her mother didn't tell the woman she was going as a missionary.

Feeling like a child, Jenny completed her check-in with her mother by her side and then walked across the terminal towards the security lines. Jenny could tell by her mother's uncharacteristic silence and tense body language that she was about to say something she had been mulling over for quite some time. *Here it comes*, Jenny thought as they passed underneath one of the antique war planes hanging in STL's terminal. Her mother took a deep breath.

"Jenny, please tell me you're making the right decision," she blurted out.

"Mother…" Jenny started, but then her mother stopped and took her by the shoulders.

"Just hear me out," she said. "You know your father and I have always raised you to love others and to do everything that you can to advance the kingdom of God. But we've also raised you to be wise and make good decisions. Now, I know that you've told me you want to do something special to help the world, but please tell me that you know what you're doing. There are many ways for you to serve people at home or in another part of the United States. Or in some other civilized country for that matter. But Africa? And the Central African Republic? I've already told you so many of the horror stories I've heard about the place. I know I'm repeating myself, but please Jenny, listen. The Central African Republic is not the place for a single, young girl to go by herself. Please, please, Jenny, won't you reconsider? It's not too late for you to change your plans…."

As her mother spoke, Jenny mentally ran through all her reasons for going, reasons she had explained to her mother countless times already. She had chosen the Central African Republic because she already knew people that would be there, and because the mission there enjoyed special protection from the government. Plus, she wasn't going completely by herself since the Sharon's would be joining her in Paris and taking her the rest of the way. She wanted to tell her mother again how she felt too sheltered in the United States where every need could be answered with a keystroke. She wanted to say how she was tired of being selfish and self-centered while others suffered in ignorance and privation. Most of all, she wanted to tell her mother once more of the special calling she felt to the people of Central Africa, a calling with which she had wrestled for months before finally submitting.

But all she said to her mother was, "Yes, Mother, I know what I'm doing. I'm doing what you raised me to do. I've trusted you with my entire life. Now I need you to trust me to make the right decision."

"You're a good girl, honey, and I respect your decision," her mother said. "But everybody needs help sometimes. Are you sure you're not just adventure-seeking?"

Jenny sighed. "No mother, I'm not adventure-seeking."

"Sure you're not just restless? That happens after college."

"No mother, I'm not just restless."

Her mother paused before she continued, thought about her next question, and then took the plunge.

"Are you sure you're not doing this for some boy?" she asked quietly.

That was a new one, and it caught Jenny off-guard. She hesitated before answering. Yes, Seth was her ex-boyfriend, but she considered that chapter of her life closed. Now, she realized that her motives may have appeared suspect. However, she knew in her heart that her choice of the C.A.R. had nothing to do with him other than that he was a personal connection in a land where she otherwise had none.

She told her mother how she felt.

"Are you sure sweetie?" her mother asked a little too sweetly.

"Mother…" Jenny replied in an exasperated but pleading tone.

She realized that others would suspect her motives, but she needed her mother to believe that she was sincere.

"I'm sorry sweetie," she replied, "I'm your mother, and I have to ask you these things. You understand, don't you?"

Jenny sighed again, but this time with a smile. Her mother was her moral compass and Jenny would have been disappointed if she had acted in any other way. She couldn't resent her mother for caring about her decisions. She gave her a big hug.

"I understand," she whispered into her ear. Her mother hugged her tightly, and when she finally let go, her eyes were wet with tears.

"I'm going to miss you so much, Jenny," she said. "What am I going to do at home with all those men?"

"Oh mother, you'll do just as fine as you always do," Jenny reassured her.

She wrapped her arm around her mother's shoulders and steered her towards the security lines where her father and brothers were waiting. Before she went through the checkpoint, her father gave her a hug and asked if she had enough emergency cash. She assured him that she did. Luke gave her the biggest hug he'd ever given her, and, for once, he didn't have a quip prepared, only a sincere goodbye. Eddie told her he would miss her, and she teased him that he might actually be taller than her by the time she got back. Her mother began to cry once again, and Jenny felt like crying too, but she held back her tears to present a confident face for her family. As she entered the security line, her mother tried to follow her from outside the security belt, but her father gently led her away. Jenny watched them as they exited the terminal, and, as the doors closed behind them, she waved goodbye one last time.

The flight from STL to John F. Kennedy International Airport in New York City was on time and uneventful. She took a shuttle ride over to the JFK international terminal, passed under an enormous hanging poster of Kobe Bryant promoting Turkish Airlines, and stood in line for her United Airlines flight to Charles de Gaulle

International Airport in Paris. Once she received her boarding pass, she was excited to see she had been marked for TSA Pre-Check, allowing her to bypass the long security lines and pass through with minimal checking. Once through, she made her way through the terminal towards her boarding gate. With over an hour until she boarded her seven and a half-hour flight to Paris, she had time to spare. She had never seen anything like JFK. The corona of lights, the massive jumbotron advertisements, the kaleidoscope of different races and ethnicities—it was almost too much for her to take in. The sheer sense of barely controlled chaos threatened to overwhelm her small-town mind already laden with worries and old memories. As she meandered through the terminal, she thought back to the fateful day when she tried to convince Seth not to go to the C.A.R. It was a painful memory, but now she realized that it had been one of the most important days of her life. She had felt so justified in her feelings, but when she brought them to Seth, they paled next to the depth of his own. The fire in his eyes, the consternation in his face as he tried to reason with her, the passion in his pleas as he bared his soul—all of it had been raw, and real. Her pitiful objections (selfish objections, as she later came to see them) now rang hollow. He was so right, and she had known it, yet she hadn't been able to bring herself to admit it.

Looking back now, she realized that she hadn't truly been selfish, but afraid. She had loved her perfect little life with Seth, and the thought of losing it frightened her. What scared her even more was the thought of embarking on the journey Seth was proposing. She wasn't ready to give up everything—her friends, family, comforts, and entire way of life—and go to a distant land and work for free. That fear was a selfish fear born out of a natural resistance to change, but at its root, it was still just a fear. Jenny was not a selfish person, but she had been so protected growing up that she could not fathom the thought of losing that protection. She had been a scared little girl, paralyzed by the weight of all her fears. The real reason that her mother's comment about Seth irritated her was because she knew that above all, she had been afraid of him too and of the depth of his passion.

Much time passed before she was able to face her fears. Seth's departure left her in shock. She wandered through life for a few weeks, going through the motions like nothing had changed. Then she grew miserable. Every day without Seth was torture, not just because she missed him, but because she missed the life they'd had together. She was hurt and depressed. She limped through the next six months, barely keeping up with her classes or fulfilling her responsibilities at church. Nothing seemed to satisfy her. Her depression turned to anger, but that only made things worse. She was angry at Seth, though she knew she had no right to be. He had left her for the most noble of causes, and her anger only showed how shallow and immature she was. But her anger remained nonetheless.

With the new year, she tried to get over her misery. She read her Bible, prayed many hours at home and at church, and sought the counsel of those closest to her. Eventually she saw and accepted that Seth had made a hard, selfless choice in leaving her to serve the people of Central Africa and that his decision had not been in response to any fault in her. However, this revelation only increased her misery because it meant that she had been selfish in trying to get him to stay. But as time passed, she began to realize that she was the one who had made a poor decision. Her pain, which she had focused outward on someone else, sank ever inward as she realized the person most responsible for her misery was herself. For several weeks she wallowed in self-pity, but, after she was through, she took stock of her life to try to root out the flaws in her character that were causing her so much pain. The process was uncomfortable. She endured many troubling days staring at herself in the mirror, but in time she was able to identify and rectify her shallowness and immaturity. Only after remaking herself was she able reconsider the choices she had made.

When Jenny finally reached her departure gate, she felt weighed down by her memories. She found a seat by the gate and popped in her headphones to distract herself. She bobbed her head, bounced her leg, and hummed along to her favorite bands. Like a balm, the familiar sounds of her favorite songs flowed into every nook and cranny of her mind, soothing her thoughts and bringing peace. She listened, read for a while, and then listened some more, until it was time for her to board.

Her journey from New York, USA to Bangui, CAR began at 2:17 pm Eastern Standard Time, and continued on for fifteen hours, with only a short two-hour break in Paris. She crossed six time zones from NYC to Paris as she traveled east, but crossed no time zones as she traveled south from Paris to Bangui. It was by far the longest fifteen hours Jenny had ever spent, yet it was magical, like a daydream, during which she was never truly anywhere on the globe, only in transit, moving from one place to another.

Her trip went according to plan except for one exception. When she landed in Paris, she had a text waiting from Sharla Sharon that read, "Call me as soon as you land." Immediately, her heart started pounding. The Sharon's were supposed to help her with the customs and visa process since it was her first time flying internationally. As she dialed Sister Sharon's number, she took several deep breaths and told herself to stay calm—there was no reason to assume anything was wrong. Sister Sharon answered on the fourth ring.

"Sweetie," she began, "I don't want you to worry, but we need to change our plans a little." She sounded calm and collected, but Jenny could hear Brother Sharon arguing with someone in the background.

"Okay," Jenny replied, trying and failing to match Sister Sharon's calm tone.

"Elias and I won't be able to fly with you to Bangui today."

Jenny's heart skipped a beat.

Sister Sharon preceded to explain how they had been at the airport in Paris all night trying unsuccessfully to persuade the Central African consulate and the French Border control to let them fly back to the C.A.R. She explained all the technical details, something about both of their visa requirements and extension times being out of order, but Jenny couldn't understand most of it. The French officers were telling them they needed to go all the way back to the United States and reapply for their visas.

"So basically, we can't get into the country today," Sister Sharon said. "It's very frustrating."

Jenny's heart sank. "I'm so, so sorry, Sister Sharon," she said.

"So are we, dear. But this doesn't have to affect your trip. We talked to the border control, and they have assured us that you will be able to get through since this is your first time traveling to the C.A.R. We just won't be able to go along with you. But I'll walk you through the entire process, and when you land in Bangui, our friends will meet you as soon as you go through security, just like we planned. Don't worry, everything else will still run smoothly."

She was right. Jenny passed through customs with barely a glance from the woman behind the counter, made her way to the next departure gate, and boarded the plane for Bangui without a hitch. But she still worried. She had always planned the trip with the Sharon's by her side, and now that things had changed, she couldn't help feeling nervous. She had come a long way in conquering her fear of the unknown, but she still had to fight it sometimes. As the plane was preparing for takeoff, she realized her heart was still thumping. She said a quick prayer, asking God to calm her nerves and to give her courage. She remembered a conversation she'd had with her pastor when she had first been struggling with what she felt was a call from God to be a missionary.

"Jenny," her pastor had said, after she'd given him all the reasons why she couldn't go to Africa, "it seems to me like you are trying your hardest to find a reason not to go. Are you scared?"

It took a few moments, but finally she admitted it, to him and to herself. She told him yes, she was afraid.

"Not afraid, Jenny," he replied. "I asked you if you were *scared*."

She wasn't sure what he meant by that, and she told him so.

"Being scared and being afraid are not necessarily the same thing," he said. "You can be scared of something but not afraid. Everyone gets scared of new things, especially if those things are significant, like being called by God. We're all scared of change because it's an unknown. But fear is something more. It's something in your spirit. Moses was afraid to follow the call of God and go back to Egypt to speak to Pharaoh because he didn't know what would happen. It was an unknown. Gideon was afraid to stand up to the Midianites because he didn't know how to defeat them. It was an unknown. God helped both men conquer their fear, and they went on to do mighty acts of valor. But that doesn't mean they weren't still scared. Imagine if you were Moses standing at the Red Sea, with the armies of Pharaoh at your back. Do you think Moses wasn't scared? I'm sure he was. But he trusted God and still did what he was asked despite the fact that he was scared. Even Jesus Christ our Savior, the greatest hero ever to walk this earth, was scared. The Bible tells us how he sweated like great drops of blood when he was in the Garden of Gethsemane on the eve of his crucifixion, and he asked his Father in heaven that the cup of suffering would pass from him. Jenny, the divine nature of Jesus, the side of him that knew all things, understood that everything would work out fine in the end. But to the human side of Jesus, *it was still an unknown.* Yet, his attitude remained, 'not my will, but thy will be done.'"

He had continued talking to Jenny, telling her how she might always be scared, but that she could still conquer her fears. He read II Timothy 1:7 to her, which says, "For God hath not given us the spirit of fear; but of power, and of love, and of a sound mind," and explained to her that those who God has filled with his Holy Spirit don't have to live in fear. Her told her a million personal stories, as pastors are fond of doing. Then he said something that resonated in her mind: "Jenny, out of all the reasons you've given me, it seems like what you're afraid of most is fear. And fear is not a good excuse not to turn the world upside down."

That had been the turning point in Jenny's battle. Thinking back to it always gave her courage. As the plane taxied to the end of the runway and lifted into the sky, she said a short prayer of thanks, and her fears subsided.

Chapter 3
Shaken

There was one upside to traveling without the Sharon's: Jenny had the entire row to herself. She raised the armrests, laid down across the three seats, and was soon asleep. The next thing she knew, the flight attendant was gently shaking her awake and telling her to put on her seat belt for the descent into Bangui M'Poko International Airport. As the big Air France plane dropped beneath a thin layer of clouds, Jenny moved to the window seat to get her first glimpse of the African continent. The first thing she noticed was the green. Even amongst the houses and buildings of Bangui, a capital city of over 700,000 people, green was everywhere, growing in alleys, yards, streets, and any other place that wasn't occupied. Untamed jungle crowded the edges of the city and stretched as far as her eye could see. It gave the country a vibrant, vivacious look.

But as the plane dropped lower, the dirt between the trees began to show. The buildings were dilapidated and the roads unpaved. Lifeless-looking cars bounced along, sat motionless in endless traffic jams, or lay burned out in lots or driveways. Pools of standing water, by-products of the temperamental Oubangui River on which the city lay, flooded many areas. The city itself was laid out in a random pattern as if it had been thrown together at the last minute. A good layer of dust coated everything, and a thin cloud of smog lay over it, painting the city a hazy brown color from Jenny's vantage point in the descending jet.

As the plane lined up its final descent onto the runway, she was shocked to see acres of shanty-towns surrounding the airport. Tents made of sheets, tarps, canvas, or palm leaves and supported by branches, rotted boards, or scrap-metal sat crammed together to form a fluttering sea of dull colors. Derelict planes of all shapes and sizes served as partial shelters and clotheslines. Smoke from dozens of campfire stoves filled the air. Children, feral dogs, thin men, green-uniformed soldiers, mothers with baskets of laundry, and hungry birds swarmed like ants on a discarded ice cream cone at a carnival. As the pilot extended the landing gear, Jenny realized the makeshift village wasn't just next to the airport, it was *in* the airport, on active runways. The plane dropped closer, and she thought they would land right on top of the camp. They dropped so close she could read the graffiti on the sides of tents and see the excited expressions on the faces of the people. Children lined the runway as the plane touched down. As it rolled away, they chased it, giggling and tripping over one another in their excitement.

The big plane lumbered up to the single terminal and stopped. Jenny knew it was a terminal because there were planes parked at it, but beyond that, it looked nothing like any airport terminal she had seen before. It looked more like a cheap, old motel, the kind where the front has a forced shine, but the backside is dirty and unkempt. She followed the other passengers through the stifling heat, across the tarmac, and into the relative coolness of the building. It was clean, but after a closer look, she saw the fraying carpet edges, the peeling paint, and the dust in the spaces in between.

Jenny's heart began to hammer. Then she heard her name.

"Jenny Clarkson!" a feminine voice called out. The voice was abrasive but cheerful and strong, with an accent straight from the American South. She didn't recognize it, but she knew there was only one person to which it could belong.

"Nanci!" she said as she turned to a stocky, attractive middle-aged woman with a warm smile and a vigorous wave. The woman ran to her and enveloped her in a bear-hug that forced Jenny's beating heart to slow and banished the apprehension from her mind. Nanci Bernard was a life-time missionary who had worked in Africa, on her own and unmarried, since she had graduated from high school. She had lived all over the continent, from Ethiopia to South Africa, and had come to help the Sharon's in the Central African Republic five years ago. Self-supported and self-sufficient, she was from a large, wealthy family in Louisiana that had been funding missions work for decades. Sister Sharon had put Jenny in touch with her months ago, and ever since then, the two of them had engaged in a steady stream of emails through which they had already gotten to know each other. This was as friendly a face as she had hoped to see.

"How are ya, darlin'?" Nanci asked. "Was the flight alright?"

Jenny assured her it was.

"You poor girl," Nanci said, "We only just learned a few hours ago that Brother and Sister Sharon weren't going to be with ya. I remembered that this was your first international flight, and thought, 'Oh, Lord, she'll be as nervous as a possum in a garbage can.' But I'm glad it was a good one, right?"

Jenny assured her again with a smile that, yes, the flight had been fine.

"Well, then the Lord answers prayers," Nanci replied. Jenny could tell that she was sincerely relieved. She blushed, but smiled.

"This is Ferdy," Nanci continued, placing her hand on the forearm of a tall, stately African man with a salt and pepper beard who had waited with a patient smile while Nanci fussed over Jenny. He stuck out a long hand and gripped Jenny's.

"I'm Ferdinand Ngoupande," he said with a reserved smile.

"But we all call him Ferdy," Nanci interrupted.

"… but everyone calls me Ferdy," he finished with another knowing smile. Nanci had told Jenny all about Ferdy. He was a native Central African who had grown up in abject poverty determined to escape his upbringings and make something of himself. Through many years of hard work, he attracted the attention of a wealthy French patron, who paid for him to get an education if he promised

21

to return and help his country. Ferdy had needed no extra incentive. He was in love with his country and his people and wanted nothing more than to help them succeed. He preceded to graduate from Oxford with honors with a degree in Medical Business. After that, he worked for a pharmaceutical company in France where he also completed a master's degree in geopolitics. After nearly a decade of training and education, he returned to the C.A.R. to lead a nonprofit organization that distributed medical supplies and drugs to citizens. He met the Sharon's not long after they came to the C.A.R. and got involved in their mission, eventually becoming an active Christian because of them. Currently, he split his time between the medical center in Bangui and the village where he helped the Sharon's minister.

"We are glad you finally made it here, my dear," Ferdy said in crisp, Oxford English. "Now we can go," he added with a dry tone and a straight face.

"Oh, Ferdy," Nanci sighed, "are we starting this already? The poor girl has just barely landed."

"Yes, she has," Ferdy replied, "and if she doesn't get her hindquarters moving, someone will steal the jeep, and she'll have to ride an elephant to Sangha."

"Oh, you know nobody rides elephants in Africa," Nanci countered. "They only do that in Asia."

"How would you know, my dear?" Ferdy snorted. "You have never been to Asia, and I have lived my entire life as an African. I believe that qualifies me as an authority on the subject."

"You've never ridden an elephant."

"Of course, I have. I have ridden elephants since my youth. In fact, my father owned one when I was a boy. She was an old mare. 'Tam-tam' is what I used to call her, and every day I would ride her to and from the market. That is, I would ride her every day that I wasn't responsible for feeding the family tiger, Winston."

"Oh, for goodness' sake!" Nanci huffed in frustration, but her eyes were smiling, and Ferdy was chuckling, a rich, deep, melodious sound. They made quite a scene as they walked through the airport bickering like an old married couple. Their antics may have been annoying to some people, but they made Jenny feel right at home.

They retrieved Jenny's luggage and exited the terminal. The return of the oppressive heat was like a smack in the face. Jenny had never been this close to the equator before, and, though northern Missouri gets its fair share of humidity, she had never experienced the legendary humidity of the tropics. It felt like someone was grabbing her around the throat and choking the life out of her. She tried to tell herself that she could handle it and that she had come here to serve despite the uncomfortable conditions, but it didn't help.

Almost immediately upon exiting the terminal, a gang of children surrounded her. A few were smiling, but most simply stared up at her with a detached expression. They crowded around her, some pawing at her clothes, and others jabbering in a combination of French and Sango, the native Central African dialect. Others smiled up at her with their hands held out, thinking or hoping that she had something to give them. Jenny smiled back at them and tried to continue on, but they pushed around her and trapped her in the center of their little mob. Fortunately, Nanci and Ferdy noticed and came to her rescue, scolding the children in their native languages, and shooed them away. The children stepped back and allowed her to pass, but they followed her despite the stern warnings from Ferdy. They made it to the jeep, a bulky, open-air, off-road model with a canvas top, but only after pulling out of the parking lot were they able to escape the children.

As they drove off the airport grounds, Nanci apologized for the treatment, and Jenny nodded her thanks, but the encounter didn't fade from her mind. Ferdy and Nanci kept up a running commentary about the city and its culture, but Jenny was only half listening. She only really paid attention when they told her how more refugees were showing up at the airport every day. Though the UN Peacekeepers kept moving them on, more always arrived to take their place. The Peace Corps had left in 1996 because of the dangers of the country and hadn't officially come back since. They talked about poverty levels and death rates, but none of those things were more interesting than the look she had seen in the faces of those kids outside the airport. They battled the city traffic for quite some time, but Jenny couldn't get those faces out of her mind. She had prepared herself for the poverty, violence, sickness, and garbage of a third-world country, but not for the desperate look she had seen in those eyes.

Once they got out of the city proper, Jenny began to breathe a bit easier and take more stock of her surroundings. What struck her most was the intensity of the jungle surrounding the city. She'd expected a gradual change from the city to the wild, with some smaller suburbs and perhaps some farmland in between. But as soon as they passed from the city, the jungle loomed over them on both sides of the road blocking any view for more than a few yards. The trees reached out from either side, and, in some places, mingled so tightly above their heads that only a faint light bled through. Here and there they passed into open spaces created by intersecting roads, or wide fields of corn, cassava, coffee, or plantains. But the jungle always grew to its fullest right up to the edges of the cleared spaces. Ferdy explained that they continually pushed the jungle back with burning to make way for farmland, or by cutting to harvest timber. But if left untended, it always grew back, ever encroaching upon the boundaries set for it by humanity. Jenny stared into it, seeing it as some unstoppable malignant force, a dark parody of sweet mother nature.

But the farther they got away from the city, the more Jenny realized that, though the jungle was dark, it also possessed a mysterious beauty. Sometimes, the sun would peak through at just the right angle and strike a tree or flower, causing it to glitter like an emerald. She came to enjoy the dim light, which decreased her view, but enhanced the colors, like a water color painting seen in a softly lit gallery. She caught glimpses of monkeys peering at her from between vines, of beautiful birds flapping amongst the trees, and of Central Africa's famous butterflies. Even driving down the road at appreciable speeds Jenny could see the colorful little insects fluttering back and forth between the flowers. Sometimes they would dart across the road, and Jenny's own heart would flutter, hoping that the jeep's windshield wouldn't smash them. They were delicate and magical, and, for a short while, they made her forget about the faces she'd seen at the airport.

During the drive, Ferdy and Nanci explained much of the country's history and current political status to Jenny. They told her how it used to be a French colony called Ubangi-Shari, and, after it had achieved independence in 1960, it had been ruled by several brutal dictators who hindered the country's development for decades. Ferdy explained that he could not leave the country until civilian rule was finally established in 1993, when he left to go study in England. He had barely been able to get back into the country in 2003 before General François Bozizé seized control. He spent the next decade struggling to bring aid to the suffering nation. His first real break-through had been after the Crisis started and he met the Sharon's. When Jenny asked what "the Crisis" was, Ferdy's face grew grim. He explained to her that General Bozizé had only seized power through the aid of several Muslim tribes of Central Africans, but after seizing control, he ignored them and never followed through on promises he made to them. Tired after a decade of Bozizé's treachery, a coalition of the tribes, which became known as the Seleka, stormed the capital and forced Bozizé to flee the country. The United Nations sent in a peacekeeping force, which persuaded the Seleka to go home but not before a predominantly Christian group called the Anti-Balaka formed to oppose them.

"The two groups have been fighting ever since," Ferdy told Jenny with a disgusted look. "Both sides have been accused of war crimes and have been outlawed by the government, but there is little the president can do to stop them. Even worse is that the senseless violence is perpetrated by neighbors who don't profess to belong to either group. Muslims kill Christians, and Christians kill Muslims, for no other reason than that they disagree about God."

"What makes it so heartbreaking," Nanci said, "is that so many sincerely believe that their god is pleased with their acts of violence. Many of them just use the religious differences as an excuse to perpetrate the violence, but some sincerely believe in it. Both sides claim that their god is a God of love, yet both sides continue to harm each other."

"There are many deep-seated wounds that afflict my people," said Ferdy. "Much of this violence is in response to these wounds that have never healed. People claim to be righting wrongs that others have done to them. But the violence only creates more opportunity for vengeance, and the cycle only grows worse."

"Even the ones who claim to be Christians and to serve the same God that we do put their desire for vengeance above their love for God," Nanci added.

"So then, your job here is doubly hard," Jenny surmised. "Not only do you have to convert people to Christianity, you also have to convert the Christians from a gospel of violence to a gospel of love."

"Exactly," said Nanci. "It's been rough, but the Sharon's, along with Seth and Ferdy, have done an incredible job here. You'll see when we get to the village."

"Do the Seleka or the Anti-Balaka ever bother the village?" Jenny asked.

"No," Ferdy replied. "Though the Sangha Reserve is nominally in an area controlled by the Anti-Balaka, they don't bother us."

"Reserve?"

"Yes, the Dzanga-Sangha Special Reserve," Ferdy repeated. "The village which we refer to as Sangha is near a tributary of the Sangha river in the Dzanga-Sangha Special Reserve. Didn't Nanci tell you?" he said as he glanced sideways at her.

"Yes, darlin'," Nanci replied with a hint of a sigh, "the village is technically located in a national wildlife park called the Dzanga-Sangha Special Reserve. It is protected by the Central African government as well as by the governments of several surrounding nations."

"Oh," Jenny said. That didn't sound legal to her. A short silence followed.

Sensing a slight build in tension, Ferdy spoke first. "We have a… special arrangement with the park rangers."

Jenny noticed the slight pause before he said "special arrangement." She wondered what the special arrangement was, but sensed that they didn't really want to talk about it right now.

"So, do the park rangers protect the village from the fighters?" she asked, trying to change the subject.

"No," Ferdy replied.

"Oh," Jenny said again. Another awkward silence.

"With them too, we have a special arrangement," Ferdy said. Jenny saw him smiling in the rear-view mirror.

"Jenny," Ferdy continued, noticing her stare, "much will become clear when we reach the village. There is much that we could tell you right now, but it won't make much sense until you see the village and experience the people for yourself. I sense that you want me to assure you everything will be safe where you are going, but I can give you no such assurance. Central Africa is an unstable place. Things can change overnight. You must know this. But I think no harm will come to you, for only a resourceful girl would have decided to come into the middle of this. And, most importantly, Our Father in heaven has his hand on you, for we have prayed that He would. None of us know what He has in mind. For now, let it suffice for you to know that the village is safe from outside influences."

Nanci waited a beat, and then declared, "Ferdinand, I bet you could make a crawfish feel safe as you were dropping him in a pot of boiling oil."

Her comment was absurd and diminished the eloquence of Ferdy's little speech, but he laughed his rich, melodious laugh anyway, and Jenny couldn't help but join in. It made her feel better.

They drove for over twelve hours after leaving Bangui. Jenny grew stiff from the hard jeep seats and the rough roads over which they traveled. They stopped several times to eat and relieve themselves, but the journey still felt much longer than any of the flights she had taken over the last few days. They arrived late in the town of Bayanga where they would spend the night in a hotel before finishing the journey to the village the next day. The hotel was small and ill-equipped by western standards, but Jenny was far too tired to care. She collapsed on the twin-size bed in her clothes and was soon fast asleep.

Only one thing of note occurred during their drive. During the summer, the Central African days grow longer, but still, darkness began to fall before they reached their destination. As the sky grew dark, Ferdy pulled off in a turn-out near a dirt road. When Jenny asked why they were stopping, he informed her that it was getting dark, and that it wasn't safe to travel unguarded at night. He flashed his lights a few times and waited. After several seconds, a man emerged from the jungle and got into the back of the jeep next to Jenny, introducing himself as George Hauser. He was friendly, with a pleasant Irish accent and a thick mustache. Ferdy announced that he was their security guard. But he was equipped more like a soldier, with a big pistol at his hip and had a nasty-looking machine gun slung over his shoulder. He made polite conversation with Jenny, but his eyes were always moving, probing the darkness. His presence should have made her feel safer, but it didn't. For the first time since she'd landed, Jenny wondered what she had gotten herself into.

Chapter 4
Hotel Paradise

They left Bayanga early in the morning and drove east. As in Bangui, they hit jungle as soon as they left the cultivated areas, only here it was thicker and darker. They passed through a park ranger checkpoint and then jostled down a dirt road for an hour. They came to a place where they turned off onto a game trail and blazed their way through the densest jungle Jenny had seen so far. Another hour passed before they reached a wide clearing several acres across where the little village of Sangha sat.

They parked near the edge of the village. Jenny got out slowly. She was unprepared for what she saw. It was a shanty-town like the ones she'd seen surrounding the airport, but up close, it was twice as shocking. She had imagined mud huts, or rough shacks, but most of the buildings weren't even that extensive. Most were little more than tents made of four sticks and a dirty piece of canvas for a roof. If they were walled in, it was by torn sheets, rusty pieces of sheet metal, old car doors, or cardboard flats. The sturdiest ones were made of sheet wood held together by a few rusty nails with an old rug for a door. She had known before she came that there would be no electricity, but she hadn't been prepared for what looked like a complete lack of proper sanitation. Tall grass grew rampantly everywhere. A pack of mongrel dogs wrestled over a bone on a dusty footpath lined with rocks and trash.

A woman hurried down one of the paths. Once she reached them, she launched into a conversation with Ferdy, speaking excitedly in French, while tugging on his sleeve and gesturing deeper into the village. She wore a long skirt and a plain blouse with her hair tied back in a white bandana. Jenny heard a sharp clack that made her jump. She looked over her shoulder and saw Hauser cocking his rifle as he listened to what the woman said. He barked a couple words of rough French at her, and once she responded, he hurried off into the village with Ferdy, Nanci, and the woman right on his heels. Forgotten for the moment, Jenny hurried to keep up.

As she hurried along, she tried not to look at the devastated shacks that stared at her on either side of the dirt street. Like a person trying to avoid the eyes of a beggar on the sidewalk, she stared straight ahead and searched for something else to occupy her attention. She tried to follow the conversation between the village-woman and Ferdy, but couldn't understand enough French to keep up. From her one year in high school and one semester in college, all she could grasp was that something important was happening. It didn't make her feel any better. She bumped into Nanci who remembered that she was present and whispered to her that everything was okay, but someone had been stabbed, which of course communicated to Jenny that everything was *not* okay. A knot began to form in her gut.

They came to the opposite edge of the village where a low, wide pavilion and several rows of rough wooden benches stood in a large open space. A crowd of villagers had gathered there. As soon as they saw Ferdy, they parted to allow him through to the center of the group where he began to whisper to a tall, trim white man with short, black hair and a thick mustache. The man was dressed in military fatigues and armed with a large handgun strapped to his thigh. He and several other armed men stood around the circle and watched coolly. Everyone's attention was focused on a small African man kneeling in the dust closely guarded from behind by another armed man.

The young man kneeling in the dust was in a heated conversation with another man standing over him. Several moments passed before

Jenny realized the man was Seth. She didn't recognize the squareness of his shoulders, the tan of his skin, the wild unkempt hair that stuck out in every direction, or the commanding way he addressed the man at his feet. But his profile—highbrowed, aquiline nose, jaw-line cut from granite—was the same. He was thinner than when she'd last seen him, but he had always been that way, thin and stringy, like a wolf. He still spoke with intensity, gesturing with his hands to punctuate every syllable. Jenny could see that his passion was still burning strong.

He spoke with the man at his feet in a mix of English, French, and Sango. They were clearly disagreeing about something sensitive to the entire village, for the villagers crowding around them were agitated and murmured to each other constantly. The village-woman whispered excitedly into Nanci's ear, and she in turn whispered to Jenny.

"Aleena says that the man on the ground tried to kill his neighbor earlier this morning and then ran into the jungle. They've all been searching and only just now caught him." She gestured to a man seated on a wooden bench several yards away with his left arm in a sling and a bandage wrapped around his ribs. "That's Nikolai, the man who was attacked," she continued. "He claims the other man stole his boots. The man on the ground is named Mohammedou Djotodia. He says the boots were his, and the other man stole them from him. He says he attacked Nikolai when he tried to take them. But that seems unlikely. Mohammedou is new here, and we don't know much about him. And everyone knows about Nikolai's pair of boots. They were a gift from some of his relatives in France. A good pair of shoes is hard to come by here. I guess it's possible that Mohammedou is telling the truth, but it's much more likely that Mohammedou is the one who did the stealing and attacked Nikolai to get his boots."

"Oh," replied Jenny. She wasn't sure how to respond, so she asked Nanci who the tall military man was.

"That's Clayton Mercury. He's a friend of the Sharon's. He leads a small mining operation in the area, but he has been very kind to us. These are his men here. They're probably the ones who caught Mohammedou."

"They're miners?" Jenny asked.

"Technically," Nanci answered.

They watched the situation proceed for several more minutes. The arguing between Seth and Mohammedou intensified. Mohammedou tried to rise several times, but each time the burly armed man behind him shoved him back to his knees.

"What are they saying now?" Jenny asked.

"Mohammedou has just been explaining to Seth that Nikolai is a Christian, an infidel who has blasphemed Allah, and so it is his duty to punish him for stealing from him. He's been quoting random snippets from the Quran to justify himself. You're seeing firsthand how the inhabitants regularly use their religion to justify their acts of violence towards one another. We've stamped it out in Sangha for the most part, but Mohammedou is new."

"There are Christians *and* Muslims here?" Jenny asked.

"Yes," Nanci answered patiently. "We don't turn away anybody who needs help, regardless of their religion." She resumed her translation. "Now Seth is telling him that even if Nikolai did steal his boots, he still has no right to assault his neighbor. His religion gives him no right to hurt others, and, in this village, we don't do things that way. He obviously doesn't believe Mohammedou's story. He's telling him that we all have known Nikolai for a long time, and we all know the story of how he got his boots. Mohammedou has broken the peace of the village and brought violence into a place of safety. Now he's scolding him because the people gave him shelter and a home here in Sangha and have trusted him, but he has betrayed that trust. He says that anywhere else in the country he would be executed brutally for what he's done."

When Seth finished speaking, silence settled onto the village. Mohammedou stared up at him, and the contemptuous look on his face slowly melted into one of fear. Seth stared him down for several more seconds and then turned to confer with Clayton Mercury and Ferdy. Jenny caught a glimpse of his face before Ferdy stepped in the way. It was darker and more rugged, but his eyes were still deep and intense, and the look of determination that fit his handsome features so well was stronger than ever. The three of them spoke in low voices. Jenny couldn't tell what they were saying, but she saw Clayton Mercury put his hand on the big pistol on his hip and say something that made Ferdy look at him in consternation. Seth apparently didn't like his suggestion, because he shook his head and said "no." Mercury pulled him closer and whispered more intently, but Seth shook his head again and said loud enough for her to hear, "I know, but we don't do things that way. The Sharon's wouldn't want it." Mercury sighed and shook his head allowing Ferdy to jump in and whisper a suggestion. Seth shook his head to that too. Mercury and Ferdy argued back and forth until Seth put in another suggestion which the other two didn't seem to like. They traded several more muffled comments to which Seth remained silent. He dropped his head and ran his fingers through his thick hair. Then, having made up his mind, he turned back to Mohammedou.

He spoke out in clear English. "Mohammedou Djotodia, by bringing violence into our village and attempting to kill your neighbor, you have violated our peace, sanctity, and unity. Because this is not a court or official tribunal, I cannot punish you as you deserve. However, I can force you to leave so that your poisonous behavior can no longer damage what we have built. I hereby banish you from Sangha, never to return." He then repeated his last sentence in French, and then Sango. The villagers, agreeing with Seth's decision, began to shout and applaud. Mohammedou blanched. The man behind him stepped away, allowing him to stand to his feet in a half crouch like a cornered animal. His eyes grew wide with fear as he watched the cheering villagers around him. The section of the circle nearest to him opened, creating a wide corridor through the crowd towards which they all pointed. Mohammedou understood that he had no other choice. He threw a look of pure hatred at Seth and then dashed down the corridor amidst a hail of rocks launched by the jeering crowd.

The villagers surged after him, shouting and throwing more rocks. As he dashed off into the jungle, they cheered and hugged each other. Jenny squeezed between Nanci and Aleena to avoid getting stepped on by the happy throng of people. Amidst the commotion, she noticed Clayton Mercury stride through the crowd to George Hauser, and, barely audible over the cheering crowd, heard him yell, "Follow him. And make sure he doesn't come back." Hauser nodded and slipped out of the crowd.

The people began to disperse after that, as Nanci and Ferdy playfully shooed them all back to their work. As the space cleared, Jenny saw Seth talking to Nikolai. He was smiling and patting his shoulder, but the injured man kept trying to get down on his knees. Seth continued to smile but would not let the man kneel before him.

"They all love Seth," Nanci said from Jenny's elbow, "but sometimes they go a bit too far in showing their affection. The Sharon's have to deal with the same thing. They've been trying for years to get the people to understand that acts of justice and mercy should be normal and are nothing to be worshipped for. But these people have been so mistreated, they don't know how to act when someone shows them kindness. They are starved for love."

As she spoke, Jenny realized she was steering her towards Seth. Her heart began to beat faster. She had only had sparse contact with him through email since he had left, and, though he had seemed happy to have her help, she began to have doubts. They had so much undiscussed history that she didn't know what to say or how to greet him. They had never had a chance to talk over the things they said during their break-up. She had figured that enough time had passed to let bygones be bygones, but, now that he was here, she began to worry.

As she approached him, Nikolai gave one last bow and hobbled away. Seth turned and laid eyes on Jenny for the first time. As they made eye contact, he froze. His lips continued to smile but his eyes widened in surprise and took on that glazed deer-in-the-headlights look. His entire body tensed and seemed to scream in shocked remembrance like a person who suddenly remembers that he has left the stove on. Jenny's heart leaped into her throat, and her stomach twisted into a knot the size of an elephant.

But the moment only lasted for a fraction of a second. Just as quickly, Seth's entire demeanor slid smoothly from surprise into comfort. He was caught off guard only for an instant. His shoulders relaxed, and his eyes brightened to match the rest of his face. When he spoke, his smile was genuine.

"Jenny Clarkson, where have you been…" he said in that relaxed, lazy tone she remembered so well.

Her face broke into a smile, and she hugged him, her anxiety already draining away. She squeezed him, a little too tightly she thought later, but he didn't seem to mind and laughed. He was happy to see her. They went through the normal pleasantries appropriate for two friends who haven't seen each other for years. They had never gone through such pleasantries with each other before, so they were awkward, but not painfully so and soon they were laughing like the old friends they were. Both sought to make the other comfortable, and the awkwardness soon passed.

But Nanci Bernard was not one to let any situation slip past without a comment. "If I didn't know better, Seth," she said with a mischievous smile, "I'd say for a second there it looked like you forgot that Jenny was coming today."

"Oh, come on, how could I forget that?" he said with another big smile, but his cheeks blushed a little. "We've been looking forward to her being here for months now. It's just that without the Sharon's here and with them getting stuck in Paris, I've been so busy and so—"

"You forgot," Nanci interjected.

"I didn't forget," he replied with more seriousness. Jenny couldn't resist piling on.

"Wow, Seth," she said with a mock sigh. "I'm disappointed. I guess I'll still have to take care of everything for you, huh?" He used to hate when she said that. She crossed her arms and pretended to be peeved.

Seth rolled his eyes and made a sound of disgust in his throat, but he had that crooked half-smile-half-smirk in the corner of his mouth. "Well, I know how you love to take care of me. I guess you're still good at it too, huh?"

"Only because I've had so much practice," she replied.

"Well, practice makes perfect, right?"

"I guess I should just expect it now."

"Then, I am happy to oblige."

"Ha. I'd love for you to disappoint me someday."

"I thought I already had."

"You've got that right."

"Come on, Jenny, you really think I forgot?"

"Yes. You should be ashamed of yourself."

"Oh, I'm really tore up about it on the inside, trust me."

They were laughing now, but Jenny could tell he actually was a little embarrassed, so she let it go and asked him what she was supposed to do next. He suggested that they get her bags, and then he would show her where she would be staying. But before they could move, Clayton Mercury called out to him, asking for a word. He directed a couple of boys to help Jenny with her luggage and then dashed off.

Nanci sighed. "That's our Seth, always on the move. I shouldn't have teased him. He really does have a lot on his plate with the Sharon's gone."

After retrieving Jenny's luggage, Nanci led her back towards the pavilion. On the way, she introduced her to the young woman who had first met them, Aleena Zoumara. Jenny liked her almost immediately. She was sweet and soft-spoken, but quite loquacious, and spoke broken but intelligible English. She and Nanci led Jenny past the pavilion to a group of nicer dwellings set aside from the others. The first one was a large, military style tent which served as the Sharon's home. The next two were smaller, but slicker camping models. One had a colorful rain cover and awning which belonged to Nanci. The other, guarded by a big Staffordshire bull terrier, was where Ferdy stayed when he was at the village. The last one was a small but functional army tent made of thick canvas. This was to be Jenny's home for the next three months or longer.

The three ladies ducked their heads and entered the little tent. They stood in silence as Jenny took it in. After a couple of long seconds, Nanci shrugged her shoulders and said, "It ain't Hotel Paradise, but I hope it'll be okay." But she misunderstood Jenny's silence. After walking through the village, Jenny had been trying to come to grips with living in one of those cardboard shacks, but now, standing in the cozy little tent, she was too relieved to speak. It had a canvas floor connected to the walls to keep out water and unwanted pests, and it was thick enough to protect against the tropical sun. It was furnished with a sturdy cot, a small end table with a battery-powered lantern, and several plastic tubs to hold her belongings. But the best thing was a funky rug that took up most of the free floor space. When she asked about it, they told her it had been hand woven for her by Aleena and some of the other village women. Jenny knelt down and felt it with her hands. It was made of thin wool fibers, a little rough to the touch, but sturdy and tightly woven. She guessed that it had taken many hours to complete.

As she rubbed her hands along the soft fibers, a lump rose in her throat, and she sniffed back a tear. Aleena knelt down beside her and hugged her. "Welcome to our lives," she said. Jenny felt like she was home.

Chapter 5
We're Not That Different

Nanci and Aleena left Jenny alone to give her time to unpack her clothes and get settled in. She only brought a large suitcase, a duffle bag, and her backpack, but after unpacking all of them, she realized she had brought too much. She would need her skirts and undergarments, but she also had a pile of t-shirts emblazoned with all sorts of iconography from college logos to superhero emblems to fast-food chains. Staring at them now stacked outside of the plastic tubs, too many to fit, she realized she only needed a handful. She decided to give one away every week until she could fit them in the tubs with the rest of her clothes.

After about an hour, Aleena returned and sat with her while they waited for Nanci. Jenny learned the young woman was only two years older than her but had already been married twice. She married the first time at only fourteen to a man thirty years her senior. The man had married her for only one reason: to bear children. He was a strict Muslim, and, when Aleena failed to provide him with any children in the first five years, he began to shun and abuse her. She was able to separate from him but her family refused to take her back. She ran away to the city where she met her current husband, Jean-Marc Zoumara. They fell in love quickly, and all seemed right except for one thing: Jean-Marc was a Christian. When Jean-Marc's family heard about their engagement, they forbid him from having anything to do with the Muslim Aleena. When he refused to comply, they cast both of them out. They lived in poverty until they met the Sharon's, who helped them settle in the Sangha village. Since that time, Aleena had converted from Islam to Christianity and was now a Sunday School teacher.

Jenny listened to Aleena's story intently. She was timid and did not readily offer information, but she seemed happy to provide it when Jenny asked. By the time Nanci returned to take them on a tour of the village, the two young women were talking and laughing like old friends.

The three women began to walk the dirt streets. To Jenny's surprise, she found them peaceful. After the earlier excitement, all the villagers had returned to their various places of interest: the men to the mining outpost, the women to their daily work, and the children to school. As they passed each home, Aleena called everyone by name—mothers at their work, old men too weak for mining, and toddlers too young for school. Each called back and greeted Jenny by name. They had been eagerly awaiting her arrival for weeks and were excited to meet her. They called her "sister" and gave her homemade gifts and other items. Jenny felt like she was returning to family.

As they walked along, Jenny studied the little village. Though the homes were little more than tents, they weren't crowded together like the ones she had seen at the airport. They were spaced in neat, even rows or grouped together in tight circles. The holes she'd seen in the sheets and cardboard walls, which had seemed random at first, now appeared intentionally placed to act as windows. The spaces between the houses were clear of debris, and the wild grass, which grew on the outskirts of the village, was short and manicured. She realized that the stones and loose items lining the paths had been placed there on purpose to act as boundaries for the rough streets. She saw little trash outside the homes, and she realized that the things she had thought were trash were actually the possessions of the villagers. In every home she saw mosquito-netting, one of the most important possessions of any inhabitant living in a land with disease-carrying insects. Every home also had a small water filtration device—cheap but vital to good health in a country with unsanitary water conditions. She saw outhouses and circular, open-topped chambers set aside from the homes near the outskirts of the village which she learned were communal showers the villagers took turns using.

They passed a long tent with both ends rolled up, which Nanci referred to as the hospital. This was where she spent much of her time tending to the sick and injured. The hospital was furnished with ten beds and several tables of supplies. Only one bed was occupied, by Nikolai, who was being tended by a large man with a shiny bald head and a gray-speckled beard who introduced himself as Sudaiq. He greeted Jenny with a blessing in the name of Allah and informed her that, in addition to serving as the chief physician, he was also the imam and de facto leader of the Muslim villagers. When the conversation turned to Seth, he told her all about how he assisted him in his duties. "That boy is not very good with remembering tasks, or medicines, or items," he said to her with a big smile, "but his smile makes everyone get better." She remembered that Seth had never been good with remembering names of drugs, bones, or muscle groups, nor at diagnosing patients, but his winning personality and bedside manner more than made up for those shortcomings.

They left the hospital and continued on towards the school, but Jenny's mind lingered on the friendly physician. Anticipating her trip, she had researched the Central African Republic and had been surprised to learn that much of the violence amongst its people was between Christians and Muslims. As an American living in the twenty-first century, she was familiar with the ideological clash between Islam and Christianity and the violence that sometimes went with it but had always seen that struggle as a Middle-Eastern problem. She would never have expected to find the same dynamic in the middle of the African jungle. Because of this, she hadn't known what to expect of the villagers. She had tried to enter the situation with an open mind, but despite her best efforts, she realized she expected to be treated with indifference or hostility by the Muslims.

But Sudaiq hadn't treated her that way at all. In fact, none of the villagers had, Muslim or Christian. So far, they had treated her and each other with nothing but kindness and hospitality. Yet, the incident earlier that morning hinted at deeper issues. She asked Nanci if there was much strife between villagers of the two religions.

"There was at the beginning," Nanci replied. "In fact, we had to separate the village into Muslim and Christian halves to keep them apart. But these people were on their last legs and had nowhere else to go. They were tired of violence and didn't have their hearts in it. I think they only squabbled with one another because that's how they'd always lived. They thought we expected it of them. But once the Sharon's told them they didn't have to fight and showed them how to live together in harmony, peace became the new norm. They can't get enough of it now. You saw how they wanted nothing to do with Mohammedou and his violent ways."

"I also saw them throw rocks at him," Jenny said.

"Well, yes, honey, you're right," Nanci conceded, "but old habits die hard. At least they didn't throw hunting spears at him, which I've seen them do before. Some of these people used to really hate each other."

"What changed?" Jenny asked.

Nanci raised her eyebrows. "Everything," she said. "These people used to just say that they were Christians and that they believed in God, but the Sharon's showed them what believing in God really means. They used to praise God and then curse their neighbor with the same mouth. The Sharon's got them to understand that Jesus is not a brutal, violent God whose wrath we must appease, but a God of forgiveness, who takes away our sins because he wants to but then expects us to act differently. When the villagers understood that God was unhappy with the way they treated their neighbors, including their neighbors of a different faith, they began to change."

"But what about the Muslim villagers?" asked Jenny. "That explanation doesn't seem like it would work for them?"

"Well, it was harder for them," Nanci admitted, "but not as hard as you might think. Most of the people in this country, Muslim or Christian, believe that they are serving the same one, true, almighty God. They just differ in how they think they are supposed to worship him. The Sharon's used basically the same argument, that the way they were treating their neighbors displeased God."

"But how did they convince them?" Jenny pressed. "I mean, that argument makes sense to me, but I've believed it all my life. How did they convince them that the violence displeased God, and that they needed to treat each other differently?"

"Love," Aleena said, entering the conversation for the first time. "Brother Elias and Sister Sharla and Sister Nanci and Brother Seth love us, just like Jesus loves us."

"Aleena is right," said Nanci with a small smile. "Brother and Sister Sharon loved everyone here unconditionally, both Christian *and* Muslim. They gave their time, their energy, their attention, and their resources to everyone. That was something that none of them had ever seen before. It took a little time, but once they saw the result of the Sharon's faith, they all listened and wanted to know how to be like them. From there, it was easy to explain to them the importance of loving one another the way Christ loves us. Like I said, it took longer for the Muslim villagers, but the proof was in the pudding: the Sharon's had peace, and that's what the people wanted more than anything else."

"Sister Nanci and Brother Seth help, too," Aleena reminded Nanci with a hug.

She smiled. "Yes, yes, and Ferdy, too. It's been a group effort, and we are making progress. But there are a few individuals who still need work."

As Nanci finished her last sentence, she inclined her head towards a small figure creeping from cover to cover towards the edge of the village as silent as a panther. Aleena sighed and shook her head in frustration. She started out after the small figure with a determined stride. Nanci giggled and followed her with Jenny close behind. As they drew closer, Jenny saw that it was a small, barefoot boy dressed in shorts and a t-shirt several sizes too big for him. The women approached quietly. They drew close before the boy noticed that he was being followed; when he did, he broke into a run. Aleena was hot on his tail, but the boy ran like a gazelle zig-zagging between shacks and garbage piles in a practiced manner. He was almost to the edge of the village when Nanci jumped out from behind a lean-to and he ran straight into her arms.

The boy struggled and squealed like a piglet, but Nanci only laughed. She planted a big, wet kiss on this cheek, after which he stopped struggling and resigned himself to his fate. Aleena reached them and smacked the boy on the head before launching into a fervent downpour of angry French. Jenny didn't catch much, but she didn't need a translator to understand the one-sided conversation. The boy was being scolded. He stood straight as a rod, with his head down, coming no higher than Aleena's elbow, and took the scolding.

Aleena was angry, but she couldn't maintain the heat of her passion long, especially in front of Jenny, who was a guest, and Nanci, who smiled like a cherub throughout the tirade. Eventually she ran out of words and her tone grew softer. She made a joke in French and tickled the boy lightly. Jenny couldn't catch the meaning, but she saw the immediate effect on the boy. He pulled his head into his shoulders like a turtle, and plastered an enormous frown across his face, the kind that children make when they're trying to cover up a smile. But he couldn't resist for long and broke out into a grin, giggling uncontrollably as Aleena and Nanci tickled him.

With the scolding now complete and the punishment dispensed, Aleena turned to Jenny and introduced the boy as Femi, her son. Jenny greeted him in French, but he ignored her proffered hand. Aleena sighed again and rolled her eyes. "Femi is very shy when he wants to be," she said. Jenny smiled and retracted her hand, and Femi still didn't look up at her. But the next time she looked at him, he was staring at her with his big, brown eyes. As soon as she made eye-contact, he glanced away. She laughed to herself.

They took Femi back to school, a clearing amongst the homes

near the village edge where the teachers taught the children as they sat in the dust. Aleena handed Femi back to his teacher, a young woman of about eighteen, who apologized for letting him escape again. She and the other teacher, an older middle-aged woman, seemed stretched to the limit to keep the twenty-five or so children in line. The age range was wide, stretching from toddlers of only a couple years, to pre-teens, a few of which already looked like adults. Aleena explained that they taught French and some English, along with math and a smattering of other subjects like history and life science. Nanci had already told Jenny that they needed her help in the school more than anywhere else. The thought of teaching young children excited her, but now that she saw the group of rowdy kids, half of which seemed to be clones of Femi, she wasn't so sure. But the more she watched them, the more intrigued she became. These children were different from the pitiful wraiths she'd seen outside the Bangui airport. Those children had looked at her with longing eyes that held no trace of hope and had already resigned themselves to a life of want and begging. But not these children. They also lived in squalor, but they were alive in ways that the children at the airport weren't. They wore the same rags, but the expressions on their faces were not those of defeated, hopeless wretches. A joy permeated their entire beings in subtle but unmistakable ways. These children had hope, perhaps unfounded based upon the circumstances in which they lived, but it was there in their eyes nonetheless. They were thriving, not just surviving.

Jenny pondered this as the two teachers paused their lessons and introduced her to the children. The children were excited to learn that she would be their new teacher and were disappointed when informed that she would not be starting for a couple more days. All of them waved goodbye to her as she left to continue the tour. There wasn't much more for her to see, and, as Nanci showed her the last buildings, she found herself thinking of the children and wanting to ask about the liveliness they had. She didn't know how to phrase her question, so instead she asked Aleena about Femi's age.

Aleena's answer surprised her. "We don't know. Jean-Marc and I found him around the time we met Brother and Sister Sharon, when we were running from our families. No one knows where he came from. Even he might not know. He is very young, so we don't push him too hard, but we think he was running away from someone or something. Jean-Marc and I have always wanted a child, and he needed a mother and a father, so we took him in."

"He's a group project," Nanci added. "Whoever said it takes a village to raise a child must have been thinking of Femi. He was a little animal before Jean-Marc and Aleena took him in. He did whatever it took to survive. We still have a problem with him stealing anything that isn't locked down. He's gotten more whippin's from more people in this village than most kids get in their lifetime, but, my-oh-my, if that boy isn't strong willed!"

"He's so adorable though! How do you stay upset with him?" Jenny said.

Both women laughed and agreed with her. "It's hard," Nanci replied, "but what else can we do? He'd still be a little animal if it weren't for Aleena, and Jean-Marc, and this village. We all might still be animals if it weren't for people that loved us enough to be hard on us."

Jenny agreed, but before she could reply, a bell rang to announce that lunch was ready. They joined a stream of people moving towards the pavilion. They arrived to find several women setting up tables and chairs and readying various kettles and platters of food. Aleena and Nanci took places behind the line of tables to serve, and Jenny, not wanting to be left out, joined them. The pavilion filled with more women and their children, and before long, the men began to arrive in twos and threes, tired and dusty from working in the mining camp. Soon the pavilion was full, but no one began to eat. As the hot food sat there and continued to cool, Jenny looked to Nanci for an explanation.

"Wait for it," she whispered.

As if on cue, the entire village turned and watched Seth appear from one of the paths and rush into the clearing. The villagers clapped and cheered as he approached and slapped him on the back when he came to the front of the line. His face turned red, but he smiled too as he apologized for his tardiness. When the laughter subsided, they all bowed their heads as he prayed for the food, cheering once more when he finished and released them to eat.

As Jenny served, she watched Seth interact with the villagers. He walked back and forth between various groups, patting people on the backs, laughing with one, arguing with another, and chasing children when they ran past him. Jenny saw how the people treated him too, looking at him with adoring eyes, laughing at his corny jokes, and good-naturedly teasing him about various things. They treated him with a deference that most people reserved for their elders or employers. Jenny saw that they not only loved but respected him, too. She could only wonder about what things he had done and what situations he had been through to earn that respect. He was so different from the smooth, dapper, prideful boy she had known. Yet, she also felt that he must have been this way all along somewhere deep inside.

The entire village passed through the line quickly, some two hundred people. The meal consisted of a thick stew flavored with curry and bits of chicken served over a bed of fufu, a dish made of boiled cassava ground into a paste with a texture somewhere between oatmeal and mashed potatoes. They also had slices of bread, which they used as spoons to eat the fufu, and to mop up the remains of the stew. The meal was simple, but hot, well-made, and filling. When Jenny's turn to eat came, she tasted the stew carefully. It wasn't the best flavor in the world, but neither was it the worst, and it grew on her the more she ate. Though she had trouble using the bread as a spoon, she finished her plate and asked for more.

She looked around for something to drink until Nanci informed her that because their only drink was water which had to be purified, they always went home and drank water purified with their individual filters. After cleaning up, Nanci took Jenny back to her tent and showed her how to use her own filter. The first cup of water she drank was lukewarm like bathwater, but it felt like glacier water to Jenny's thirsty body.

Before the workers returned to the quarry, Aleena introduced Jenny to her husband, Jean-Marc. He was of average height and thin but with a firm grip and a wide smile. He was jovial with a wicked sense of humor directed mostly at his wife, though he was also very affectionate with her. Jenny sensed a connection between them that went far beyond that of a normal husband and wife. They had been through the fire together, and the bonds of love forged between them were strong. Jenny sensed this was a common theme running throughout the village. The villagers were bound by a love that had been built and strengthened through fire.

After the men returned to the quarry, Aleena excused herself so she could return home and prepare dinner. Jenny offered to help, but she insisted that she continue getting to know the village and the people. Nanci agreed, stating that she would have plenty of work to do soon. Jenny didn't mention that she was absolutely exhausted; in addition to her two days of travel, her internal clock was telling her it was six o'clock in the morning, and that she had stayed up far too late. She looked up at the sun, which was high in the sky. It was too hot to sleep, but she felt like dropping anyway. She longed to try out the new cot in her tent, but Nanci, whose source of energy seemed inexhaustible, led her out of the village towards the fields.

Along the way, they talked about agriculture. Nanci told her the village had several farmers who cultivated different crops and taught the other villagers how to raise them. Since they were living in a protected wildlife reserve and couldn't cut down any trees without agitating the park rangers, they had to grow their food in natural clearings. This meant the fields were of various shapes and sizes and located at different distances from the village itself. The fields next to the village were mostly cassava and corn, but further away they had fields of okra, yams, peanuts, rice, and garlic. Maintaining the fields was hard work. Jungle soil is notoriously low in nutrients and minerals, and the farmers had to work the land hard. Several of them also lived in small shacks next to the fields to protect them from nighttime foragers like antelope and monkeys. Their tools were rudimentary, their knowledge of farming even more so, but the fields were crucial to their survival in the jungle. The villagers owned and shared all the crops, for without them, they would have to depend on regular shipments of food from a nearby town for survival, something they could not do and keep their way of life secret.

Jenny wanted to ask Nanci why their way of life needed to be so secret but decided against it. A few things didn't add up, but she chalked it up to her inexperience with the culture. She assumed that everything would make sense in time.

When they reached the closest fields, Jenny was surprised to see that ninety-five percent of the field workers were women. Nanci sensed her confusion and reminded her that the men worked in the quarry all day, leaving most of the farming to the women. She explained that the men received wages from Clayton Mercury, part of which they paid into a communal fund for the crops, farming equipment, and other bulk supplies. They used the rest to buy individual items and supplies which Seth or Ferdy picked up from the villages on regular trips.

They spent the rest of the afternoon traveling between the different fields helping where needed. By the time they returned to the village, dinner was approaching, but Jenny was too tired to care. Jet-lag had taken her with a vengeance, and all she wanted to do was crash somewhere and sleep for hours. But as they walked between the homes, waving to the women preparing their meals, an assortment of appetizing aromas tickled her nostrils, and she realized that she was hungry too. She wondered how meals would work for her and was about to ask Nanci, when they rounded a corner and entered the small circle of tents that made up their shared neighborhood. There in the center of the ring of tents, on a picnic table underneath an awning, a beautiful feast was laid out. Fresh fish sizzled in a skillet next to a large pan of chicken sautéed in garlic and cumin. A mountain of cassava fufu over-shadowed dishes of fried okra and yams. A basket of fresh bread was set to the side with a plate of fried bananas for dessert. Standing over it all, beaming like the last rays of the setting sun, was Aleena.

"Surprise," she said, and Jenny understood why she hadn't let her help prepare.

Jean-Marc and Ferdy joined them by the time they'd finished washing up, and, several minutes after they said grace, Seth rushed up, apologizing once again for his tardiness. They ate leisurely, savoring the tasty morsels Aleena had spent hours preparing. Judging by the way the others relished each individual dish, Jenny decided that it must have been a special meal. She liked everything, but her favorite dish was the fried bananas. The six of them talked and laughed long after the meal was over, drinking cups of Folger's coffee from Elias Sharon's private stash. As the sun slipped below the surrounding jungle, Ferdy lit several torches, and they continued to fellowship, talking about any topic that came to mind. The sun continued to set, plunging the world beyond the torches into shadow and giving the illusion they alone were the sole inhabitants of the earth. The nocturnal birds and insects emerged, invisible in the darkness outside the ring of torches, but making themselves known by their unique sounds. It was the most memorable meal Jenny could remember. She only wished she had been awake for more of it. She nodded off only twice during the meal, and by the time the torches were lit she couldn't keep her eyes open. Several times she started awake to see them all staring at her. They smiled and tried to get her to go to bed, but she wanted to be as accommodating to them as they had been to her. She resolved to stay until the end, no matter how many times she fell asleep.

Near the end of the evening, while the ladies were cleaning up, Jenny did catch a conversation, one she suspected she was not meant to hear. She had been dozing again, sitting at the table with her head propped up on her hands. She awoke once more but didn't open her eyes. As she drifted off again, she heard Ferdy speaking to Seth. Something in his tone caught her attention.

"Colonel Massi is back."

"What? How? I thought you got him suspended weeks ago."

"No, Seth, I said I would report the information to contacts I have, who would then pass it on to the President's advisors. I never guaranteed the colonel would be suspended. Evidently they were only able to get him transferred to another post."

"What, you mean child slavery, accepting bribes, and outright murder aren't enough to get a man suspended from the army?"

"Seth, you know that the government is still weak. There are massive limitations to its ability to affect change, and, more importantly, its ability to back up change. And don't forget that some of those bribes Massi takes are our own."

"Yes, but the only reason we bribe him is because he's a brutal savage and if we don't, he'll come marching down here with a battalion of troops and demand to know what's going on. And we can't have that, especially if the reports you've heard about him being tied into the Anti-Balaka are true."

"Oh, they're not reports anymore. I have firm proof that Colonel Massi is a high-ranking member of the Anti-Balaka."

"Well, why is he still in the army if he's a member of a dissident militia?"

"Because he is an experienced soldier, and we don't have many of those left in the C.A.R. Most of them have fled or turned mercenary. It pays more."

"That must have been why Clayton told me to increase our bribes to the park rangers."

"He told you to increase the bribes? When?"

"Today after the business with Djotodia. He said that if the park rangers get a whiff of what's really going on here, they'll sell us to the Anti-Balaka in a heartbeat."

"I'd like to believe in my fellow countrymen more than our

Canadian mercenary does, but I can't say I disagree. We'll just have to be more careful, Seth."

"I know, I know. Oh, God I miss the Sharon's. They're still stuck in Paris?"

"Yes. And they have no timetable to give us for when they'll be back."

"Okay. We'll just have to keep going as we are for now."

Ferdy paused before continuing. "Are you okay boy? You've been working non-stop for weeks now. You look exhausted."

"I am. But there's just so much to do, especially with the Sharon's gone."

"True, true. But you'll be no use to anyone if you run yourself into the ground. Don't forget to stop and breath."

Jenny decided that she had eavesdropped enough and stirred before opening her eyes. Seth and Ferdy, standing several yards away, looked at her, perhaps to gauge how much she had heard, but she pretended not to see them. She yawned and told everyone she was finally giving in and going to sleep. The men thanked her, the women fussed over her, and they all thanked her again for being there. Right before she entered her tent, Seth caught up to her.

"So, how was your first day, girl?" he asked her.

"It's been insane! So much to take in and learn. I don't know how you do it all. But I'm really happy to be here."

"Good, because we're all happy to have you here. You're going to be able to help us so much. We've needed good help like you for a while now." He said "us," and "we," like a king speaking in the royal we.

"Thanks Seth," she replied. "I can't wait to do something useful." She began to duck into her tent.

But Seth had one more thing to say. "Hey, seriously, sorry for forgetting about you getting here today. I didn't forget that you were coming, I just briefly forgot that it was today."

"Don't worry about it, Seth. You seem like you have a lot of responsibilities."

"I do. But I had planned to be a little more present on your first day. It's just with the Sharon's still gone, and with the whole business with Mohammedou and Nikolai, I was just running ragged today. I'm sorry."

He danced back and forth from one foot to the other like a boy trying to apologize for something he didn't want to admit he had done. She had never seen him like this before and would've found it funny if she hadn't been so tired. She tried to soothe him.

"No, Seth seriously, it's not a problem. I want to be a help here, not a hindrance. Besides, Nanci and Aleena took great care of me. I've had a wonderful day."

He looked relieved. He thanked her once again for coming and then bid her goodnight. Jenny zipped her tent shut and got ready for bed. She could barely keep her eyes open long enough to change her clothes. But despite her fatigue, sleep eluded her. The unfamiliar setting, the mosquito-netting, the strange sounds outside the tent, and the events of the day were conspiring to overcome her jet-lag. She needed help. At home, she would listen to music before falling to asleep. She hadn't thought she would need it tonight, because she was so tired. Apparently, she did.

She popped in her headphones and selected a slow country ballad. She wasn't much of a country music fan, but this song had struck her the first time she'd heard it, at a time in her life when she was still struggling with the call she felt in her heart to go to the C.A.R. It seemed appropriate. The sweet sounds of the strings and piano carried her swiftly to sleep. Just before she lost consciousness, she thought about the conversation she had overheard between Ferdy and Seth. In her drowsy state, she could only remember that it had alarmed her. But then she thought of all the people she had met and the love they had shown her. It didn't erase her worries, but it did make her feel like she could handle whatever Africa had in store for her.

Chapter 6
Heavenly Sounds

Jenny slept in the next morning and almost missed a delicious breakfast of eggs, fresh fruit, and corn bread prepared by Nanci and Ferdy. Seth came late again for the meal, rushing in with his hair wet from the shower. When he excused himself to go work on his sermon, Jenny realized she had lost track of the days—Sunday had already arrived. She had heard many stories about the lively African church services and was excited to experience one for herself. But then Nanci asked her to teach one of the Sunday School classes. "Don't worry darlin'," she assured her when she began to protest. "It'll be easy for you. You'll have nothing to worry about." Jenny thought of a few things to worry about like the fact that she spoke only basic French and zero Sango, but she reminded herself that she had come to serve. If they needed her to teach Sunday School, that's what she would do.

After breakfast, she helped Nanci clean up, and then they headed over to the pavilion where the villagers had already begun to gather. The service hadn't started yet, but the villagers were already deep in prayer, from the youngest child to the oldest grandparent. Some prayed together in small groups, while others prayed alone, pacing the aisles or kneeling in the dust. They were loud, louder than any group of worshippers Jenny had ever heard. She followed Nanci to a place near the left side of the pavilion where several dozen log benches sat and knelt to pray. However, she didn't do much praying.

She tried hard to focus, but the people around her constantly drew her attention. Several times she caught herself staring. An older woman was kneeling with her face in the dust rocking back and forth all while crying out in a language Jenny could not identify. Another woman lay on her back, groaning to the heavens with sounds that weren't in any language at all. A man squatting near the back shook like he was having a seizure, but made no sound. Two young boys paced the center aisle and rambled in French and Sango, oblivious to the two small girls praying for each other over which they stepped. Jenny had been in many prayer meetings, but here she found a fervency and a passion she'd never experienced.

The atmosphere intensified as more people arrived and added their prayers. Later, Jenny learned that the Muslim villagers met at the same time in one of the fields for their sabbath meeting, and that a handful of the villagers didn't attend either meeting. But there was still over a hundred people gathered under the pavilion. As the minutes ticked by, Jenny realized there was no official start time. All they did was gather and pray. By the time Seth arrived (last as usual) the pavilion was in a roar as over a hundred voices cried out to God. Seth joined right in. After several minutes, he walked over to a corner of the pavilion to retrieve a stool and a beat-up guitar. In response to a silent signal, several of the villagers, two boys and three women, moved to the front and turned around to face the group. Seth set the stool next to them and began to tune the guitar. As he did, he looked out into the crowd. His eyes lit up as they settled on Jenny, and he headed straight towards her.

"Jenny, you can still play guitar, right?" he asked when he reached her.

She froze for just a second. It was true, she could play the guitar a little, but she hadn't played much in front of other people. She reminded Seth of this.

"Yeah, but you were always better than me," he replied. That was also true. They had both messed around on the guitar back in the day, and Jenny had always been better than Seth. But the difference had been only slight; neither had been very good. She had kept up on the instrument since he had left, but only for her own amusement. "All you have to do is play what you know," he said. "They don't really care what it is as long as they can worship to it. I'll sing if you play."

Jenny didn't want to do it, but she reminded herself one more time that she had come to serve.

"I'll do my best," she replied.

"Great!" he said. "Start with 'How Great is Our God.' They love that one."

There was no time for Jenny to rehearse. As soon as Seth finished talking, he motioned her to follow him to the front. She sat on the stool and picked up the guitar. Little pieces of wood were chipping off, and the strings looked ready to pop at any second. Words in various handwritings and inks had been scrawled across the body and the back of the neck. It didn't look capable of playing a single note in-tune. But she didn't have time to worry about that. As soon as she sat down, Seth motioned for her to play. As she strummed the chords to "How Great is Our God," the congregation quieted down a little and transitioned from prayer to worship. To Jenny's ears, the chords sounded harsh and off-putting, but the villagers didn't seem to notice. Seth led them in the familiar words of the song, and they all joined in, some singing and some just worshipping with hands lifted toward heaven.

Backed by the five singers, Seth led them in a seemingly random mix of the song's verses, chorus, and bridge, in English first, then in French, and then in Sango. He signaled for Jenny to keep playing over and over so many times that she hesitated to look at the audience for fear of seeing annoyance on their faces. But the villagers didn't seem to care. They worshipped with no regard for the music or the singers. For them, the music only facilitated what they had already been doing. Jenny couldn't help but feel self-conscious, especially as the song dragged on, but her mind moved from what she was doing into a more spiritual place. She found herself singing the familiar words with a new sense of praise–not just repeating sounds, but sincerely expressing worship unto God. When the villagers began to sing in Sango, the atmosphere under the pavilion became so tender that, even though she couldn't understand the language, she had to blink back tears. She hadn't been that affected by a song in a long time.

After they finished the song, Seth whispered to her that they wanted a fast song next. The first that came to her mind was "I Am Free" made popular by the Newsboys. With only that one beat-up guitar, the song lacked all the bells and whistles Jenny was used to, but the villagers, who had never heard the song before, loved it. They particularly liked the call and response format of the chorus, so Seth repeated it many times. The people jumped and danced to the music, and some of them even ran around the area. Every face was smiling, including Jenny's.

After "I Am Free" the people wanted another slow song, so Jenny played "Lead Me to the Cross," another new one for the villagers. After the song was over, Seth stood and exhorted the people to worship though they needed no encouragement. There was nothing they liked better than praising their God. They danced and jumped and shouted more without the music than they had with it. It was crazy, but Jenny couldn't help but join in. She had always been a reserved worshipper, but there was something infectious about the way the people showed their love for Jesus that pulled her to her feet and prompted her to shout louder than she ever had in a church service.

Once the congregation settled down, Seth thanked them all for coming and dismissed them to their Sunday School classes. The adults stayed under the pavilion where Ferdy was to teach them about the importance of baptism. The children broke up into several groups based on age and scattered around the fringes of the open space. Each group had one or two teachers and five to seven students. Aleena took Jenny's hand and led her over to the group she taught. It was made up of two girls and five boys including Femi, all aged eight to ten. The boys were rowdy, but Aleena quieted them down with one sharp word. Then she told them that they had a new teacher called "Miss. Jenny" who would be helping her teach the children the stories of the Old Testament. Then with no warning at all, Aleena announced that Jenny would now teach them the story of Daniel in the Lion's Den. Fortunately for Jenny, it was an easy story she had read many times, and she told it with as much enthusiasm as possible. But the children sat stone-faced and stared at her throughout most of it, only showing interest when she mentioned the lions.

The children looked confused when she finished the story until Aleena began to talk to them in French and Sango. Jenny realized they didn't understand much English, just as she'd feared. From the little French she knew, she picked up that Aleena was retelling them the entire story. She felt embarrassed until Aleena came to the part about the lion's den. Then the children leaned forward with wide eyes, occasionally looking Jenny's way and understanding what she had been saying. At the climax of the story, Aleena emphasized the word "lion", which in French sounded like "lee-own." She repeated the word and directed the classes attention to Jenny. They stared up at her. Not knowing what was expected of her, Jenny raised her hands like claws and gave her best roar. The children gasped and began to jabber amongst themselves as Aleena laughed.

After that, they loosened up while Aleena finished retelling the story. At the end, she asked Jenny what they should have learned. She told the children something like "if you love God, no matter what happens, he will always take care of you." The impact of her own words struck her as she remembered that she was in a war-torn, famine-ridden country, where lives were threatened every day. She began to draw a connection between the stories in the Bible and the look of hope she saw in the eyes of the children. It made her realize just how crucial her work would be.

After about half an hour, the adult class broke up and the people left to get a drink or to relieve themselves. Soon, everyone gathered back underneath the pavilion, and Seth asked Jenny to play another song. The people clambered for "I Am Free," so she played it again. The people sang and praised God with the same vibrance they had the first time. Once Seth ended the song, he exhorted the people to worship, and, once again, they worshipped harder than they had with the music. As the volume died down, Seth opened his Bible and began to read. The other singers quietly made their way back to their seats, so Jenny did too, realizing that Seth had begun his sermon. He had given no segue to warn her. Some of the older and younger ones sat down, but many did not and shouted back words of encouragement at Seth each time he raised his voice. Jenny couldn't find a seat on any of the benches and had to stand off to the side of the pavilion. As the service continued, she grew tired and sat down in the dirt with the children, who were just as interested in the preaching as the adults were.

Jenny had never heard Seth preach before and was blown away with how accomplished he was. His words, already eloquent and coherent in English, were made more impressive because he had to translate many of them into French or Sango depending on whether the audience understood him. He spoke with clarity and confidence. His thoughts were well-formed, poignant, and effective, betraying a wisdom beyond his years. To her amazement, he preached without notes and only looked at his Bible to quote passages. She could hardly believe he was the same person. The only thing she recognized, was his passion, which exploded out of him like a geyser.

Seth preached for almost an hour about surrendering to the will of God. He used Matthew 26 as his text, where Jesus prays that the cup of suffering would pass from him, but accepts it if it be God's will. The villagers kept up their enthusiasm throughout the whole sermon. Jenny's stomach began to growl, as did the little tummies of the children surrounding her, but no one left, and no one fell asleep. As Seth began to wrap up his sermon, he motioned for Jenny to come up. She grabbed the guitar and returned to the stool where she played background music as he finished. He had been talking for some time about how it was the duty of every person to accept God's will and give up their own.

"… And one of the main ways we act out the will of God," he continued, "is by treating each other correctly. How we treat our neighbor determines whether we have the love of Jesus inside of us. Fighting amongst ourselves does not show the love of Jesus. Hurting each other does not fulfill the will of God. 'But what about when someone hurts me?' you may ask. 'What about the people who have burned our homes and killed our families?' Jesus gave us the answer. He said, 'I say unto you, love your enemies, bless them that curse you, do good to them that hate you, and pray for them which despitefully use you and persecute you.' The only way to fight violence is with love. If we want to change this country, we need to love people as Christ loved them."

By this point, many of the people were weeping and kneeling at their places. As Seth ended, many of them came to the front and prayed with one another, or asked Seth to pray for them. They cried out for God to show them his will and to help them accomplish it as Jesus did.

Through it all, Jenny sat on the stool and played as the cries of the people tugged at her heart. As she listened to the heartfelt cries, she thought about all the things the people lacked and all the hardships they endured just to survive the destructive forces raging around them. That they were asking God to show them how to help others, rather than praying for God to help themselves, smote Jenny's heart to the core. The logical part of her mind could not fathom how they could be so selfless in such a selfish world. But the other part of her mind, the spiritual, loving, emotional part of her mind, instinctively grasped the situation and joined in, crying out to God in response. She began to pray, asking God to help her have the same selflessness in fulfilling his will.

The people prayed for quite a while. No one kept track of time. There was nothing else scheduled for the day, and they were already doing the most important thing. Eventually the intensity of the prayer tapered, at which time Seth returned to the front from where he had been praying with an old man and addressed the people. His remarks were short and consisted of him reminding the congregation that waiting for them in heaven was a home where there would be no more violence, sickness, famine, or pain. As the congregation cheered and leaped for joy, he took the guitar from Jenny and began to play. The congregation cheered louder as they recognized the song he was playing. The song was called "He Bled for Us," and it went like this:

> *He bled for us, He bled for us*
> *We bleed for each other*
> *As He bled for us*
> *Jesus my savior, He bled on a tree*
> *I'll bleed for my brother*
> *My brother loves me*

The song had four similar sections that used the same melody and only changed the words. Like with the other songs, the whole congregation sang each part multiple times in multiple languages. It was colorful, upbeat, and infectiously positive, despite the heavy themes of death and sacrifice with which it dealt. As they repeated the same lines over and over again, the lyrics sank into Jenny's heart. The villagers seemed to inhabit the song deeply, for, like Jesus, they had literally bled and died for each other, and were now declaring their willingness to do so again. For just a moment, Jenny felt tiny, dwarfed by that gigantic possibility: greater love has no man than he who lays down his life for his friend. A lump formed in her throat and throbbed until she thought she couldn't bare it. Then she realized where she was, and that she, too, might be called upon to give up her life for a friend in this wet, smelly, dangerous, lovable country so far from her home. She knew she wasn't ready to face that yet, but she was getting there. The lump shrank and disappeared, and her heart soared as she joined in with the villagers in their song.

When they finished singing, Seth quieted them all down and introduced Jenny as their new teacher, guitar-player, and neighbor. The people cheered and clapped their hands while those closest to her gave her a hug or a pat on the back. Then Seth gave her a scare by asking her to greet the crowd. The lump in her throat grew, and she choked her way through a "thank you" and a "glad to be here." Thankfully, Seth stepped back in and thanked the crowd for giving Jenny such a wonderful introduction to how they did church. Then the villagers did something that wrenched Jenny's heart and caused that lump to grow into a full-fledged mound. Before Seth could finish speaking, they lifted their hands and thanked God for sending Jenny to them. She lost control then and began to cry great big tears of thankfulness and joy as Nanci and Aleena hugged her. The village of Sangha was quickly finding its way into her heart.

Once the service was complete, the entire congregation dispersed to their homes only to return with pots, pans, and silverware. Soon their Muslim neighbors returned from their services in the fields and joined in making dinner. The meal consisted of bread and fufu again, but with lamb and rosemary stew this time, instead of chicken and curry. It was a meager meal, but in consistency only; in passion, compassion, and gratefulness, it was a bountiful feast enjoyed by all. The villagers ate and laughed throughout the late afternoon and into the evening, heedless of the mosquitos and humidity. As the sun dipped below the horizon, and darkness began to fall, the jovial throng broke up, the children scampering off to chase butterflies, the women gathering their pots and pans for washing, and the men rearranging the tables and benches. Jenny helped in any way that she could, and then walked back to her tent with Ferdy, Nanci, and Seth. Once there, they sat at the picnic table and talked into the night, continuing to laugh and tell stories, most of which centered on Seth. There was the time when he left his tent unzipped one night and monkeys got into his clothes. The next morning some nosy children found his underwear scattered across the lawn and wore them all over the village. It took hours for Seth to get them all back. Another time he let Femi borrow his hat, and the precocious boy wore it down to the river where he accidentally dropped it in a crocodile nest. The hissing mother refused to let anyone close enough to retrieve it. They had to wait until her eggs hatched and her young were old enough to leave the nest, at which point the hat was hardly worth wearing. Jenny added her own story of a time when they were in college and Seth stayed up too late at her house on the night before a test and didn't have time to study. He went home and studied all night but was so tired in the morning that he went to the wrong class. After finding the right room, he had only half a class period to do the test. The worst part (in Jenny's opinion) was that he still aced the test while she, who had studied plenty and gotten a good night's rest, received an A-minus.

They had great fun that night but Jenny couldn't make it to the end. Her jet-lag was still catching up with her, and, instead of trying to stay up like the night before, she thanked them all and excused herself. Nanci and Ferdy soon followed her lead and retired to their tents. Seth lingered for a moment to thank Jenny for playing the guitar for him at the service.

"You've been practicing, haven't you?" he said.

"A bit," she replied. "I've played in church a few times, but I never thought it would be useful here."

"You should play from now on."

"Really? Are you sure?"

"Totally," he said, drawing out the long 'o' in *totally*. "It's one less thing I'll have to do. Plus, you did way better than I usually do. Did you see the people? They loved it."

"You mean they're not always like that?" Jenny asked, a little self-consciously.

"Well, yeah, they are. But I could tell that they were excited to have you there and to hear you play."

Jenny sighed. "These people are so wonderful. I can't even begin to imagine how they can be so happy and hopeful and live like this.

And for them to be happy just for someone like me to be here? It's so humbling."

Seth paused and shook his head before replying. "Yes, they are wonderful," he said. "I've never met any people like them before. They seriously believe that God has blessed them beyond what they deserve, and that those blessings are reason enough for them to share everything they have with each other. And you know what? They're right. They *are* blessed, as are we all, and, because they are blessed, they *should* share everything they have. I imagine this is what the early church must have been like. They held everything they had in common, not because they were forced to, but because they wanted to, and they believed that they should. These people have come so far, and it's really not anything that I or the Sharon's have done. It's the people themselves. Take away the negative influences, point them in the right direction, and they head towards righteousness on their own. It's not what we would think of as a utopia, but it's getting there. It's like a tiny glimpse of what living in the kingdom of heaven will be like."

"I can't believe that I get to be a part of it," Jenny said.

"Yes, and they're happy to have you here. Aleena told me you taught Sunday School, too. You're already making a difference. I will have to teach you 'He Bled for Us' though."

"Yeah, I'd love to learn that one. The villagers loved it! But I've never heard it before. Who's wrote it?"

"Yours truly."

"Really? You wrote a song?"

"Kind of. The villagers like to make up their own tunes and sing random lyrics. One time I heard some of them singing a tune with 'he bled for us, he bled for us' over and over. I sat them down, picked out a few chords, wrote some more lyrics, and then taught it to them. We sang it in church, and it was a massive hit. We sing it almost every service now. Even some of the Muslim villagers sing it too."

"It's a serious song, but they sing it with so much life."

"That about sums up the attitude of the entire village. They live amidst serious circumstances, but they're full of life. Rather than be depressed, they're optimistic. Seriously, they're unquenchable."

He gave a huge yawn as he finished his last sentence and rubbed his eyes. Jenny smiled.

"Wow, you seem more tired than me, and I'm still on Missouri time," she said.

He groaned in mock anguish. "I am exhausted, Jenny. With the Sharon's gone, I've got to do all the church stuff, plus a hundred other things that I didn't know they did. I cannot wait for them to get back. Hopefully, they'll get all that customs stuff figured out soon."

He bid her goodnight and shuffled off into the darkness. She entered her tent and zipped it up tight. She felt exhaustion closing in as she dressed for bed. This time, as she laid down, she put her headphones in immediately to ease her sleep. The first song that popped-up on her playlist was an upbeat worship tune, not a good sleeping song, but she let it play anyway. It made her think of the villagers lifting their hands and singing praises to God together in one mind and one accord. She smiled as she thought about the wonderful blessing that had been given to her: an opportunity to experience the love and peace of God in a tiny village hidden deep in the jungles of Africa. As the chiming guitar melodies and ambient background noises faded towards a close, she had just enough time to hit pause on her phone before she fell asleep.

Chapter 7
Like a Lion

Monday started early, before the sun was up, with a boisterous wake-up call from Ferdy. For breakfast they had reheated fufu (Jenny would be sick of it by the week's end) and cinnamon sauce washed down with a glass of lukewarm water. She was becoming apt at using the small filter to clean her water but was still tempted to drink it unfiltered. But Nanci told her a story how she had drunk the water once in haste without filtering it and spent the next two weeks in bed with infectious diarrhea. Jenny continued to filter her water.

After breakfast, Ferdy asked her to come with him to fetch the day's supply of water from the river. On the way, he explained that each family was responsible for the well-being of its members, but they all lived in little groups or "neighborhoods" of two to four families that shared larger duties such as collecting supplies and slaughtering livestock. Jenny's new neighborhood consisted of herself, Nanci, Ferdy, the Sharon's, occasionally the Zoumara's, and Seth. "That boy needs five mothers," Ferdy chuckled.

To fetch the water, they had to walk to the river, a tributary of the Kadéï River, itself a tributary of the larger Sangha River which empties into the mighty Congo River far to the south. The villagers had built a crude dock in a small cove on the bank of the river through which a gentle eddy flowed. They had cleared many of the bushes and reeds away, but Ferdy still warned her to watch out for crocodiles. When they reached the dock and filled their buckets,

Jenny noticed the only other people getting water were men. She soon found out why. The distance from the village to the river wasn't far, no more than a couple hundred yards, but to a girl carrying a five-gallon bucket of water it felt like a mile. Jenny struggled along with one bucket, while Ferdy carried one in each of his strong arms without so much as a strain. He outpaced her and returned to carry her bucket the rest of the way. Nanci looked confused when they returned to their neighborhood but began to giggle and scold Ferdy when she realized what he had made Jenny do. Ferdy simply stated, "Now, she knows where the water is." Jenny rubbed her sore arms and laughed sarcastically at his little joke.

Next, Nanci sent them to get supplies, along with a stern warning to Ferdy about not letting Jenny carry items that were too heavy for her. Ferdy chuckled to himself as he led Jenny toward the center of the village to a large military tent that covered a large assortment of crates and boxes. While they waited in line, Ferdy told her how each month he collected a portion of the villagers' mining wages and then drove to Bayanga or to Nola to purchase basic supplies like salt, water filters, soap, and shoes. The supplies were then rationed out to the villagers each week or passed out as needed. Jenny asked him how smoothly the system worked. Ferdy shrugged his shoulders. "It has problems. Everything always does. But it is the best system we have, and it keeps the people from having to go into town themselves. Most outsiders think I am buying the supplies to distribute to many villages in this area, and I do spread a bit around to keep up appearances, but ninety-nine percent of the supplies are for this village."

When they got to the front of the line, they were greeted by a short, round, middle-aged woman named Maria whose job was to protect and administer the supplies. Her two tall teenage sons, Peter and James, helped her. Her husband Sébastien worked in the quarry with the other men but helped her during the mornings. As Maria gave them their supplies, they heard raised voices at the other end of the tent. Sébastien, a large potbellied man, was yelling in French at a short, mousey-looking man. Much of the conversation was too fast for Jenny to catch, but she recognized "voleur", the French word for "thief," several times. After a minute, Sébastien ran the smaller man out of the tent. Maria went back to him and they spoke to each other in harsh tones as she led him to the front of the tent. Sébastien scowled at his wife, but his face broke out into a massive grin when he caught sight of Jenny and Ferdy. He gave Ferdy a bear-hug and would have enveloped Jenny in one as well if Ferdy hadn't steered her away with a cordial "au revoir."

"The other man was trying to get one more ration of lard than everyone else," Ferdy said as they walked back, "or so Sébastien thought."

"I see," Jenny replied.

Ferdy chuckled. "Sébastien does not tolerate dishonest people. He is like the gorilla: fierce, but gentle with those he loves."

Jenny gave him a strange look. "Fierce *and* gentle like a gorilla?"

Ferdy chuckled once again. "One day I will take you to see the gorilla, and you will see that he is both a madman *and* a gentleman."

After they returned to Nanci, Jenny helped her prepare food for the rest of the week which consisted mostly of grinding cassava to make fufu. Then it was time for school. She followed Nanci back to the clearing they had visited on her first day and taught reading for the next three hours. It was exhausting. She had never taught children to read, a herculean task. To make matters worse, she taught the same age group that had barely been able to sit still during her half-hour Bible story the day before. By the time the second hour began, the adolescent boys were quivering with suppressed energy. To their credit, they tried hard, but they couldn't suppress their restlessness for long. At least Aleena was close by at all times to settle them down, but her efforts were only a delaying tactic. Jenny spent most of the time corralling the boys, especially Femi, who, though he barely spoke a word to Jenny, was quite the clown with his friends. She grew frustrated and wanted to lash out at them, but her anger softened each time by the memory of the children she'd seen at the airport. At least these youngsters had something to be excited about.

Around noon, the classes broke for lunch. Jenny wanted to go find a place to lie down and rest, but Aleena directed her to the pavilion once again to help serve lunch. They arrived just as the miners were returning. Lunch once more consisted of a spicy stew but served over imported rice this time instead of fufu. After lunch it was back to school where Jenny taught for another three hours. When she finally released the children, they bolted from the clearing like a bunch of wild zebras, screaming and snorting in utter glee. Despite her fatigue, Jenny smiled at them. They had been hard to corral but seeing the life inside of them made it all worthwhile.

After helping the other teachers clean up the area, Jenny once again set her mind on finding a place to rest. But her work wasn't finished. Aleena took her to the animal pens where they kept the goats, chickens, and one old donkey and gathered their daily allotment of eggs. Then she showed her a secluded spot on the river where the villagers did their laundry. They joined several other women and washed clothes in the river. After that, they trekked back to the village and hung them all out to dry, finishing just in time for Nanci to find and take them out to the fields where they worked for an hour gathering their ration of vegetables and grains for the week. Nanci introduced Jenny to dozens of people all while pointing-out various plants, farming implements, and rare insects. Nanci, who had grown up on a farm, took great pleasure in educating others about farming, and, before Jenny knew it, they were helping the field workers till the fields. She was far too tired for farming, but she refused to give in to her fatigue. She attacked the work she was given with as much energy as she could muster. But by the time Nanci exclaimed that they'd lost track of time and hurried her away, she was more than happy to retire.

They hurried back to their camp where they started to prepare dinner. Ferdy joined them before long, and Seth arrived just as they were sitting down to pray over the meal. With him was Clayton Mercury, who joined them for dinner. No one made any particular remarks, but Jenny sensed that his presence was out of the ordinary.

Mercury was quiet and aloof, but once he began talking, he seemed comfortable. Still, she was a bit intimidated by him at first, especially by the big gun he carried on his hip and the curt, militaristic way he conducted himself. She wasn't sure how to treat him, so she mostly kept quiet and listened while the others talked. The first several minutes of polite conversation consisted mostly of Nanci and Ferdy asking Mercury about how the mining operations were going and him answering in vague terms. Then the conversation turned to Jenny's first day of work. They laughed and teased her as she told them how tired and clumsy she had been. To her surprise, Mercury joined in with the banter. As the night progressed, she found him to be an engaging conversationalist, with a wicked sense of humor and a laugh that made his mustache dance up and down. She quickly became comfortable around him.

Seth was silent throughout most of the meal. He stared down at his food as he shoveled it into his mouth like a grazing buffalo, speaking only when spoken to and giving brief responses. To Jenny, he looked as tired as she was. She realized that she hadn't seen him all day, which surprised her, considering the small size of the village. As the meal began to wrap up, Nanci commented that Seth looked like he was "fixin' to fall asleep with his head in his food" and asked him where he had been all day. Mercury answered for him, telling the others that Seth had been at the quarry helping him settle disputes between the villagers and his men.

"Sometimes my boys can be a bit rough with the workers," he said cautiously. "Apparently there was a dispute with one of your villagers, and he got fed-up and slugged one of my men. Tensions ran high, and it was all I could do to keep them from having an all-out brawl. Seth seems to be the only one who can keep your villagers in line, so I sent a runner for him and got him there just in time. We diffused the situation, but then my guys wanted to fire the villagers involved in the scuffle, and some of the villagers wanted to quit outright. But Seth and I were able to negotiate with both parties and get everything back to normal. Everyone kept their jobs and their heads, and we even had a more productive day than I predicted."

"What was the specific nature of the dispute?" Ferdy asked. "Were our men getting paid too much?"

Mercury snickered. "No, there was a dispute about the product," he said, and Jenny thought she saw his eyes flicker towards hers before they jumped back to Ferdy's face. He offered no other information.

After a short pause Nanci, thanked him for keeping the workers. "We appreciate it. Your kindness has always–"

Mercury cut her off. "Kindness nothing," he said with a cold look. "We need those workers. My boys aren't miners." He neglected to say what they were, if not miners. Nanci nodded her head and looked away, her eyes settling on Jenny's. There was a small smile on her face and a knowing look in her eyes.

"Anyway," continued Mercury, "I'm glad Seth was there. Not sure how he can get those stubborn men to work. You must have a way with animals, eh Seth? Seth?"

Everyone turned to the end of the table. Seth's head was drooping against his chest, and his forehead was only inches from his plate.

The rest of the table began to chuckle. Ferdy reached over and palmed Seth's head with his big hand to raise it back to a sitting position. Seth jerked awake, almost falling out of his seat. They all laughed as he gave a sheepish grin and stretched before apologizing. Nanci began to clear the dishes and told everyone not to go too far because she would have a special dessert ready soon.

Jenny wandered over to her tent in a daze. The sun was going down, the fire was lit, her belly was full, and she felt just as tired as Seth. She opened the flap to her tent, saw her cot, and decided that she would lie down for just a minute, lest she fall asleep at the table, too.

Jenny awoke slowly, savoring the comfort of her pillow. It would be another long day.

She sat up with a start. It couldn't be morning yet. What about dessert? She looked through the open flap of her tent and saw no light except for the dull glow of the dying fire. Her phone clock confirmed it for her: she'd slept through dessert. A sigh escaped her lips as she lay back and wondered what Nanci's surprise had been. She zipped up her mosquito netting and snuggled back into her bedding without even changing her clothes or closing the tent flap.

She was almost asleep again when she heard voices. They sounded like they were right behind her tent. She tried to ignore them and almost succeeded, but then she heard her name.

"Why didn't you want to talk in front of Jenny?" That one sounded like Seth's voice.

"Because this is a sensitive operation. The fewer people who know, the better." She was sure the second voice was Clayton Mercury.

"Oh, come on Merc, everyone knows what you're digging up out there. You obviously can't hide it from the men, who can't hide it from their wives, so the whole village knows."

"Yes, and that worries me. The only reason they know is because I need the workers. No one else needs to know."

"But Jenny is a part of the village now."

"She's still one too many. It could get out at any time."

"But no one leaves the village. And even if they did, they all hate the government, the Anti-Balaka, and the Seleka. Just out of spite they would never tell about it. The secret is safe in the village."

Jenny was awake now and listening with both ears.

"Oh, yeah?" Mercury's voice grew quieter, but more intense. Jenny had to strain to catch his words. "What about that swine Mohammedou Djotodia? You think he'll keep his mouth shut? I know firsthand that he's got some shady contacts that he's already gotten in touch with since your little bout of mercy, and now he hates you. I have good reason to believe he's ex-Seleka, too. If that's true, then we're only a step away from having them beating down our door. If the Seleka come into this area, Colonel Massi and his Anti-Balaka thugs will be right behind them."

"Look, what else could I do? I will not become an executioner or a jailer, and I already told you that by showing mercy to Mohammedou, I believe that he will keep this place a secret."

Mercury swore. "Then you're a fool, boy."

There was a tense silence and then Seth spoke again.

"Wait a second, how do you know that Djotodia has already been talking to his shady contacts?"

Mercury swore again, stronger this time. "I make it my business to know things like that."

"You had him followed, didn't you?"

"Of course I had him followed! You can make whatever little judgments you want, Seth, but I have an operation to run here. I had my boys track him all the way into Nola, but they lost him once he made contact with his old friends. They could have been Seleka for all we know. He's lucky he got away, because I would have made sure that he wouldn't be able to tell anyone our secret. Ever."

"I don't want to hear that!" Seth nearly shouted. Mercury hissed at him to keep his voice down, and he continued in a lower voice, albeit one that was still too loud. "You do whatever you want, Clayton, but we are not mercenaries like you and your men. We're in the business of helping people, not getting rich. You involve me in something like that again, and I will pull all of our workers out of your camp!"

"Don't be foolish, boy. You know good and well that your little science project here can't survive without me and my men. You can't survive without our guns and wages, and we can't do our mining without your workers. Elias Sharon understood that, and so should you. We have a symbiotic relationship, you and I, and we both have to do our part to make sure it survives."

Seth didn't respond, so Mercury continued in a more conciliatory tone.

"We've got a hungry lion by the tail, Seth. We're feeding Colonel Massi and his men just enough to keep them away, but we have to control all other information that leaves this jungle. If word gets out to anyone, Anti-Balaka, Seleka, or the government, everything we've built here will come crashing down. Our goals are aligned: neither of us want anyone coming out here and figuring out what's going on. That means you have to trust me with security matters. Have I ever steered you wrong before?"

He said it as a statement, not a question. Seth sighed, and, in it, Jenny heard a hurricane of weariness and stress.

"You're right. I'm sorry, okay? None of this is going according to plan anymore." He sounded so tired.

"Keep it together, eh kid? None of us need you unraveling right now. Look, you keep the girl as close as you need to, all right? Talk to her, share a tent, whatever. Just remember what I said."

Jenny heard the big man turn and walk away. Several moments passed before Seth did the same.

She laid back and reeled. This was the second conversation she had unintentionally eavesdropped on, and both had been about this Colonel Massi. Who was he, and what did he have to do with Clayton Mercury? Seth had referred to Mercury and his men as mercenaries. What were mercenaries doing running a mining operation? And what were they mining that was so special they couldn't let any word of it get out? She tried to sleep, but slumber would not come. She was tired, but her mind refused to rest. What was going on?

Jenny's eyes snapped open, and she exploded out of bed, entangling herself in the mosquito netting. She had fallen asleep again without realizing it. But something had awakened her violently. Her tent flap was still open and flapping in the wind, but this time the fire had died. She lay on the floor of her tent, her heart pounding against her ribcage.

Then, she heard it again. The sound started with a loud moan that rushed down into a series of rumbles like a waterfall crashing to rocky depths below. To Jenny's racing mind, it sounded like a monster clearing its throat. She heard it a third time. The hair on her arms stood on end. She heard it a fourth and then a fifth time. The sixth time was followed by a repeating series of rough coughs, like a panting horse but faster, deeper, and more violent. It was uncanny—familiar, yet unlike any sound she had ever heard before. The village dogs began to voice those half-serious half-nervous yelps dogs use whenever they are frightened. Distant voices called out to one another as the village awakened in confusion. All the while the chilling roar, for that's what it was, continued to resound. It was an animal, it was big, and it was close.

Jenny pulled her shoes on and scurried out of her tent into the humid night. Blackness surrounded her, but she could see the soft glow of distant torches towards the center of town. She turned her feet towards the torches, tiptoeing through the damp grass. Every shape in the darkness loomed out at her like some malevolent attacker, and every sound made her twitch. She was so nervous that she almost ran into a tall, dark figure standing at the village edge that seemed to spring up at her from out of nowhere. She froze for several seconds until she recognized Clayton Mercury calmly smoking a cigarette.

Without turning towards her he voiced a single word: "Lion."

"Lion?" Jenny squeaked, not sure if she had heard him right.

He must have nodded, but she couldn't tell in the dark.

"Lion, come down from the North. Chad, or Cameroon. He's way out of his range."

Jenny came up next to Mercury, and they listened to the lion as it continued to roar. She could see the mercenary's eyes in the dim light cast by the distant torches and the glow from the cigarette between his lips. They were wide and intense, and they stared out into the jungle roving to and fro, searching, and perhaps penetrating the all-consuming blackness.

"Are we…" Jenny began.

"We're fine. He's just letting us know that he's here."

Seth rushed up. Still the big mercenary did not turn. He seemed frozen in place, his gaze ensnared by something only he could see.

"Leopard?" Seth asked.

"Lion," he replied.

"What? There are no lions here. How do you know?"

"You ever hear a leopard roar in the night, kid?"

"No."

"That's because they don't. Leopards only roar when they're angry. They don't announce their presence. This guy is announcing his presence. He's letting us know that he's in town."

Mercury fell silent. They stood in the darkness and listened to the big cat roar. Now that Jenny knew it was a lion, the sound became less and more frightening.

"He must be old, or sick," Mercury said, mostly to himself, "or he wouldn't be this far out of his home range. I've never heard of a lion coming this far south. He must really be desperate, or he wouldn't have come into the fields."

"How do you know it's in the fields?" Seth asked, still not convinced.

Mercury ignored him and continued to smoke his cigarette.

"What are you doing out here..." he whispered into the night.

"Well, maybe it's a leopard, and it's angry at something," Seth ventured.

"It's a lion, Seth," the big man said, finally tearing his eyes away from the jungle. "We saw his tracks this morning in the jungle and in the fields."

"Oh," Seth replied. "And you didn't think we needed to know about that..."

Mercury tossed his cigarette on a bare patch of dirt and ground it out with the heel of his boot. "You don't need to know everything, Seth," he said with a smirk. "Don't you trust me?"

He chuckled and began to walk away.

"Where are you going?" Seth called after him.

"Back to my camp."

"For guns?"

"No, to sleep, boy."

"Wait a second, what are we supposed to do?"

"About what?"

"Uh, the lion!"

"Tie the dogs up and put a couple more armed sentries around the livestock. But you probably won't need them. He'll stop marking his territory in a minute and slink off to somewhere. Stop worrying."

"Stop worrying? There's a lion on the loose!" Seth shouted after him, but the mercenary had already disappeared into the night.

Seth gave a disgusted sigh. "That guy drives me crazy sometimes."

Jenny smiled. "I like him," she said, and she meant it. Though he had intimidated her at first, she was growing fond of his rough sense of humor and the deep sense of mystery that he exuded.

Seth gave another sigh, but it sounded more like a laugh. "Go to sleep, Clarkson," he said with a snicker, "and don't forget to say good night this time."

"Good night, 'boy'" Jenny said with a smile and Seth shook his head.

By the time she reached her tent, the adrenaline in her system had faded and exhaustion had crept back in. She checked her phone, found that it was only eleven o'clock, and crawled back into bed. She was almost asleep when she remembered her mosquito netting. Untangling and zipping it up took several minutes, but she finally got it done and laid down once again. Sleep took her in seconds.

She woke up one final time that night. She had been dreaming that she and Seth were being chased by someone through the jungle, while at the same time they were chasing someone else she couldn't identify. After many twists and turns, they finally came to a clearing where Clayton Mercury rode up on an enormous lion. They asked him for help, but instead he charged them on the lion. She woke up just as she felt the lion's claws dig into her skin. Sitting up, she noticed that once again she had left her tent flap open. She untangled herself from the mosquito netting and got up to shut it. As she zipped it shut, she thought she heard a snort. All the events of the night rushed back upon her and she froze.

But then she heard Nanci cough in the tent next to her. Breathing a sigh of relief, she made her way back to her bed and fell asleep.

Roar

*T*he old lion crouches in the tall grass at the edge of the clearing and watches. All around him is the scent of man. He is still hungry, hungry enough to eat man, but man still walks, this way and that, guarding his territory, protecting it from the beast he cannot see, but knows is there.

The lion coughs softly and drags his great bulk to his feet. Big, old, slow, and ponderous, he is still a silent stalker, moving like a wraith through the night. He is a creature of terror, that much he knows, and so, he is not surprised to sense terror all around him. The salty smell of sweat, the muffled yelps of the dogs, and the silent vibrations caused by stamping livestock are all signals to him: fear has come to man's territory.

Yet, the old lion is not a wraith, but a creature of flesh. He knows that he is not immortal and so he fears man just as man fears him. His flesh cries out for meat, but his instincts, which have never failed him, drive him to caution. As he slinks between the tall, evenly spaced crops in the fields of man, he does not do so as the king of the savannah, but as an intruder, a foreigner in these savage jungles he does not know.

He continues to circle man's territory, always keeping just in cover. He moves slowly, cautiously, almost leisurely. For him, time is only the rising and setting of the sun, the coming and the going of the rains, and the slow deterioration of his once proud body. What once was mighty is growing weak, but nothing else has changed. He will hunt, he will kill, and he will eat, whether tonight, tomorrow, or the day after. Next month, next year, it makes no difference. The pain in his belly has *always been there, and he does not expect it to leave now. It will drive him out, again and again, until one the day it will finally stop once and for all.*

The lion slips around to the far side of man's territory and once more settles in at the edge of the grass to watch. The scent of man is hot in his nostrils, but in the mind of the old lion, the scent is more accurately represented as boy. He knows that boy is here, but he cannot distinguish his scent from the rest of man that surrounds it. To him, it is all the same. He will find the boy and he will eat him. There is no shame in this act. If eating boy is what he must do to survive, then he will eat boy.

The stalker of the night continues to watch until the sky reveals the first hint of dawn. He raises his wicked head, coughs once more and makes his way back into the depths of the jungle. Day is coming, but night will soon return.

Chapter 8
We Learn to Bend

The days passed in quick succession for Jenny. She worked tirelessly for the village of Sangha, making food, tending the fields, teaching school, playing guitar, and helping wherever else she was needed. She began to toughen up; her hands grew rough, her skin tanned (after burning for several days), and she became more comfortable with her accommodations. Her cozy tent gave her few problems except for the mosquito netting. The netting was annoying at first, but she came to appreciate it for it was her only refuge from the clouds of voracious insects. Showering in the stalls shared by the villagers was an adventure until she learned to use as little water as possible, since she had to carry her own water from the river. Her taste buds got used to the different foods, and she came to enjoy many of them. (Except for fufu. She could never do more than tolerate it regardless of what it was served with). For the most part, her body reacted well to the foreign foods, though she spent one night sitting next to the outhouse. She had been too adventurous and tasted some fried monkey that a villager had caught and prepared. One of the many lessons she learned was to be gracious to all but to not accept everyone's generosity, especially involving food.

The lack of electricity annoyed her, not because she missed her hairdryer or microwave popcorn, but because it meant she had fewer opportunities to charge her iPhone and extra batteries. She tried to conserve power as much as possible, and even cut back on her music-listening, but she still felt like she was constantly shutting off her phone to save power. She still called her mother every day, but cell service was very poor in the jungle. If her phone wasn't working, her only other option was the Sharon's satellite phone. Eventually George Hauser gave her a partial solution to her problem. Every few days when he did a security check of the village, Jenny would give him one of her batteries which he would charge at the generator in the mining camp and return to her on his next visit. Jenny found the burly Irishman gruff and uncouth, but friendly. He never forgot to pick up one of her batteries before he left. But her problem grew worse when one of her batteries went missing. She looked everywhere and even enlisted several of her new friends to help, but the battery did not turn up. Jenny couldn't help but suspect thievery, though she hesitated to accuse anyone, or even to suggest that the battery had been stolen.

However, with only a few exceptions, her time in Sangha was positive. There were one or two individuals that seemed to dislike her, but everyone accepted her. Most of them loved her and with good reason. Jenny was a wonderful girl, upbeat, sensitive, and quick to please. The villagers learned before long that she was not some shallow tourist who wanted to make herself feel good. Like Seth, she had come to help and asked for nothing in return. Day after day, as she worked alongside the people from sunrise to sunset, she proved her commitment to them, and they came to respect and admire her. She never asked for a break nor refused a request for help. The villagers didn't have a hard time falling in love with her.

Jenny loved them right back. They were good people—simple, prone to frustration, and quick to anger, but also forgiving, quick to love, and possessing an inner strength that defied the circumstances in which they lived. The village was small enough for her to learn the names of most of the villagers. Most of them spoke fluent English, and she polished up her French enough to have extended conversations in only a few weeks. Sango was harder to master, but she kept at it, and was able to recognize enough to understand the occasional word thrown into a conversation. The people giggled at her attempts to learn the language, but they loved her for trying and assured her she was learning twice as fast as Seth had. They were quick to instruct her, and she was a quick learner. One of the most special things they taught her was how to sing and play "He Bled for Us." Several of the teenagers took it upon themselves to teach her the song one day when she paused to watch a few of them as they sang and strummed the old guitar. Jenny didn't even realize she was staring until the youngsters began to give her weird looks. When she apologized, one of them, a big-boned sixteen-year-old girl named Johnna-Marie, offered to teach her the song. The impromptu lesson was a little awkward at the beginning, especially because the other children stood apart and watched with stony faces. But as they watched Jenny laughing and talking to their friend, they softened and sauntered over to give their own advice. Soon, the entire group was laughing and singing along as Jenny learned the song.

The young people were Jenny's favorite. After the impromptu music lesson, she began to develop a closer relationship with the village teens. They loved to sing while she played music, especially when she taught them her favorite songs. Many of the extra t-shirts she gave away ended up in their possession, and they wore them with pride. Sometimes they would get her to play soccer, a sport that only interested her because they played it. The kids were all naturals at the sport, schooling her day-in and day-out and exhausting her though they didn't seem to break a sweat. Jenny thought she was only embarrassing herself, but the fierce respect that showed in their eyes was impossible to miss.

She built a special connection with the younger children too. She continued to teach the same age-group every day except Saturday, and on Sunday she taught them Sunday School. Each child had a unique personality and disposition. There was Momo, a large ten-year-old boy who Jenny thought of as a bully until she realized that he only picked on the other children because he was desperate for their attention. The other boys ganged up on him in fights and arguments which ended with bruises on the other boys and big tears of sorrow in Momo's eyes. Benji and Markie, two inseparable brothers, were followers and did whatever the other boys did. They were easily molded by Omar, a pleasant but devious boy whose Muslim mother was raising him alone. He had never met his father, a French soldier in the U.N. peace force stationed in the center of the country. The boy was never serious and had a knack for playing pranks that sometimes crossed the line between goofy and mean. His half-sister Uzma was best friends with the other girl in the class, Sally. Uzma was quiet and painfully shy, preferring to let her brother, or the loquacious Sally speak for her. Sally was a tall, bright girl with a beautiful smile and an adorable laugh. She was the oldest person in the class and never let the others forget it. She was the first person to raise her hand to answer a question and the first person to congratulate herself whenever she got the answer right. Jenny had to hide her face to keep from laughing on numerous occasions.

Jenny came to love all the children, but she had a special spot for Femi. The boy was an enigma. Precocious to the point of rudeness but serious as a bloodhound, he hated to be laughed at, especially when he was in earnest about something. Jenny never knew how to respond to his outrageous questions and ideas. He might remain silent for an entire day and then raise his hand right before class was over and ask why the river was wet but the leopard was dry even though they both roared. Or he might talk to Sally throughout Jenny's entire Sunday School lesson and then ask if Adam and Eve were black or white. He was constantly thinking up inventive ways to circumvent rules and get what he wanted. Once he asked to go to the bathroom but didn't return for almost twenty minutes. Jenny went to look for him and found him hiding under a sheep-skin rug in the goat pen. He would have gotten away if he hadn't sneezed. She also had to watch him carefully because he couldn't control his itchy fingers. Anything not tied down was fair game for him. Aleena and Jean-Marc constantly disciplined him with spankings, tongue-lashings, and confiscation of his things. After such occasions, he was usually sullen and unresponsive for a day or two, but he always asked for forgiveness in the end. He was wild like an untamed colt, but he had a good heart, and Jenny loved him.

Besides teaching and working in the fields, Jenny also assisted Sudaiq in the medical clinic. Her biology degree and experience working in a hospital were invaluable to the big medicine man, who had no formal medical training and only the most basic medical supplies with which to work. What he had was a big smile, a bigger heart, and a love for people worth more than all the medical knowledge in the world. Almost. They had several close calls. Most of the patients were workers injured in the quarry with injuries that Sudaiq could treat. But some were sick from consuming under-cooked or rotten food and needed medication, something Sudaiq knew little about. Once or twice Jenny had to stop him from giving the wrong drug or dosage to a patient. She hesitated to interrupt the much older man, but he always accepted her help with thanks and a desire to learn more. Jenny came to love and respect the kind, jolly man for his humility and compassion. She always looked forward to working with him and volunteered to help whenever she could.

Many times Jenny helped Sudaiq because Seth could not. Sudaiq told her that Seth usually assisted him every morning with the care of patients and upkeep of the facility, but with the Sharon's gone, he had less time to help. Mercury needed him more and more at the quarry to act as an intermediary between the mercenaries and the villagers, who often quarreled with one another. He also had to fulfill Elias Sharon's role as de facto judge and mayor of the small village, mediating disputes and dealing with issues of a more municipal sort, like making sure the paths were kept clean and the supplies were shared equally. Every couple of weeks he would accompany Ferdy into town to purchase supplies and take care of other issues. Any other time he had left over he spent praying and studying for his sermons. Jenny rarely saw him except on Sundays at church when she played while he sang and at dinner every night. But he was always so preoccupied and tired that they often spoke little more than a few polite words to each other. This disappointed Jenny, not only because she had wanted to get to know him again but also because she had many questions to ask him. She was enjoying her time in Sangha, but several things still bothered her. The legal status of the village was still unclear in her mind, and she still didn't know what the mercenaries were mining or why they were mining the jungle in the first place. She also wanted to ask who Colonel Massi was and why his name seemed to cause a shiver to run up her spine.

One day she grew tired of waiting for a chance to talk to Seth and took her questions to Aleena and Nanci. The three of them were preparing a dinner of rice (instead of fufu this time) topped with a goat and mushroom sauce. Jenny wanted to ask her questions casually but couldn't seem to find a way to begin. She got her chance when Aleena began to tell Nanci about an incident at the quarry Jean-Marc had related to her. Jenny waited for a pause and jumped in.

"What exactly are the mercenaries mining for?" she asked without looking up.

Aleena cast a sideways look at Nanci, but the other woman just smiled. "We don't rightly know," Nanci said. "The mercenaries just hire us. They keep whatever it is they find to themselves."

Jenny kept her eyes focused down on the mushroom she was slicing and said nothing. She was too polite to ask her obvious follow-up question: *how could you all be working there and* not *know?* Her temper flared. She had worked with these people for weeks, and they still wouldn't trust her?

The silence continued for several moments until Jenny noticed that both Nanci and Aleena had stopped working. She cast a quick glance at their faces. They were both looking at her and smiling.

"What?" she said, a little harder than she meant to. The two women giggled.

"That's what we're supposed to tell anyone who comes around asking," replied Nanci, "but as you can see, it isn't a very good reply.

But it's good enough for the park rangers who look the other way and for the occasional stranger that might stumble upon the village. Folks like that understand that we want to keep our business to ourselves and won't ask any more questions."

"But," Aleena broke in, "a smart girl like you would see there is something more."

"Your suspicions are correct, Jenny," said Nanci, "something more is going on, but it's nothing to worry about."

Jenny wanted to scream in frustration, but she settled for something less outrageous. "It sure seems like something to worry about," she said, looking Nanci in the eye.

Nanci swallowed. "Jenny, sweetie, I won't lie to you and say that everything here is all hunky-dory and that you have nothing at all to worry about. But I never told you this was going to be a cakewalk. This ain't Missouri, dear. This is Africa. It is dangerous here. We're in the middle of a dangerous area on government land in a make-shift village that isn't sanctioned by anyone. This is a precarious position. We could be discovered at any time and kicked out. Or worse."

She let her last statement hang in the air before continuing. "Fortunately for you and I and Seth, we're Americans, so the government probably won't touch us, but the rest of the villagers could be arrested, imprisoned, or shot. They're living in constant danger. But they go about their lives like nothing is wrong and like what they've built here will last forever. They don't worry so we don't either. In the end, what else can we do?"

"I understand that," Jenny said trying to stay patient, "but why are mercenaries here in the first place? Why all the cloak and dagger stuff? And who is Colonel Massi?" She hadn't meant to ask that last question, which she shouldn't have known about, but neither Nanci nor Aleena seemed to notice.

"Colonel Massi is a wicked man," Aleena said with deadly seriousness. "He kills, he steals, he rapes, and he destroys. He has no reason to come here unless he finds out what the mercenaries are mining."

"And what are they mining?" Jenny asked.

"Gold," said a deep voice behind them.

The three women turned to see Ferdy stride up followed by Jean-Marc.

"Gold?" Jenny asked as the two men sat down at the table.

"Gold," Ferdy replied.

"Lots of it," Jean-Marc added.

"Now, we don't actually know for sure," Nanci started to say, but Ferdy cut her off.

"Ah, but we do know for sure. Jean-Marc has seen the gold with his own eyes, though Clayton Mercury tries to hide it."

Jean-Marc chimed in. "I was a miner before Aleena and I came here. I know what I am looking at when I see it. This area has an unusually high concentration of mineral and ore deposits. Whenever we strike something that looks like it could be gold, we are to tell Clayton Mercury at once. Then his men take over and remove the ore away from prying eyes. But he cannot hide from us what he finds, and if he cannot hide what he has found from us, he cannot hide it from the rest of the world either."

"I am more worried about Colonel Massi finding out than I am about the rest of the world," Ferdy said.

"Who is Colonel Massi?" Jenny asked.

"Colonel Massi is the local chieftain or dictator of this area, depending on who you ask. He also happens to be the local Anti-Balaka leader, but he uses the cloak of their ideology as an excuse to perpetrate acts of violence and brutality. If he finds out what Clayton Mercury and his mercenaries have found, he will come and burn everything we have built here to the ground."

Jenny listened to them talk with a stony expression on her face, but inside, her heart was beating like a drum. Everything they told her made sense with what she had seen, but peace did not come with understanding. All the warnings that her mother had given her about traveling to Africa rushed back to her. For a second, she panicked on the inside.

"Why don't we do something about it?" she blurted out.

"What can we do?" Ferdy asked her.

"We can go somewhere else away from the mercenaries where we won't be in danger from Colonel Massi," she replied.

"We have nowhere else to go, my child," he replied. "Besides, here with the mercenaries we have work and protection."

Jenny almost began to hyper-ventilate, but she caught herself just in time. This was too much for her to handle. She hadn't signed up for gold, and mercenaries, and brutal warlords. She started to regret ever leaving home and coming to Africa. Her heart beat faster.

But then Ferdy said something that reminded her of her pastor back home.

"Jenny, we have much to fear, but we do not. We can fear or we can live. We have only two options."

She looked around at the kind, understanding faces and saw they weren't worried for themselves, but for her. Once again, she felt the overwhelming compassion that permeated these people. Even in the midst of their own trials they still worried about her needs before their own.

Nanci squeezed her hand. "Like I told you before, darlin', it ain't Hotel Paradise, but it'll be all right. We learn to bend."

Jenny felt like crying, but for her Seth rushed up just then, apologizing in his usual way for being late. He sat down in a rush but then, noticing that everyone was staring at him, asked if he had missed anything. The others chuckled but didn't reply.

After her talk with Ferdy, Nanci, and the Zoumara's, Jenny began to see Seth in a new light. Not only was he overburdened trying to fill in for the Sharon's, he was also dealing with an illegal gold smuggling operation and trying to protect a village of people from a brutal murderer. At first, she was upset that he didn't seem to have time for her, but now she felt sympathy for him and the extraordinary circumstances in which he found himself. She began to pray for him and for the village every morning during her devotions, asking God to protect and strengthen them all.

One day, about six weeks into her stay, she was working in the fields and saw Seth wandering at the edge of an okra field in the shadow of the jungle. He looked dejected. She was too far away to see his face, but his posture told the story: shoulders slumped, head down, hands shoved deep into his pockets as he trudged along. Her heart went out to him, and, in that moment, she wanted nothing more than to cheer him up or relieve his weariness.

She called out to him three times before he heard her. He looked up at her as she waved and smiled but continued walking with the same dejected posture. Jenny sighed, again wishing she could cheer him up.

"That is not how a woman calls a man," said a voice beside her. She turned and saw one of the villagers, a large woman called Keke, working two rows over. "Make him feel important," she said with a wink, and returned to her work.

Jenny was confused by the woman's remarks but shrugged her shoulders and called out to Seth again, beckoning him over. "I need your help," she yelled to him. At once, his whole demeanor changed. His shoulders squared, his back straightened, and his aimless wandering turned into a determined stride as he marched down the rows of tall okra plants. When he reached her, he stood at attention ready to aid, but Jenny continued working. After several seconds, he began to look around in confusion, until he caught the smile that Jenny couldn't keep from slipping onto her lips.

"Wait…" he said slowly, "you don't need help with anything…"

Jenny gave an embarrassed chuckle, but Keke burst out in laughter as did some of the other women working nearby. Seth looked around in confusion at the giggling women. "Why did you call me over?" he asked.

Keke made a miffed sound with her lips. "As if a woman needs a reason to speak to a man," she said in mock annoyance. The women giggled again. "What you got that so important, boy?"

"I have a lot of things to do," Seth began, "because–"

"Yes, you look like you doing so much over there with your chin in your hand," Keke broke in, and the women laughed again.

"Keke, you know good and well what I do all day."

"Hear that girls?" Keke asked, ignoring Seth's reply, "Sounds like this man can't do a woman's work." The laughter increased, and this time Jenny couldn't help but join in. Seth sighed and glared at her, but she just shrugged her shoulders.

"I should have known you'd all turn on me one day," he said to Keke in mock anger. "I guess I haven't been tanning your hides enough lately."

Jenny froze. That last comment seemed way over the line, but the women roared with laughter and began to fling dirt at Seth. He grabbed a shovel to shield himself, laughing just as hard as them. Jenny was right in the line of fire and ducked down to avoid being hit by a stray dirt clod. The women chanted in Sango as they pelted Seth, who began to knock the clods back at them. Eventually it was too much for him, and he fled down the rows of okra as the women cheered in mock triumph. After going about fifty yards, he came back acting wounded, but his eyes were smiling. He pretended to be hesitant about coming within range again, brandishing the shovel like a weapon until they all assured him of his safety.

"You got that shovel in your hand, now use it boy," Keke yelled to him. Seth smiled and fell in line next to Jenny and got to work. Over the next hour the two of them talked and laughed like the old friends they were. It was the first extended conversation they'd had since Jenny had arrived. They talked about all the things Jenny had experienced since arriving, then about Seth's two years on the mission-field, Ferdy's amazing life story, and about people back home. But when Jenny mentioned the Sharon's, she saw Seth's face drop. Thinking she had reminded him of all the work he had to do in their absence, she changed the subject and began talking about okra. But Seth was no longer paying attention to what she was saying. In the middle of one of her sentences, he broke in.

"The Sharon's went back to the States," he blurted out.

Jenny stopped short. "What? When? *Why?*" she asked in disbelief.

"I just found out from Ferdy a couple hours ago. I understand why they did it. They've been trying to get back into the C.A.R. for weeks, and they don't have the money to wait around in Paris forever. They've decided that the best thing they can do, is go back to their family and raise more money for the mission. They'll keep trying to get back in, but they have no idea when that will be."

Jenny was stunned. The only reason her parents had supported her decision to go to Africa was because they had met the Sharon's in person and they had assured them they would take good care of their daughter. The only reason *she* had even considered going was because the Sharon's would be there. She had come to rely on them from a distance before she'd even set foot in Africa just as she had with Nanci. Now, there would be no official oversight by anyone experienced from the United States. Nanci was a wonderful, talented person, but she was not a licensed minister and required supervision from an official missionary. Besides, she wasn't equipped to be the leader of a village. Jenny felt her fear rise once again, a fear that had lain dormant inside of her for the past six weeks as she waited for the Sharon's to return. Now, that layer of security would not be coming.

She wanted to tell her fears to Seth, but after a look at his dejected face, she said instead, "Seth, I'm so sorry. I know you've been under a lot stress while they've been gone."

"Looks like that stress isn't going to go away now," he replied.

"I'm so, so sorry. What are we going to do? What can we do?"

"Well, we've both got updated visas, so we shouldn't have any problems staying in the country. And the Sharon's are still technically missionaries here, even though they aren't present in the country, so we shouldn't have any problems with the organization they are a part of. And Ferdy has good relationships with the government and with the World Health Organization, so I don't think anyone will come after us."

He stopped and looked at Jenny, hoping for a reply.

"So, do we just sit tight and wait it out for a while?"

"I think that's all we can do," he replied, in a more optimistic tone. He seemed pleased that she had suggested that they stay. "We can't just leave these people, right? This is all they have, and I don't think they are ready to do this all on their own."

Jenny nodded. "You're right. I came to help and I want to stick it out as long as possible."

He smiled and thanked her.

"But," she continued, "you need to start sharing some of your load. You'll kill yourself if you don't. Let me help. Or some of the villagers, like the Zoumara's. Somebody else can teach or preach sometimes or mediate disputes between the villagers. And I've been helping Sudaiq a lot at the hospital lately, so you don't have to be so concerned with helping there. If there's anything more that I can do, please, let me know."

"I will Jenny," he said with sincerity. "Thanks. I should go right now, I really do have things to do." He smiled and handed her the shovel, waved goodbye to all the women, and walked back towards the village. As she watched him go, Jenny said a silent prayer for him.

"See, you help him already," Keke said, and she winked at Jenny.

That night, Jenny stayed up late and called her mother, catching her as she was waking up. Her mom was sleepy, but grateful that she had called. Jenny summarized the past few days like she normally did, and her mother reprimanded her for not calling often enough, which was also normal. Jenny was excited to tell her mother all the things she was doing to help the village, but Rachelle only replied with sleepy grunts and asked about her health. She was especially concerned about her bowel movements and eating habits. She sighed and for the umpteenth time assured her mother she was fine.

"I'm sure the Sharon's wouldn't go there if the water wasn't safe to drink," Rachelle said. "How are they by the way?"

Jenny wanted to tell her the Sharon's would go to any country regardless of the safety of the water if it meant that they could help people, but instead she said, "I think they're fine, Mom."

"You think?" her mother replied. She was a stickler for grammatical details.

But this time Jenny hadn't misspoken. "Yes, I *think* they are. But I don't know for sure because they haven't gotten back into the country yet." She had explained all this to her mother before, but she wasn't keen on telling her that the Sharon's wouldn't be getting in any time soon.

But Rachelle kept pushing. "Jenny, this is getting serious. Why won't the authorities let them back in? The only reason your father and I allowed you to go was because the Sharon's assured us they would take good care of you. This makes me think that perhaps they aren't as experienced as they led us to believe."

Jenny wanted to tell her mother that she was a grown woman and they couldn't have stopped her from going even if they had wanted to. But instead she defended the Sharon's, telling her mother that they had decades of experience and that it was hardly their fault the authorities wouldn't allow them back into the country.

"Jenny, it's been six weeks. If they aren't there in the next few days, I think you need to come home."

Jenny swallowed. She wasn't going home, not yet. She didn't want to tell her mother that, but she knew she needed to tell her that the Sharon's were stuck outside the country. Her mother would not like it.

"Mom," she began in a calm tone, "like you just said, it's been six weeks, and I am fine. I can get along without the Sharon's if I have to. Their presence won't make me more or less safe. The people here are great, and they've been helping me in every way possible." She swallowed again and took a deep breath. "Besides, I just found out today that the Sharon's went back to the States. They probably won't be getting into the C.A.R. for a long time."

A slight pause, and then the storm broke.

"WHAT?!?!" her mother roared, now fully awake. "You mean to tell me that the missionaries abandoned my daughter in the middle of a third-world country and just made their cozy way on home to safety?"

"Mom…" Jenny tried to interject, but Rachelle was having none of it.

"That is the laziest, most irresponsible, inappropriate thing I have ever heard! How dare they leave you there by yourself when they promised that they'd take care of you? That's it. Your coming home on the next flight. I've had enough of this worrying to death about your safety.

"Mom," Jenny tried again but her mother didn't stop.

"I'm getting you a ticket right now. Doesn't matter what it costs. My baby is not staying in a foreign, violent country by herself, I don't care who I have to throttle to get you here. I want you to start packing right now, and call me every few hours, just to make sure everything is okay. I'm getting on the computer right now to find you a ticket, and then I'm going to go get your dad and make sure he clears his plans for the next couple of days so he can be available to pick you up from the airport. This is ridiculous."

Jenny knew what her mother was about to do. She'd seen her do it many times. She was about to take control of the situation and steamroll everyone until she got what she wanted. "Mom," Jenny said more forcefully, but it still had no effect.

"Don't worry, Jenny, I'll take care of this. Let's see, there are two AirFrance flights tomorrow, but not until the afternoon. That's ridiculous. Hmm, let's see nothing else is leaving until later in the week. Oh, wait, here's one early in the morning, 6:00 am your time. What time is it there right now? Will you have time to get to the airport by then? Oh, I can't believe this is happening to us Jenny, but we'll take care–"

"Mom!" Jenny shouted into the phone.

"What honey? What is it?"

"I'm not going home."

"What do you mean? Of course you are, we'll get you here even if I have to rent a plane myself–"

"No, I mean I'm staying here. In the C.A.R."

There was a pause on the line. "Jenny..." Rachelle began, but this time her daughter cut her off.

"Mom, I gave my word that I would stay here for at least three months. I will finish out my term."

"You absolutely will not, Jenny. This is not a matter of preference. This is about your safety."

"I'm fine, Mom! I'm not in any danger." Jenny's mind flashed to Colonel Massi for just a second, but she pushed that thought away.

"Jenny! Who in the world will take care of you?"

"I'm twenty-three years old mother, I can do this. Besides, I have Nanci Bernard here, and Ferdy, who works with the W.H.O. and the villagers, and Seth–"

"Oh, you mean that boy who dumped you? Jenny, you're not getting involved with him again are you? Oh, I knew this was a bad idea–"

"No, Mother! I am not here for Seth! But I'm also not here for you!" That grabbed her mother's attention, so she continued.

"Mother, this has nothing to do with you, or Seth, or even me. It's all about what I feel God wants me to do. Can you please understand that? These people here are wonderful, vibrant, and full of love. But they need help. And I'm helping them, mother. Really helping. Haven't you been listening to all the things I've been telling you? For once in my life I'm really doing something for someone else, something that is bigger than me. I feel like I'm doing good in the world. Isn't that what we're supposed to do? Isn't that what you and Dad taught me and what I've learned about in church all my life? To love my neighbor as myself, to love them like Jesus loves me?"

There was another pause on the line, a long one this time. Finally, her mother spoke.

"Jenny, I'm proud of you for what you're doing, I really am. But this is about your safety now. You are coming home."

Jenny's heart sank. But she had made up her mind.

"Then, I'm sorry to disappoint you, Mother. But I'm staying here."

Her mother begged and pleaded with her for several more minutes, but with tears gathering in her eyes, she held her ground. Eventually, with a frustrated sigh, her mother gave up. She told Jenny she loved her and made her promise to call every single day from now on, told her she loved her again, and then hung up. Jenny put the phone down and buried her face in her pillow. Her heart ached for her mother, but also for the choice she had made. The call to follow Jesus she had seen as a blessing now felt like a burden. It weighed on her like an airplane full of stones and threatened to crush her underneath its weight. But she was proud of the decision she'd made. She thought of the scripture when Jesus told his disciples "If anyone comes to me and does not hate his father and mother, wife and children, brothers and sisters, yes, and his own life, he cannot be my disciple." It gave her courage. Still, she couldn't stop a few tears from falling.

Several minutes later, she heard someone call her name from outside her tent. It sounded like Seth.

"Jenny, you awake?" he whispered. She wiped her tears and pulled on a skirt before unzipping the tent flap.

"Hey," Seth said. "I didn't wake you, did I?"

Jenny shook her head no. She didn't trust her voice right at that moment.

"Oh, good," he replied. He swallowed awkwardly. "I just wanted to say thank you for earlier today. I really needed that. I've been so caught up with everything that I haven't given you enough time lately. Thanks for taking my mind off my troubles."

"You're welcome," Jenny said, smiling into the dark even though she didn't feel at all like smiling.

Seth must have noticed something in her voice. "You okay?" he asked after a short pause.

Jenny had every intention of assuring him she was fine, but the words stuck in her throat. She felt tears forming in her eyes again. Sensing her struggle, he put his arm around her shoulders.

"Hey, it's all right," he said gently. Jenny leaned into him and began to tell him all about her conversation with her mother, about her worries, and about the burden that weighed on her shoulders. Seth listened without interrupting until she was finished.

"I got some of the same stuff from my parents too," he said when she had finished. "I had a hard time getting them to understand that this went way beyond thrill-seeking for me, and I still don't think they get it completely. But my pastor told me before I ever left that most people wouldn't understand the burden God had placed on my shoulders. That's a hard thing to come to grips with, but you know what's even harder? Sometimes I don't understand it myself. But I trust God. Even though I've questioned myself a million times since coming here, I've never once felt I was in the wrong place."

"What do you do when you doubt yourself?" Jenny asked him.

"I crack open my Bible or hit my knees and just talk to God and let him remind me that He is still in control."

Jenny smiled. This wise, thoughtful, comforting Seth was *not* the Seth that she remembered. But she liked this Seth better.

"Thanks, Seth," she said. "I needed that. I guess you got to return the favor."

"I did, didn't I?" he replied. "You know I'm free to talk whenever you want, Jenny."

"Ha, no you're not. You barely have time to think."

"True, but for you I'll make time."

"Thanks. Goodnight, Seth."

"Goodnight, Jenny."

And he disappeared into the night.

Chapter 9
Journey to the Heart

O ver the next week, Seth was busier than ever, but he seemed to have more time for Jenny. Instead of rushing in late for meals and leaving before everyone else, he showed up early and lingered afterwards to engage her in conversation. He seemed to show up wherever she was, whether she was out in the fields, teaching school, or helping Sudaiq in the hospital. Jenny enjoyed spending more time with him, especially because he appeared to be in better spirits. Things in the village were going well too: the crops were healthy, relations between the mercenaries and the workers were improving, and three former Muslim villagers were baptized in the name of Jesus on Sunday.

But in Africa the weather changes quickly. Monday morning dawned gray with clouds and before breakfast was over, they began to empty themselves in a typical African rainstorm confining the villagers to their homes. Jenny spent much of the next two days bored. The only break in the monotony came when Seth invited her to eat lunch with him on Wednesday in his tent. They had just finished eating when Clayton Mercury appeared and asked to speak with Seth in private. Seth smiled at Jenny and told the mercenary leader that anything he had to say to him he could say in front of her. Mercury gave a poorly concealed sigh and an almost imperceptible shake of his head but began anyway.

"My sources in the capital tell me that Colonel Massi has been in contact with an ex-Seleka leader called 'General' Abdul-Azeez. They've been sending discreet messages back and forth for about a month now."

"Okay," Seth with a smile. "As long as he isn't sending messages about us, we shouldn't worry, right?"

"You should when you hear who his main courier has been." Mercury paused to allow Seth and Jenny to venture a guess. When they remained silent, he continued.

"It's none other than our old friend Mohammedou Djotodia."

Seth's smile grew stale as understanding dawned on him. Jenny's heart sank as she too understood.

Mercury continued. "I shouldn't need to tell you that if Djotodia told Azeez about our operation, you can bet that Colonel Massi knows too. They're onto us. There's no other reason for an Anti-Balaka captain and a former Seleka leader to contact one another. Azeez will need Massi's permission to move around in his territory. You can bet they're discussing a partnership: Massi gives permission, and Azeez gives the location of our ore. Win-win, right? Except this unholy alliance will mean the end of all we've built here."

He paused again, but Seth was still processing the information. Jenny looked back and forth between the faces of the two men.

"Seth, I don't have enough men to protect us from Massi *and* Azeez."

"It may not come to that," Seth said. "We don't know anything for—"

"Don't be an idiot, boy!" Mercury hissed. He had a strange habit of whispering when he was angry. Most people grew louder the angrier they got, but Mercury grew quieter. When his rage was at its hottest, he would whisper. It was unsettling. "They could be knocking down our door with assault rifles tomorrow for all we know."

"But what about the government? Or the United Nations? Can't we appeal to them for help?"

"Oh, like all the help they've given the people of this country so far? The government is weak, and the U.N. won't get anything done fast enough to save us. And besides, have you forgotten that we're all squatting in this national reserve illegally?"

"Well maybe we can talk to Massi and let him have the quarry in exchange for leaving our people alone. That seems like—"

"You can't reason with these sorts of men, son. We aren't talking about rational people. We're talking about religious zealots and men so greedy they'd sell their own children into slavery. They'll slaughter you, your little girlfriend here, and everyone in this village to get what they want, and no one will be able to stop them. Not you, not me, not the U.N. and certainly not the Central African government. Trust me, I know these things."

Jenny stared at the mercenary. For the first time, she noticed a dark, jagged scar across his collar bone peeking out the top of his unbuttoned shirt. She realized she knew next to nothing about this man and his vague past.

"No, this is the beginning of the end for us," he continued. "If you care about your people, you'll get out of here before it's too late."

Seth's face grew angry.

"What are you suggesting?" he asked.

"It's time for you to move on. I'm packing up what ore we have and moving out. I suggest you do the same with the village."

Seth was shocked. "What?!?" he asked in disbelief. "We can't move again! Where would we go? We have no place to go to."

"Anywhere would be better than here," Mercury said, louder and less angry.

"We only came here because there was nowhere else!" Seth shouted.

Mercury grabbed his arm and hissed at him to keep his voice down. "Look, I still have my contacts in the cities," he whispered. "They say that, so far, nothing concrete has been nailed down between Massi and Azeez, but that could change at any time. They'll let me know if anything comes our way, which means we may have a few days to work things out. Think about what I've said. But

Benjamin D. Copple

regardless, I'm putting my men on alert and getting everything ready, just in case. I suggest you do the same."

He released Seth's arm and stepped back. "Try to talk some sense into him, Jenny," he said as he turned and walked away.

After watching the mercenary disappear behind a shack, Jenny turned to Seth. He was staring off into the jungle with a determined expression on his face.

"What are you thinking?" Jenny asked with apprehension in her voice.

He looked outside the tent. The rain had stopped falling for the moment. "Get your boots," he said. "Let's go for a walk."

Seth wandered out through the muddy fields and Jenny followed. They walked in silence until they reached the jungle, where Seth began to talk, releasing a torrent of words that must have been raging inside him for months. When he had talked to her before, Jenny had always sensed he was holding things back, but now he spoke without inhibition. He gave her the entire story going all the way back to his first day in Sangha. He told her how he had arrived pure-hearted and energetic, but soon discovered his naïveté. The work had been brutal, the villagers uncouth, and not a single person other than the Sharon's showed any desire to help. He had expected to feel so spiritual and righteous all the time, but he only felt exhaustion, apathy, and cynicism. He was disgusted by the bribes the villagers had to pay and by the perceived avarice of Clayton Mercury and his men. The Sharon's were wonderful but so busy that they had little time for him. For a while, he questioned his decision to leave home and come to Africa. Over time, he understood why the bribes were necessary, and that, for all his gruffness and cynicism, Clayton Mercury was a decent man. After many weeks of homesickness, back-breaking labor, whining villagers, and stomach issues getting used to the food, he began to see fruit from his labor. The villagers grew on him, and what he had seen as roughness revealed itself as fear. That was in the early days, when terror and trembling still ruled the villagers. But over time, the Sharon's love and wisdom affected the villagers, and they started to turn themselves around. Seth started involving himself in their lives and to make real connections with each of them. After that, it had been impossible for him not to fall in love with them.

That first year had been a crucible for him. He saw the darkest side of humanity but came to learn that anyone was capable of changing. He watched people living in the worst situations pull themselves out of the darkness thanks to the love shown to them by someone else. He watched a group of people refuse to be destroyed by the worst circumstances. As a result, his own walk with God survived the trials and came out as solid as gold. His second year in Central Africa was a year of personal triumph and growth. The circumstances of the villagers were still poor, but their attitude towards them began to change, as did Seth's attitude toward his own situation. They found that as their outlook improved, so did their circumstances. That year, they saw an increase in their crops, an increase in their personal wealth thanks to the wages from Clayton Mercury, and an overall increase in the camaraderie between each other. They had only sporadic disputes with the mercenaries, and the park rangers were satisfied with the bribes they received. Things had gone well.

"I finally started to think we could succeed here," he explained, "but in the past few months things have changed. I don't want to say it, but it seems like things are unraveling. We've had to increase our bribes to the park rangers three times to keep them from going to the government or to Colonel Massi. We've had more labor disputes with the mercenaries than ever, and we have to be more secretive than ever to keep outsiders from discovering what's really going on. That whole business with Mohammedou is the first time in years we've had to banish someone from the village. The kind of violence he committed is something I thought we'd gotten rid of. And now the Sharon's can't return to the country? I don't know. What if Merc is right? Massi is asking more and more questions, and we won't be able to keep the mining stuff quiet for much longer. Maybe we *should* leave."

Jenny spoke for the first time. "What's so terrible about leaving?"

Seth sighed. "If I only had to worry about myself, I'd be out of here tomorrow. That's the smart thing to do, and it's what my parents would want. But you have to understand, these people have nothing. *Nothing*, other than this village. This is their home now, and they won't want to leave. Do you ever wonder why so many people stay in violent countries like the C.A.R.? It's because it's *home*. They won't leave their home. And if I left them here, it'd be like running away. I don't know if I could do that."

They stopped walking. During Seth's story, they had walked a full circle around the village. Jenny stared back across the fields at the little village of Sangha and thought about how fragile it truly was. She voiced the question she had wanted to ask Seth for a long time.

"Seth, what are the mercenaries digging up that is so valuable?"

Seth looked her in the eye but said nothing.

"Ferdy and Jean-Marc told me it's gold," she said when he didn't reply.

"It's not just gold," he replied. After a brief pause, he said, "I've got something to show you. Come with me."

He led her to a rough path that led into the jungle, twisting this way and that around rocks and huge tree trunks. This was the first time Jenny had gone into the forest since arriving at the village. She had been apprehensive about exploring the dense jungle for fear of getting lost or bitten by some strange insect, but now she regretted not doing so. It was fascinating. The path was narrow, just wide enough for a jeep to squeeze through, and the jungle grew close on either side. It was like walking through a tunnel, but a tunnel filled with many sights and sounds she couldn't identify. Seth, so used to the flora and fauna, strode through without a glance to either side, but Jenny made up her mind that later she would explore more on her own.

After about fifteen minutes, Jenny heard loud, mechanical sounds like that of heavy machinery. The sounds grew louder and soon the trees parted to reveal a tall, imposing gate set in a metal fence with barbed wire at the top and slats in-between the links to keep people from seeing in. The gate was unmarked except for a sign the read "DANGER KEEP OUT" in English, French, and Sango. Jenny did not have to be told that this was the mining camp. Seth led her to the left of the gate, and they followed the fence for several more minutes. Through breaks in the slats, Jenny caught glimpses of large machines, huge piles of rock, and a massive, irregular pit, which must have been the quarry.

Soon they came to another gate and a path that led back into the jungle. Taking it, they left the mining camp and its roaring machinery behind. Once they could hear the sounds of the jungle again, Jenny commented on how dark it was. The rain clouds were dulling the late afternoon sun, but even so, the jungle was darker than she had expected. Seth laughed and told her the jungle liked to keep its secrets. She asked him what he meant, but he just smiled mysteriously and keep going.

Soon the sounds of the camp were replaced with the sound of running water, and, before long, they came to the river where a small dock sat. Seth explained that this was where the mercenaries brought everything they couldn't transport over land. He turned off the main path and headed upstream. Even though they followed the course of the river, their way was much harder than on the path. Seth told her they were following a game trail, but they still had to shoulder through bushes, climb over fallen logs, push aside vines, and go around massive trees. Spider webs and creepers clung to her hair, mud soaked her boots, and she had to be careful where she put her foot lest she disturb some hidden creature. On one occasion, she almost stepped on something that exploded from beneath her feet in a hasty retreat. Jenny was wet and bedraggled, but her heart beat with vigor beneath her chest. She felt like she was on an adventure.

After toiling for about half an hour, they stopped to rest on a large rock. They whispered to each other at first but soon fell silent in reverence to the mighty jungle. It surrounded them with a presence that was almost tangible, rising high above their heads and pressing in on every side. As they stared up at the great trees and insatiable foliage, they were forced to contemplate their insignificance compared to nature. The jungle had existed long before the two children ever dreamed of setting foot on the continent, and it would exist long after they left. There was something spiritual about the deep jungle beauty. The raging crises of African life paled next to the grandeur of God's creation. The thought occurred to Jenny that perhaps Eden had looked like this, eons before mankind invented countries and religions. For the first time in her life, she was awed into silence.

After several minutes, above the deafening silence of the jungle, she heard the soft patter of feet. Seth pulled her behind the rock, and together they watched the trail. Soon a small figure emerged from the brush walking along and humming softly. Seth recognized the person first. As soon as it drew even with their rock, he jumped out and grabbed it. The little figure squirmed and screeched like a banshee.

"Femi!" Seth shouted.

The little boy stopped struggling when he heard his name.

"What are you doing out here?" Seth scolded him. "You know you're not supposed to leave the village by yourself, and you promised to never come here without me!"

Femi hung his head and stared at the ground.

"You promised," Seth said, crossing his arms. "Now what am I going to do? Tell your mother?" Femi didn't answer.

"What should you say?" said Seth.

Femi continued to stare at the ground.

"Femi," Jenny said in a patient tone, "what did we learn about last Sunday in Sunday School?"

He looked up at her with a quizzical look in his eye. Jenny had taught on forgiveness and on asking for it from others. Femi thought to himself and then spoke.

"I'm sorry, Sef," he whispered.

Jenny smiled to herself. The little boy still hadn't learned how to say Seth's name properly. "Now what should you say, Femi?" she asked.

"Will you forgive me?" the little boy asked.

Seth looked like he was trying not to smile. "Of course, I will, Femi," he said, but then continued in a more serious tone, "but promise me you won't come here again by yourself. Remember, this is our little secret."

"But you bring Miss. Jenny," Femi said, almost like an accusation.

"Well, Miss. Jenny is special, isn't she?" Seth asked. "And she's your teacher too. Don't you think it would be okay for us to show her?"

Femi nodded and Seth patted him on the back.

They continued along for a short distance and then turned off the trail at the base of an enormous tree. After pushing through some dense foliage around the base of the tree, they broke into a little clearing that faced the river but was closed in on three sides. They were deep in the jungle now, and the only reason the clearing existed was because large, flat rock made up the floor and inhibited the foliage from growing. The limbs of the enormous tree stretched out over it to form a ceiling just high enough for Jenny to stand. The little room was very secluded and could only be seen from across the river.

"Wow, it's so peaceful," Jenny said.

"Yes, it is," Seth said. "Occasionally I come here to read my Bible and meditate. But this isn't what I wanted to show you."

Jenny heard a rustle behind her and turned just in time to see Femi disappear beneath the roots of the giant tree. She gave a cry and rushed over to find a small crevice down which the boy had disappeared. It was too small for her to fit through and would have just accommodated Femi's small frame. She shouted his name, but Seth told her not to worry.

"That's where we're going too," he said.

"We can't fit in there!" Jenny exclaimed.

"Not that way," he replied and walked over to the edge of the flat rock, which sloped down several feet to where the river, swollen after the recent rains, flowed swiftly below it. He took off his shoes and socks and dipped his feet into the water. "Now, we swim," he said with a smirk.

"What?" said Jenny. A quick image of a crocodile dragging Seth into the mud flashed across her mind.

"Look, just take your shoes and socks off," he said.

"But… but…" Jenny stuttered, too confused and nervous to form a sentence.

"Come on Jenny, you've got to *live* a little," he said with that crooked smile. Then he slipped over the side of the rock into the water.

Jenny rushed to the edge of the rock, but Seth had already disappeared under the greenish water. She waited several moments, hoping to see him resurface, but he didn't. She called out his name several times in a panicked tone. On the third time, she heard him answer, but his voice was muffled and came from *behind* her.

"Where are you?" she said, relieved but confused.

"Over here, by the tree trunk," his muffled voice said. Jenny, looked all over the massive tree, but she still couldn't find him.

"Is this some kind of magic?" she asked Seth's disembodied voice.

"Look down."

She looked down into the crevice through which Femi had disappeared and saw the faint outline of Seth's face. He was smiling like the Cheshire Cat.

"How did you do that?" Jenny asked him as he laughed.

"It's easy, girl," he said, "all you have to do is swim down two strokes until you feel the bottom, then swim backward two more strokes towards the riverbank until you feel the side, and then swim up. It's super easy."

Jenny did not fancy a swim in dirty, crocodile-infested water, and she told him so.

"*Come on*, Jenny," he said, "you'll only be in the water for five seconds, tops. Trust me, it'll be worth it."

She sighed. He knew she would do it. He had always been good at getting her to do things.

"Oh, and don't open your mouth," Seth added. "You don't want to swallow any of this water."

"What?" Jenny said but his face had already disappeared.

"I'll be waiting," he said from somewhere under her feet.

Jenny walked to the edge of the rock and sighed. She did not want to do this, but she also wanted to see what all the fuss was about. She took off her shoes and socks and stood at the edge. The distance between her toes and the water was only about two feet, but it looked much higher from her perspective. She sat down and dabbed her foot into the water. It was warm and thick. She felt something solid flow past and touch her toe, which caused her to jump and pull her feet out of the water. That image of the crocodile returned to her mind, only this time it was her being dragged into the mud. Her heart began to pound.

She finally built up her courage enough to put both her feet into the water, first dipping a toe and then her entire foot. Then, growing bolder, she took a deep breath and slide over the side of the rock into the river. She gripped the edge and let herself get used to the current. It was strong, but she was a strong swimmer. Still, she was nervous. After several deep breaths to build up her courage, she used the edge of the rock to push herself down into the water, hoping her feet would touch the bottom. They didn't. She struggled against the current to stay in one place, afraid to abandon the security of the rock. But then she thought of crocodile's again and realized she was hanging there like a fish on a hook. *Time to let go*, she told herself. She continued to lower herself until the water was up to her neck. As the green water closed over her head, she let go of the rock and swam down.

She couldn't see a thing in the murky water, but thankfully her feet touched the bottom. She pressed her toes down into the mud and pushed forward. The current pushed her sideways, and she began to flail about with her arms as she tried to stay on course. She took two awkward strokes forward but didn't feel the edge of the riverbank. She took another stroke forward. Still she didn't feel the edge of the bank. She fought to keep from panicking and took one more desperate stroke. She almost broke her nose on a hard, rocky surface, but she didn't think about it and clawed her way upwards. Sooner than she thought, her head broke the surface of the water and she pulled herself into a dark, enclosed space and onto a dusty patch of dirt. Once on dry land she took several deep breaths, her heart beating like a drum.

After a second, she looked around. As her eyes adjusted to the dimness, she saw she was in a small grotto. But this was different from anything she had imagined. Several rays of light from the setting sun entered through crevices in the rock overhead and illuminated the walls of the chamber which shown brilliantly wherever the light touched it. She looked closer, and realized that long, wide veins of gold covered the walls. But embedded within the veins was something else that outshone the gold. Her foot brushed a stone at her feet. She reached down and picked it up. It was a diamond.

Jenny's eyes grew wide as she lowered herself to her knees. As she did, a ray of light struck the diamond in her hand and refracted into a million fragments which rebounded off of the walls of the chamber, making them sparkle like a billion stars. Jenny gasped as she realized that the golden walls were covered with diamonds. It was the most dazzling sight she had ever seen.

From a corner of the grotto Seth whispered, "Welcome to the Heart of the Jungle."

Chapter 10
Changed But Stronger

As Jenny sat and stared at the wealth of natural beauty around her, everything about the little village of Sangha started to make sense: they weren't just mining gold, but diamonds, too. This was a diamond smuggling operation. Now she understood why the mercenaries were here and why they needed the villagers. The secret conversations, the bribes, and the paranoia fell into place. Even to her untrained eye, she could see that the contents of the grotto were worth several fortunes. Never in her wildest dreams had she imagined that something so valuable could exist in the heart of the wild African jungle. She shuddered when she thought of what people like Colonel Massi might do should they learn the truth.

Seth guessed her thoughts. "Now you know why this operation has to be so secretive," he said, his voice serious. "If anyone finds out what the mercenaries are actually digging up, our way of life will be over."

For a moment, Jenny was too stunned to speak. "Wow," she whispered.

"Yeah, I know," he replied. "I'm sorry that no one told you before, but we can't risk it getting out. This is part of the reason why the Sharon's are trying so hard to get back. They have connections with the French, American, and Central African governments, including an official charter from the French Customs Office to run a missionary work in the country. Their presence stops most people from messing with us."

The Sharon's. Jenny wondered how they could have let her come here when the situation was so dangerous. Her parents would have tried to stop her from going if they had been aware of the true situation. She wondered if she would have come had she known.

Again, Seth guessed her thoughts. "The Sharon's would never have let either of us come if they didn't have special immunity. And, to their credit, they tried hard to persuade me not to come because of the danger. I'm sure they did the same for you."

They had. When she had first contacted the Sharon's and told them about her desire to help them, they had been supportive and grateful, but had explained to her in great detail the dangers of the Central African Republic. At the time, Jenny had been more worried about diseases than domestic troubles and hadn't given much thought to dangers that seemed far removed from her own life. Now, she realized that, like Seth, she'd been naïve.

Seth continued. "The Sharon's didn't understand the full extent of the mining operation when it began, but they were very open with me without getting too specific. When I found out about the gold and diamonds, I was still too naïve to understand the gravity of the situation. I thought it would be a big adventure. But now I've seen enough to realize that we're balanced on the edge of a knife."

"Does Mercury know about this grotto?" Jenny asked.

"No," replied Seth, "so far the only people who know about this place are Femi and me. But this place must be part of the vein that the mercenaries are working. I'm afraid it's only a matter of time before they find it."

Jenny nodded as she scanned the diamond encrusted and gold streaked walls. She agreed with Seth—it was only a matter of time before someone else uncovered the grotto's secret. The village of Sangha was balanced on the edge of a knife and if it fell, they would all be cut to pieces. Their situation was dire. Jenny's stomach should have been in a knot, but she felt no fear. She should have been afraid, but instead she felt peace. Perhaps the seven weeks spent laboring under extreme conditions alongside wonderful people had refined her. Or maybe the incredible scene in which she found herself was putting her mind at ease. It was hard to be afraid when surrounded by such raw natural beauty.

"Wow," she said again, "this place is *stunning*."

"I know, right?" Seth replied, thankful for the change in subject. "Femi and I call it 'The Heart of the Jungle.'"

"I can see why," Jenny said as she got up to inspect the exquisite walls. They had both begun to whisper, as if the sound of their voices might damage the surrounding beauty. "How does a place like this even happen?"

"It has something to do with pressure, and heat, and the volcanic soil in the area," Seth replied. "I'm sure Ferdy could tell you all about it."

"How did you find it?"

"I didn't. Femi did."

She remembered Femi for the first time since entering the little cave. She looked around and saw him in a corner with his back to her rummaging around between rocks and tree roots.

"I think we've found our little thief's hiding place," Seth said with a smile.

He stood up, hanging his head to avoid bumping it on the roof of the cave, and went to kneel behind Femi. When he said the boy's name, his little frame tensed, and he made a slow turn to look at Seth with a guilty expression on his face. Seth asked him what he was doing but received no answer. He looked around the little boy and began to move the rocks, leaves, and tree roots out of the way. In amongst the detritus were little odds and ends, pieces of clothing, knives, crumbled bits of paper, and several shiny objects.

"Femi…" began Seth in a scolding tone, "are these things yours?" No reply.

"Did you steal these things?"

Again, no reply. But the look on the boy's face was confession enough.

"Is it right to steal?"

Still no reply. Seth sighed.

"Femi, you know it's wrong to take things that aren't yours. That's called stealing. How many times has your mother told you not to steal things? Do you remember what she said would happen next time she caught you stealing?"

At the mention of his mother, Femi gave a small gasp and stared up at Seth with scared eyes. Jenny had to turn her face to hide a smile.

"I should tell your mother I found these things here," Seth said as he cleared his throat to keep from laughing, "but I won't on one condition. You have to give everything back to the people you stole from. Does that sound fair?" The little boy gave a vigorous nod, and Seth smiled. "Now, I want you to gather up all these things and give them back before dinner time, okay?" Femi began gathering the things up. "And I will check that you gave them back, got it?" Femi gave him a quick 'okay' sign with his hand and resumed gathering the stolen items, placing them in a plastic bag. When he had them gathered up, he slithered up the little hole he had used to enter the grotto and disappeared.

As soon as they were alone, both Jenny and Seth released the laughter they had been holding in.

"Oh, my goodness, he's so funny!" Jenny said between giggles. "How do you keep a straight face?"

"You saw how well I did," Seth replied with a chuckle. "He's such a sweet little boy, but he's got issues! We can't get him to stop taking things."

"Is he going to be all right by himself out there?"

"Yeah, he'll be fine. He knows this jungle better than anyone. Plus, he's a resourceful little guy. He's got no fear. One time a crazy bull elephant in musth during mating season found his way into the village. He whipped everyone into a panic smashing homes and trampling crops. Someone found Mercury, and he brought his big elephant gun and to shoot it, but Femi got in the way. Walked right up to the crazy elephant and stared him down. The big guy wasn't playing around though, and he charged. It was a false charge—the first one always is—but Femi didn't flinch. Seriously, not even a twitch. The big bull stopped right in front of him. It was so crazy. Femi looked like a rabbit next to him. But he held his ground, and crazy enough, the elephant backed down. We were able to shoo him away after that. Shooting him would have been risky with this being a national park, so Femi really saved us. It was one of the most incredible things I've ever seen."

"Wow. How did he get so brave?"

"We don't know. We have no idea where he came from. Aleena and Jean-Marc don't think he's even from the C.A.R. We've tried to ask him before, but he either can't remember, or doesn't want to. So, we don't ask him anymore. But he had obviously been living on the streets for some time before we found him. He was like a little animal living with stray dogs and cats. It is a miracle he even survived and even more of a miracle how far he's come since then."

"He's a special kid. You seem to have a special relationship with him."

Seth nodded and stared at the far wall of the grotto with a distant look in his eyes. "Yeah, he's my little buddy. I'm not his father or brother or anything, but I feel responsible for him. In fact, that's how I feel about all the villagers. I guess this is what it feels like to be a pastor or something, to be responsible for people's lives, their personal growth, and their souls. It's a strange, disorienting feeling. I never meant to be a pastor, but I guess I kind of became one. This must be what I'm supposed to do, what God wants me to do."

He turned and looked at Jenny as he finished. She smiled and elbowed him. "Look at you sharing your feelings," she teased. "When did you get so sensitive?"

Seth chuckled, but he still had that faraway look in his eyes. "It's so weird Jenny, it's like ever since I've come here, I've become a totally different person. But at the same time, I feel like this is who I've always been. Like somehow I was pretending to be someone before, but now that pretense is gone and my true self has emerged. I don't know how to describe it."

"I get what you're saying," Jenny assured him. "I feel like the same thing has happened to me. It's like I'm a butterfly emerging from a cocoon. Whoever I was before was still me, but now I'm changing into what I was always meant to be."

"Yes!" Seth exclaimed, "that's exactly what it's like! It's like all my life has been some sort of lesser existence, but now I'm finally living the life I'm supposed to live. I guess this is what it's like to be fulfilling your purpose in life. Now I'm the butterfly that I'm supposed to be." He began to laugh. "Wow, I've never compared myself to a butterfly before."

Jenny laughed with him. "You're so different now," she said with a smile. He turned and looked at her with a curious expression on his face, and she felt self-conscious. "But you're still you," she added. "I can see how the butterfly you are now came from the caterpillar you used to be."

They both started laughing again. "You're a lot different too," he said when they finished. "We both used to be so different. What did we care about back then?"

"Nothing that mattered," Jenny replied.

"Sometimes I feel like we wasted our time. We only thought about ourselves. We had no concept of what it means to give our lives for Christ. Now I look back and think about all the things we could have done differently to help others had we only known of what we do now. We could have done a lot of good instead of wasting our time."

He fell silent. "Not that being with you was a waste of time, Jenny," he added after a moment. "I would never wish that that hadn't happened. I enjoyed every minute of it. And I wouldn't change any of it."

He fumbled for his words. "Perhaps we needed to go through all that to get to where we are today," she said attempting to help him.

"Right," he said.

They fell silent again, both occupied with their own private thoughts. They sat side by side against a sloping rock at the back of the grotto. For several moments, they enjoyed each other's company in silence.

"You know, I never blamed you for not coming with me," Seth said, breaking the silence.

Jenny turned to look at him. He was gazing at her with his deep brown eyes. For the first time she realized how close they were sitting next to each other.

"What do you mean?" she asked.

"I mean I never blamed you for not coming with me here the first time," he clarified.

"Really?" she replied. "I thought you would. I blamed you. I thought you were destroying the perfect life that we had together."

Seth shrugged his shoulders. "I don't blame you for blaming me either. At first, I was disappointed that you didn't want to come with me, but after I'd been here a few months, I realized the enormity of what I had asked you to do. And, well, I guess I never really asked you either, did I? I just assumed that you would come with me. I guess I took you for granted, Jenny. I'm sorry."

"Seth, don't apologize," she said. She hadn't intended for this to turn into a conversation about their past. She had always hoped to discuss these things with him, but now that it was happening, she realized she wasn't ready. "You did nothing wrong by leaving me. I understand that now. You were doing what you believed God wanted you to do, and I was too wrapped up in myself to see it. It took me awhile to see things the way you did, but I'm here now, aren't I?"

"Yes, you are," he said with a smile. Jenny looked at him. He no longer had that faraway look in his eyes. Now he looked straight at her. Again, she noticed how close they were to each other. Something stirred inside her heart. A flame she had thought was long dead began to smolder.

Seth shifted his position, touching her hand as he did so. He crossed his legs underneath him and shifted to face her. He leaned forward and looked her straight in the eye.

"What if I had asked you now? Would you have come with me?"

Jenny smiled. He said it in a serious voice, but she detected a hint of that quiet, confident smirk in his features. She was about to answer but was interrupted by a distant sound. It was faint, but it sent a shiver down her spine. She had heard it before. It was a lion's roar.

The charm of the little grotto faded, and Jenny realized how dark the cave had become. The sun must have gone behind the trees. "It's getting late," she said.

Seth looked at his tattered watch. "Yeah, you're right," he said with a big sigh. "We'd better head back. Trust me, we do not want to get stuck in the jungle at night. You up for another quick swim?"

Jenny wasn't ready for another swim because her clothes had only just begun to dry, but there was no other way. "Let's get this over with," she said.

Seth went first, leaving her alone in the strange little grotto. She glanced around and sighed. This was a magical place, but she felt like some of its magic had been sucked away. She had that longing feeling that comes from a missed opportunity. She sighed once more and plunged into the water.

Chapter 11
Nothing Is Immediate

The walk back to the village was uncomfortable. Seth chattered nervously, which wasn't like him. He seemed to be on a mission to avoid silence, lest it grow awkward and give either of them time to think about what had passed between them in the grotto.

"We should be fine," he said as they turned back onto the path that led from the river to the mining camp. "The lion sounded pretty far away, and I know a lion's roar can carry several miles. He's probably miles from here. But that's on the open savannah where lions normally live and we're here in a thick, wet jungle which would absorb the sound a lot better. So, it might be closer than we think. But we've got more reason to worry about leopards than we do lions. They're so much more cunning, and, believe it or not, they're known to be a lot more aggressive than lions are. Lions usually leave people alone unless they're directly threatened, but leopards are more likely to attack a person. And they're much more active in the dark, which is why we keep those torches burning all night. Which also means we'd better get back to the village before dark."

They heard the lion roar again. It sounded like it was still far away.

"Since when did you become an expert on big cats?" Jenny asked, trying to do her part in the conversation, though she didn't feel up to it.

"When I first came here," Seth replied. "I worried about lions too, but I was quickly informed that there aren't many lions in the C.A.R. They usually live on the savannah or in the bush and almost never in the jungle."

That was interesting to Jenny. "Wait, lions don't live in the jungle?" she asked.

"Not according to Ferdy."

"Then why do they call the lion 'The King of the Jungle?'"

"That's a good question. I'm not sure. Maybe it's because people associate both lions and jungle with Africa. But we've never had a lion in this area since I've been here. In fact, I don't think there's ever been a lion in this jungle since the village was founded. That's why this one is such a big deal."

"So that's why you didn't believe Mercury when he said it was a lion?"

Seth snorted. "Yeah. I still can't tell the difference between their roars or tracks, but I guess Mercury knows. He's been all over the continent of Africa and hunted in the jungle, the savannah, the bushveld. He's the one who taught me most of what I've learned about the wildlife in the C.A.R. He and Ferdy, that is."

There was a pause in the conversation. They were passing the mining camp, which was silent now that the work day was over.

"Hey, you know what we should do?" Seth said, filling the silence. "We should go on a safari! We've both been working hard lately, and we deserve a break. Mercury and Ferdy can take us around for a day and show us the jungle. We've done it several times before. There's so much to see in this area we can reach in one day. We can pack a big lunch and have a picnic. We'll go to see the elephants, and, if we're lucky, we'll be able to find gorillas too. Trust me Jenny, it'll be awesome."

"I would love that," Jenny said, and she meant it. She had worked nonstop for the past seven weeks and hadn't had time to explore the country.

Seth was pleased. "I'll talk to Clayton the next chance I get."

After Seth's suggestion, the tension between them loosened.

They spent the rest of the walk planning the safari and talking about all the different animals they might see. By the time they reached the village, the last glow of the sun had disappeared and twilight had almost passed. As they walked through the fields, they heard the lion roar again, but this time it didn't sound so far away.

They found many of the villagers gathered at the edge of the village in a nervous mob. They were murmuring between one another, but Ferdy was talking over them all. Mercury was standing next to him with his arms crossed and an annoyed look in his eyes.

"… but so far, he hasn't come into the village, nor has he attacked us or our livestock," Ferdy was saying. "We have no evidence to suggest he means us any harm, so the best course of action is to leave him alone."

"What's going on?" Seth asked Mercury.

"Where have *you* been?" he asked.

"On a walk," Seth replied.

The mercenary raised an eyebrow. "Just the two of you?"

Both Seth and Jenny shrugged their shoulders. Mercury looked at them, sighed and shook his head.

"In case you haven't heard," he said, "there's a lion on the loose. Ferdinand and I are trying to stop the villagers from going on a boar hunt to slaughter it."

"What's wrong with that?" Jenny asked.

A man in the crowd interrupted Ferdy. "The lion is still a danger to us and our children," he shouted. "Why should we wait for him to attack us?" Several voices rose in support.

"Because we don't know that he *will* attack us," Ferdy said. The people began to argue.

"What's wrong with that?" said Mercury, turning back to Jenny and addressing her question. "First off, the lion has done nothing except roar. Now I'm all for hunting and for protecting yourself, but a lion doesn't deserve to be shot just for roaring. Second, a hunt for a big cat isn't a walk-in-the-park. It's long and grueling. These people are farmers, not hunters and are not equipped or trained to stalk a lion."

"Couldn't you catch the lion?" Seth asked.

"Yes, I *could*," Mercury said in a sarcastic tone, "but I *can't*, the reason being that I don't want to. The lion hasn't hurt anyone and probably won't, and I don't have the time nor the patience to go on a lion hunt right now. Besides, we've got bigger problems to deal with, and a lion hunt will only attract more attention to us than we need at the moment."

"Listen, listen," Ferdy said calmly in his loud, commanding voice, "We are not in danger from the lion. He is lost and afraid, as any of you would be if you were far from home. If we leave him be, he will leave us be."

"Actually," Mercury whispered to Jenny, "if the lion is this far out of his range, he's probably old, or wounded and can't catch normal prey. He might be starving. Starving lions are the ones that become man-eaters."

"We have leopards in this jungle too," Ferdy continued. "They are as dangerous as this lion, yet we do not hunt them. This lion is a new creature for us, but he is no more dangerous than a leopard. He should not disrupt our lives any more than a leopard should. Listen to the hunter, Clayton Mercury. He is in agreement, that we should not hunt the lion."

"Ferdinand is right," Mercury said as he stepped forward to address the crowd. "The lion is not a threat to us. We do not have a good reason to shoot him. However, that doesn't mean we shouldn't be cautious. Make sure to light a few more torches every night and tie up all the animals so they can't get loose. You also should be more careful about straying from the village, especially at night. As usual, everyone should be back in the village before the sun goes behind the trees." He turned to look at Seth and Jenny and raised an eyebrow.

"Please, everyone, go back to your homes and finish your dinner," Ferdy said. "Nothing needs to be done tonight."

The people still didn't act convinced, and some of them began to protest, until Seth called out: "You heard the man. Forget about the lion. Go eat your dinner." He started shooing them away. They begrudgingly moved back into the village.

"Of course," Mercury began as the area cleared, "the real reason we can't shoot the lion is because this is a national park and we'd have the French government all over us if they ever found out."

"We do not need government involvement here," Ferdy agreed.

"Still, the villagers will be uneasy until the lion is caught or leaves the area," Nanci said as she walked up. "Are you sure there's nothing y'all can do to ease their worry? Maybe just do a quick look for the big guy?" Mercury grunted and rolled his eyes.

"I've got an idea," Seth said. "Why don't we take a little game run and see what's out there? We could take a survey of the area and see if we can find the lion. We'd also get a good look at any other animals around here. You know how skittish the villagers are about leopards. This might make them feel better."

"Oh, you mean like a little safari?" Mercury said.

"Sure," Seth replied, not picking up on the mercenary's tone. "Jenny and I have been wanting to see the wildlife, and this might be a good opportunity. We'll alleviate the villagers' fears and enjoy ourselves at the same time."

Mercury took a step towards him. "You think now is a good time to have a safari?" he asked, his voice dropping.

"Why not? We've done them before, and, like you said, we don't really have anything to fear from the lion. We don't have to search for him that hard either, we just need to ease some of the villagers' fears."

Mercury took another step. "You think now is a good time to take a safari," he said. It was a question, but this time he phrased it like an accusation.

Seth paused for a second. "Yes, I do," he said.

"You think, after all we've talked about, that right now is a good time to leave your village and my camp undefended and go running around in the jungle where anyone could find us?" Mercury was whispering now, and he fixed Seth with a glare that could have crushed granite. "Have you been listening to anything I've been telling you boy?"

Seth bristled under the mercenary's withering stare. His shoulders straightened, his jaw clenched, and his chin stuck out in defiance. "All I'm asking is for you to take a game run and let us come along. It wouldn't take more than a day and—"

"Not a chance," Mercury interrupted. "I don't have time to babysit you on a potentially disastrous trip. I've got a million other things to worry about, and so do you. It's too dangerous right now, and I will not take that chance. You all do what you want, but you're on your own." He turned and strode out of the village.

Seth sighed and rolled his eyes in disgust as he watched the mercenary depart. "You still think you like him Jenny?" he asked.

"Maybe he's right," she replied. "Maybe he's just worried about our safety?"

"The only thing he's worried about are his profits," Seth said.

"I fear you are right," Ferdy agreed.

"Now, now you two," Nanci said, "Clayton Mercury may be a prickly porcupine on the outside, but deep down he really does care about what happens to us. But I'm wondering why he's so uptight right now. Did something happen recently to set him off?"

"He found out that Mohammedou Djotodia is probably in cahoots with the Seleka," Seth replied. He sounded so tired again.

"What's so bad about that?" Nanci asked.

"Mercury thinks Mohammedou will tell the ex-Seleka about our village out of revenge or to persuade his superiors to rob the mercenaries."

"Then Clayton Mercury is right to be nervous," Ferdy said. "Mohammedou is not our friend. I would not be surprised to find out he has told all sorts of stories to get back at us for banishing him."

The little group of people were silent for a moment as the reality of their situation settled upon them. In the jungle behind them, insects chirped like everything was right with the world.

"Well," Nanci began, breaking the silence, "all we can do is hope and pray that Mohammedou won't give us away, or that the Seleka won't believe him. This won't last forever. We'll be able to do a safari again sometime. We'll just have to wait a bit. Let's stop worrying about it and go finish dinner."

They walked back to their neighborhood where dinner was getting cold and tried to enjoy each other's company. But for Jenny the evening had been ruined, and she could tell by the stilted conversation of her companions it had been ruined for them too. They bid each other an early goodnight as the distant lion roared one last time.

The next day was a supply run day, and Seth tried to cheer Jenny up by inviting her along. She was thankful for the break in her routine and for the change of scenery. They left early in the morning in one of the mercenary supply trucks—Jenny, Seth, and Ferdy, with George Hauser in the driver's seat. Today, instead of his combat fatigues, tactical vest, and array of weapons, Hauser was dressed casually in cargo pants, a baseball cap, and a blue t-shirt that stretched to contain his broad shoulders and deep chest. Jenny wondered whether he was a normal presence on these supply runs, or if he had been added because Mercury was worried about their safety. She resolved to ask Seth as soon as they were alone.

The road to Bayanga was as rough as it had been seven weeks ago, but once again, the scenery fascinated Jenny. She was able to identify a few of the plants and animals now that she had spent time in the jungle, and she pointed things out and asked questions which Ferdy answered with enthusiasm. The more she saw, the more she wanted to see. But more than once Hauser mentioned that his orders from Mercury were clear: he was to take them straight into town for supplies and come straight back. Jenny tried not to be disappointed.

Once they arrived in Bayanga, they dropped Ferdy off near the center of town where he would conduct his business and then headed towards the shops and market. Seth produced a list of supplies they needed and they spent several hours finding and purchasing them, occasionally making trips back to the truck and driving to new spots as needed. They ate lunch at a modern restaurant where Jenny had a cheeseburger for the first time in two months. It was hot, juicy, and delicious. She topped it off with French fries and a chocolate Magnum ice-cream bar which she shared with Seth. They laughed at each other as the ice cream melted in the intense heat and ran down their fingers and onto their sleeves. Jenny was having too much fun to care. However, when Seth tried to lick the melted ice cream off of his hand, she slapped it away and gave him a napkin. They may have been living in a jungle, but they would not act like savages.

After lunch they walked to an area of the town which had lots of shop stands, an open-air food market, and lots of touristy shops. Since they had already purchased most of the supplies they needed, they lingered in the area while they waited for Ferdy to get done with his business. The two of them browsed aimlessly, trying on hats and shoes, tasting foods, and examining odds and ends while picking up the obscure knick-knack from their list. As they shopped, Hauser followed from a distance, ducking in and out of shops and looking at random items, but Jenny suspected that he was only pretending to shop. He frequently placed his hand on a suspicious lump in one of his pockets as if he was reassuring himself that, whatever it was, was still there. He didn't say much throughout the day unless they spoke to him, which was why it was unusual for him to approach them at a sunglass stand and speak to them in a low voice.

"Do you see that man over by the potatoes?" he asked in his Irish brogue, "the one with the hooded sweater?" Jenny started to turn, but he stopped her and made as if to show her a pair of sunglasses, pointing into a small mirror next to the stand. She and Seth looked into the reflection and saw a thin man in a cap and a sweatshirt with the hood pulled up to conceal his face.

"Little warm for a sweatshirt," Seth remarked.

"Exactly what I was thinking, lad," Hauser replied. "He's also been following us since lunch." He continued to browse through the sunglasses and then turned to a table of shirts and pants. "He's also not very good at it. Watch." He led them from table to table as if they were just shopping. Each time they moved, the hooded man moved too. He was never more than three or four tables away.

"What do we do about it?" Jenny asked as she held up a shirt to measure it against Seth's shoulders.

"We lose him, right?" Seth said as he stole a glance at the man over his shoulder.

"No," Hauser said as he stretched, flexing his muscles like a big cat. "We find out what he's up to. Let's split up and see who he follows. If he follows you, I'll circle around and watch him. You two stay together and keep shopping but keep moving." Without waiting for a response, he sauntered off as if nothing was wrong. He disappeared from sight after several moments, lost amongst the crowd, but the hooded man didn't follow him. He continued to shadow Jenny and Seth as they shopped. They drifted out of the market and into the streets, looking in windows and entering shops, but the hooded man was always in sight somewhere along the street. As the afternoon faded, they ducked into a crowded tourist shop and watched him through the window.

"This is getting ridiculous," Seth whispered. "Where's Hauser? Have you seen him?"

Jenny shook her head and looked at her watch. "We have to meet Ferdy soon. If George is going to make his move on that guy, he'd better do it soon."

"Let's help him," Seth replied. He took Jenny's hand and pulled her through the crowded shop, past the counter and down a hall towards the back door. A sign in plain English stated that the door was not to be used as an exit. An employee appeared from a door way to their left.

"Is it okay if we go through here?" Seth asked innocently. "We're trying to cut through the alley." The young woman gave a brief sigh, then nodded as she opened the backdoor and let them out.

They emerged into a narrow alley formed by the backsides of

two rows of shops. The alley was long, straight, and branched off into several other alleys.

"Now what?" Jenny asked.

"Now we wait," replied Seth. "If this guy is serious about following us, he'll panic and come looking for us after we don't come out. Then we can get a good look at him and ask him why he's following us."

Jenny looked around at the deserted alley. She saw one problem with Seth's plan.

"What if he tries to hurt us?" she asked. "Maybe he's been sent to abduct us or something. There's nobody else around. You got a weapon on you?"

Seth paused. He hadn't thought of that. "Then I hope Hauser is close by," he said. He led Jenny around the corner of the shop where they could watch the back door they had just left. Seth peered around the corner and waited.

They had been waiting for about ten minutes when Seth jerked back behind the cover of the shop and motioned for Jenny to remain silent. Then, with Jenny right behind him, he inched his face back around the corner and watched. After several seconds, Jenny felt his body stiffen. She looked at his face and saw his eyes widen in surprise. But then his brow furrowed. He gave a shout and dashed around the corner.

Jenny rushed after him and saw their stalker sprinting down the alley, hood streaking behind him, with Seth right on his heels. Jenny raced after them, but she was too far away to be much help. Seth ran like a cheetah, but the other man was faster. Seth chased him around a turn in the alley, hiding them from Jenny's view. By the time she saw them again, they had far outpaced her. They were almost to the end of the alley and would soon exit into one of the main streets. With a sinking feeling, Jenny realized that their pursuer would reach the street before Seth could catch him. Once there it would be easy for him to lose himself amongst the people and shops.

But then a short, stocky form smashed through a fence to the man's left and barreled into him, body-slamming him against the wall with a thud that shook the entire row of shops. The much thinner man crumpled to the ground. When Jenny and Seth reached the scene a dust and woodchip covered George Hauser was standing over the groaning man. Hauser picked him up in his meaty hands and slammed him against the wall again, knocking off his baseball cap in the process.

"Well, well, well, what do we have here?" the Irishman said.

It was Mohammedou Djotodia.

Mohammedou struggled in Hauser's vise-like grip, but the Irishman shook him like a rat until he stopped.

"What are you doing here, Mohammedou?" Seth asked, still gasping for breath. "Why are you following us?"

Mohammedou sneered and spit in Seth's direction. Hauser pulled a pistol out of his suspicious pocket and jammed it into his gut, knocking the wind out of him for the third time. The mercenary wasn't playing games. He growled at Mohammedou: "Talk. Now."

A look of genuine fear slid across Mohammedou's dark features. He spat out a word in Sango that Jenny didn't recognize but assumed was a curse word.

"General Abdul-Azeez sends his regards," he snarled.

"And who might that be?" Hauser asked, shoving the gun deeper into Mohammedou's gut.

Mohammedou grimaced but continued to speak. "He is my leader, and he knows all about you and your infidel village. He will come and take what you steal from our land, and he will destroy you all for what you have done." He glared at Seth with a snarl on his face as he spoke. Jenny had never heard anyone speak with such hatred before.

"Is that so?" Hauser asked, twisting the pistol even deeper into Mohammedou's body. The African man gasped in pain.

"That's enough," Seth said, placing his hand on Hauser's shoulder. Hauser stared at him for a moment, but Seth stared right back. Finally, Hauser released the man, who collapsed to the ground holding his stomach.

Seth looked at Mohammedou, a sad expression on his face. "I don't know what we ever did to you to make you hate us so much, Mohammedou," he said, "but I am sorry that you do. We took you in and tried to help you, but you betrayed our trust and brought violence into our home. I saved you from being killed by banishing you, and now you've repaid me with betrayal of an even greater magnitude. You may have doomed us all."

A moment of silence passed where Seth just looked at Mohammedou, but the other man couldn't meet his gaze.

"Well, I know how to fix some of this," Hauser said. He lifted Mohammedou to his feet with a rough jerk and pressed the barrel of the gun into the nape of his neck.

"No," Seth said in a commanding voice.

"This is the only way to stop any of this," Hauser replied. "If he's dead, he can't tell General Abdul-Easy anything else about where we are."

"No," Seth said again, louder this time. "We will not be executioners."

"Speak for yourself, kid," Hauser replied.

"This makes us no better than they are. It goes against everything we teach in our village."

"I'm not a part of your village."

"This is village business, Hauser. His crimes were against us, and we don't do things this way. Put him down."

"This is mercenary business. I'm protecting the interests of my employer, and you, and the village too. You don't have to be a part of this. It's not your fault."

Hauser's face was set in stone, but so was Seth's. Mohammedou tried to look tough, but he couldn't hide his terror. Jenny broke in.

"George, this country and these people have seen enough violence. If you kill him, you only add to that violence, and you make us no better than him and those other murders. Can't we please take him to the authorities or something?"

Hauser looked like he was wavering. He turned to face Jenny, shifting the position of his gun a fraction of an inch.

Mohammedou seized the opportunity. He jabbed his bony knee up into Hauser's groin and twisted away from him like a monkey escaping a python. Hauser doubled over for only an instant, but it was long enough for Mohammedou to escape down the alley. When he reached the street, he melted into a crowd of people and disappeared.

"Why didn't you grab him?" Hauser barked at Seth. He didn't reply, just stared down the alley after Mohammedou. Hauser swore and began to limp back the way they had come. "Come on," he said, "let's get Ferdy and get out of here."

Seth looked at the ground in dismay. Jenny put her arm around him and led him through the alley and back into the sunlight.

On the way back to the village, Ferdy listened to their story in silence, an unreadable expression on his face. When Jenny finished, he rubbed the stubble on his chin thoughtfully. All he said was, "We can only pray that Colonel Massi's hatred for the Seleka will outweigh his lust for gold." But he didn't sound hopeful.

The rest of the trip was quiet. Hauser drove straight to the mining camp to report to Mercury while the others waited in the truck. No one spoke while they waited. Ferdy closed his eyes and rested while Seth stared into the jungle, his chin in his hand. Jenny wanted to say something, but couldn't think of anything, so she stayed silent.

Hauser came back after about fifteen minutes. Jenny expected Mercury to come with a stern look and a dozen new security rules, but Hauser came alone. They all looked at him in expectation. He got behind the wheel of the truck and drove towards the village.

"Mercury says this General Abdul-Azeez is a chieftain from up north," Hauser began, "where the Muslims have control. He says he is probably ex-Seleka. He says we have to be even more careful than we were before, and he says again that it's time for us all to move out. We don't know for sure if Abdul-Azeez has contacted Colonel Massi yet, but the fact that Mohammedou is back in the area is good reason to believe that he has."

The others were silent for a moment as Hauser's words sunk in. "Did Clayton have any new security advice?" Ferdy asked.

"Nothing except that we need to be even more careful," Hauser replied. "Oh, and one other thing: he said that if you still want to do a safari, he's okay with it."

"Really?" Jenny asked. She was excited, but she hadn't expected Mercury to concede the safari, especially after the day's events.

"He said if you must go, now is as good a time as any. Things sure won't get better any time soon. He said to knock yourselves out."

"Wait," Seth said, "he won't be joining us?"

"No," Hauser replied. "I'll be taking you. He said we should be okay for the next few days; the military takes forever to do anything here. If anything is going to happen, it won't happen for a while."

"Okay, whatever he says," Seth replied. He still looked skeptical, but now there was a new light in his eyes. It looked like excitement. "This will be just what we need to take our minds off of all of this stuff, Jenny."

"When would you like to go?" Hauser asked.

"What do you think Ferdy?" asked Seth, turning to him.

Ferdy stroked his chin and glanced at Hauser with a curious look on his face. He paused before he spoke. "We Africans live in danger every day," he began. "If this unholy alliance between Colonel Massi and General Abdul-Azeez is coming to destroy us, it makes no difference if we are on safari or in the village." He continued to stare at Hauser, who didn't meet his eyes.

When the mercenary didn't respond, he continued. "As far as when we should go, one day is no better or worse than the next. However, it is too late for us to be ready to leave tomorrow. We must get up quite early if we want to catch the bongo."

"The bongo?" Jenny asked, confused.

"Bongo are a type of large antelope," Seth said. "They're beautiful but very skittish and secretive. If we want to see any, we have to go very early. They're only active at night or dawn."

Jenny nodded. She remembered coming across a picture of a bongo when she had been researching her trip. Seth was right about them being beautiful. The reddish-brown coat and white stripes along with the long, spiraled horns had entranced Jenny, and had helped paint a romantic picture of Africa in her brain. Her work amongst the poverty-stricken Central Africans had mostly destroyed that picture, but the mention of the bongo brought it to her mind once again.

"I can handle an early morning," she said, "if it means getting to see a bongo."

"Even though we are in a wildlife reserve where the animals are more used to human interaction, many of them still avoid us," Ferdy replied. "The bongo like their privacy and rarely allow people to see them. But we will try. Saturday, two days from now, should give us enough time to prepare."

"It's settled then," Seth said. "Saturday is Safari Day." He smiled at Jenny and gave her a wink.

Chapter 12
The Rains in Africa

Despite Jenny's excitement, Saturday morning came too early for her. She had spent another boring Friday cooped up by the rain with nothing to do but daydream about the safari, but when her phone alarm went off at 4:30 am, she groaned and rolled over to hit the snooze. But Nanci unzipped her tent before she could fall back to sleep and greeted her in a voice far too loud for 4:30. Through the crack between the tent flaps, Jenny saw nothing but darkness. She forced herself to rise. Even though she knew the early morning was necessary, part of her still wanted to remain asleep. She stumbled out of bed, fumbled with the zipper on her mosquito netting, and struggled through the motions of getting ready.

By the time she had washed up, dressed, swallowed a quick breakfast of bananas and imported crackers, and brushed her teeth, her phone clock read 5:28. She grabbed her backpack and hurried to the northeast corner of the village where the rest of the small safari waited next to a large idling jeep. She was the last to arrive—for once Seth had arrived earlier than her. They did a quick inventory of their supplies and then loaded up to go.

The sky was a soft purple behind the black silhouette of the jungle as they rolled onto the bumpy trail leading out of the village. Ferdy, their resident tour guide, sat in the front with the driver, a Frenchman with a thin goatee named Jacques Bigot who worked as one of Clayton Mercury's scouts. Between them sat Femi, who slumped against Ferdy's big shoulder and snoozed. In the middle row sat Nanci, Aleena, and Jean-Marc. Jenny and Seth sat in the back next to George Hauser who carried a big shotgun this time in addition to his usual assault rifle. After their run-in with Mohammedou Djotodia, he wasn't taking any chances.

As they drove along several rough game trails, penetrating deeper into the jungle, Jenny's excitement grew. She focused all her senses into the darkness, straining to catch some hint of life. But the jungle was too dark, and the rumble of the jeep too loud. After about forty-five minutes of bumping along, they stopped. Bigot shut off the engine and killed the head-lights. The darkness enveloped them like a slap in the face. Jenny had never experienced such extreme blackness. With no ambient light, the blackness became a tangible thing, pressing into her eyes and smothering her like a thick blanket. Somewhere the sun was bringing dawn, but it wasn't high enough yet to illuminate the depths of the jungle. In the early morning hours, the darkness reigned supreme.

No one spoke. The absence of sight amplified every sound a hundred times. Frogs croaked in a thousand different voices while a million insects whistled and sang in a chorus that rivaled any symphony. Birds twittered, cawed, and screeched back and forth to one another. A monkey punctuated their conversations with a booming call. The last few bats, still hunting for their dinner before settling down to sleep out the day, squeaked and fluttered overhead. Ferns and vines rustled against each other in the gentle breeze. Water dripped from leaves soaked from a night rain, and, somewhere behind it all, the river flowed quietly and steadily like an ambient musical pad in a rock ballad. It was mysterious, chaotic, and confusing, but undeniably enchanting.

Jenny sat still in the backseat of the jeep and listened to the wonderland around her. As her eyes adjusted and dawn drew near, she began to pick out shapes and silhouettes. Slivers of purplish light trickled down, outlining the shapes of massive tree trunks, tangled creepers, and dense bushes. Occasionally a dark shape—perhaps a bird or a bat—would flutter over her head. But other than that, the jungle remained still.

Then, a new sound joined the chorus of ambient jungle sound effects. It was short and soft, perhaps a body brushing against a fern or a foot stepping on a leaf. Jenny froze. She scanned the dim forest, searching for any sign of movement. After several tense minutes passed without incident, she started to wonder if she'd imagined the noise. But then a shadow moved to her left, interrupting the dim light passing between two trees. The moment was brief but long enough for Jenny to glimpse a large shape tiptoeing across their path. It disappeared in the blackness and Jenny strained into the darkness to pick it out again. After several minutes, she feared the moment had passed. But then she felt Seth nudge her gently. She stared into the darkness once again and was rewarded when she saw movement. A head with wide ears, a long muzzle, and tall, spiraled horns materialized out of the darkness. It rotated, scanning the area. The ears stood out, alert for any warning sound. As Jenny stared, the rest of the creature began to take form. The delicate head was connected to a thick neck that flowed down into a large body supported by four agile legs. A short, furry tail held tight to the animal's rear completed the picture. Seth leaned into her ear and ever so softly whispered one word: *bongo*.

A thrill ran through Jenny's body as she stared at the silent creature. For several moments it stood still, watching and listening. The people in the jeep held their breath. Jenny could hear her heart pounding in her ears. The bushes to the left of the trail rustled and a second bongo stepped out of the foliage. Then a third emerged and then a fourth, followed by several small calves too young to have horns. They all huddled around the first bongo, which was larger than the others and seemed calmer. The bongos sensed the people, but they couldn't see them in the dark morning jungle.

As the jungle grew lighter, Jenny could pick out more of the bongos' features, like the jagged lightning-bolt shaped stripes on their backs. But the coming of the sun also revealed the jeep to the skittish mammals. They all seemed to notice it at once, freezing suddenly. They remained in place for several seconds, and then, at some silent command, they hurried across the trail and into the bushes where they vanished without a sound.

The people in the jeep all let out a collective exhale and began to whisper to one another in excitement. Ferdy told them that the big one was the matriarch of the herd, since bongo herds only consisted of females and younglings while the males lived a solitary life except during mating season. Bigot was about to start the jeep again when the trees rustled again and another bongo, bigger and statelier than all the others strode onto the trail. It had enormous elegantly twisted horns that crowned a grand head held erect in honor. Ferdy whispered that this was a big bull, but Jenny didn't need to be told. She recognized the wise, old stag of the forest.

The male bongo regarded them with mild interest. After a staring contest that lasted several minutes, he ambled towards the jeep and off to the left side. He stopped at the back and stared at Seth and Jenny. He was only a yard or two away. By now the sun had risen high enough to send some of its rays to the forest floor where they struck the big male, illuminating his chestnut coat and black face. He was a handsome creature to behold. For several long moments he stared into Jenny's eyes. She stared right back, captivated by the gaze of this majestic forest ghost.

But then the bongo decided to move on. He continued around the back of the jeep and into the jungle to the right of the trail. Before he disappeared, he paused and looked back, twisting his head around to look past his rump, and to stare at the humans one last time. Jenny blinked, and he was gone.

The people in the jeep began to laugh and chatter amongst one another. They had been lucky enough to witness a rare thing: a herd of bongos and a solitary male bongo in one morning. Bigot started up the jeep, and they continued down the trail. Jenny couldn't believe what she had just seen.

"Wow," she breathed, "that was… so… magical…"

George Hauser gave a chuckle to her right and muttered, "You haven't seen nothin' yet."

At that moment they burst from the darkness of the jungle into a wide clearing blazing with sunlight. At one end of the clearing was a low cliff over which a waterfall flowed, dumping a thin strand of white water onto a herd of elephants taking their morning bath. They splashed and sprayed one another, filling the clearing with a fine mist that mingled with the morning fog just beginning to rise and burn off in the sunlight. The run-off from the waterfall spread out across the clearing in dozens of streamlets that turned the ground into a muddy paradise before coalescing back into one stream and flowing back into the river. At a safe distance from the elephants, a mother hippopotamus and her baby played in the mud. Several small herds of antelope drank from the streamlets. Cattle egrets speckled the scene with spots of white. Long shadows cast by towering trees at the edge of the clearing painted everything with long, dark striations. The trumpeting of the elephants and the low hum of the waterfall filled the air.

As Jenny gazed at the gorgeous scene with her mouth wide open, Aleena turned around and smiled.

"*This* is Africa," she said. Jenny felt like she had finally arrived.

They sat and enjoyed the tranquil scene for quite some time. When the elephants began to move into the cool jungle to escape the heat of the rising sun, Ferdy directed Bigot to move on. They followed the river downstream at a slow pace, allowing Ferdy to point out various types of flora and fauna. They startled a flock of cranes that took flight, gangly wings moving in long, laborious strokes. They observed several small splashes which Ferdy identified as crocodiles sliding into the water. Once, they saw one floating lazily in a spot where the flow of the river was almost imperceptible. Jenny mistook it for a log until it jerked its jaws out of the water with a wriggling fish clasped between them.

Eventually the jungle growth hindered their progress beside the river, so they crossed to the other side via a bridge set up by the park rangers. On the other side of the river, they headed upstream until they came to a herd of African forest buffalo blocking the path. The reddish buffalo gathered together in a tight cluster, lowing softly. Bigot brought the jeep to a stop and turned off the engine. For several minutes the two groups observed each other, the buffaloes shifting and stamping in agitation, and the humans staring in fascination. Jenny counted thirty-two buffalo. They were small, no larger than an average milk cow. In fact, they looked very much like red cows and nothing like their much larger and more aggressive savannah cousins, the Cape buffalo, which are feared by predators and native farmers alike. She understood why these animals were also known as "dwarf buffalo."

After several minutes the buffalo built up enough courage to move forward. They approached the jeep cautiously, ears back and eyes wide. The herd parted when it reached the jeep, and the buffalo passed on either side. Up close, Jenny noticed how soft and fuzzy their fur was, and she had to fight the urge to reach out and touch one. As they passed the jeep, the buffalo merged into one herd again and hurried away.

Bigot started the jeep up again, and they continued roaming the jungle looking for more of the beautiful wildlife. When the sun reached its zenith, they stopped for lunch. They chose a small clearing at the top of the waterfall below which they had seen the herd of elephants bathe that morning. They unpacked baskets of bread, goat cheese, dried meats, fresh fruit, and filtered water which had been prepared by Nanci, Aleena, and Jenny the night before. They spread out blankets at the edge of the clearing in the shade of a massive okoumé tree and lounged as they ate. Below them stretched the magnificent Central African Rainforest, an undulating sea of greens broken only by the river. Jenny took photo after photo of the gorgeous panorama. From her vantage point at the top of the overlook, she could see none of the violence, poverty, or hatred which plagued the country. Here, nothing but wild, green, untamed jungle greeted her eye. She was reminded again of the potential the extraordinary country held if only more people would dedicate themselves to preserving instead of destroying.

After lunch, Ferdy led them on a walking tour through the nearby jungle. They stayed close to the tributary stream, following its course as it flowed between the trees. Because the animals had been cooped up for several days by the rain, the jungle buzzed with activity. Here, Ferdy proved to be a veritable encyclopedia of information. Every tree, flower, buzzing insect, and bird call was only a pinprick into his great reservoir of knowledge. He mimicked the call of a grey-cheeked hornbill as it chased a group of De Brazza's monkeys away from its nest and explained the social behavior of a mantled guereza as the black and white primate cleaned its fur on a tree branch over their heads. He discussed the keratin composition of the scales of the armored pangolin as one labored up a tree and pointed out the differences between several species of mangabey scampering through the canopy. He could even tell the difference between the types of antelope tracks that crisscrossed the mud beside the river.

"I thought Ferdy's degrees were in medical business and geopolitics," Jenny whispered to Seth during one of Ferdy's non-stop lectures. "Why does he seem to know everything about everything?"

Seth smiled and shook his head. "The man is a genius," he replied. "He reads whatever he can get his hands on and doesn't forget a thing. He's got the attitude that everything is a lesson. I can only imagine what he would have achieved if he'd been born into a modern country like England or the United States. He'd probably have twelve doctorates and be a billionaire."

"Or he might have ended up doing exactly what he's doing right now," Jenny said. "He seems like he was born to help these people."

"You're probably right," Seth agreed. "I guess the biggest reason why he knows so much about this country is because he loves it more than anything else."

As they continued walking through the jungle, Jenny understood more of the passion Ferdy had for the Central African Republic. The country wasn't just beautiful, it was *enchanting*. Every bend in the trail hid something more extraordinary. She saw a mustached guenon, a colorful monkey with a stark white stripe of fur under its nose that looked like a mustache. She snapped a photo of the bright-red backside of a Central African colobus monkey as it scampered away from her and caught the endangered African grey parrot as it cracked open a nut. The famous butterflies of the C.A.R. fluttered around her head, resplendent in a dozen different colors and a hundred different patterns. Ferdy showed her the tiny tracks of a blue duiker, a shy forest antelope no bigger than a Boston terrier. Once, they heard the cry of an African fish eagle, and Jenny glimpsed it through a break in the canopy as it soared high above them. The majestic bird looked remarkably like a bald eagle right down to its dark-brown body, yellow beak, and white head. Most thrilling of all was what she discovered at the base of a massive tree. Several deep gashes scarred the trunk at about chest height. She called the group over, and they gathered around her while Ferdy examined the bark. After several quiet moments, Ferdy smiled and patted Jenny on the back. Without saying a word, he moved aside the bushes at the base of the tree and pointed. There in the dirt, almost too faint to see, were leopard tracks. The shiver that went up Jenny's spine wasn't from fear, but exhilaration. Somewhere in the back of her mind the worries of life still festered, but for now, she felt nothing but wonder.

They trekked through the undergrowth in a big circle, arriving back in the clearing after an hour. By the time they made it back, Aleena, Jean-Marc, and Bigot, who had stayed behind, had repacked the jeep and prepared to move on. They drove for another hour, heading deeper into the jungle. The terrain sloped up and grew rougher as they left behind the more touristy areas of the reserve and entered regions only the park rangers visited. Here there were no roads, just rough trails made rougher by the rains. The jeep splashed through mud puddles and crunched through fields of tall grass.

Several times they had to backtrack because the undergrowth was too thick. The further they drove the more curious Jenny became. Nobody mentioned where they were going, and, though she was dying to know, she refrained from asking Ferdy who was busy helping Bigot navigate the terrain in front of the jeep. He seemed to know where he was going, but in a general rather than a specific way. He constantly glanced at the sky, checking for rain clouds Jenny assumed. So far, the sky had been empty, but Jenny now knew from experience that weather conditions changed quickly in the African rainforest.

Eventually they came to the edge of a thicket of medium-sized leafy plants which were shorter than the foliage of the jungle but too dense for them to drive through. As soon as the jeep stopped, Ferdy stood up in the seat and began to study the field through a set of binoculars. As he looked through the binoculars, he spoke in low tones to Bigot and to Hauser. A thick bank of clouds rolled in, blocking the sun and casting the bright green thicket in a dull hue. The three men stuck their heads together and whispered to one another. They came to a decision, and then Ferdy told everyone to get out of the jeep.

"We walk from here," he announced. "Single file. Everyone stay together. Move slowly and don't make a sound."

They lined up with Ferdy in the lead and Hauser in the rear. Bigot stayed behind with the jeep again. Jenny was bursting with curiosity and tried to stay calm. Her eagerness must have showed on her face, because Ferdy looked back at her and smiled his big, mischievous grin. He bent down and whispered in her ear: "Now, I will show you a real gentleman."

The little band moved into the thicket. Behind Ferdy walked Femi, followed by Jenny and Seth, then Aleena and Nanci, with Jean-Marc in front of Hauser and his big shotgun in the rear. The moist thicket soaked their clothes as they walked. They pushed through as quietly as possible, trying not to trip over logs or become entangled in vines that dangled from sporadic trees. Jenny, who wasn't tall enough to see over the big, leafy plants of which the thicket was primarily composed, had no idea where they were going. It would remain a mystery until they reached it.

After several tense minutes of quiet trekking, Ferdy motioned for them to stop and get down. He squatted down and gathered them all together in a huddle.

"Stay calm," he whispered. "Do not make any loud noises or sudden moves. Do not approach her. If she approaches you, stay very still and let her do as she pleases. She will be gentle if you are."

Jenny's heart beat against her ribcage like a boxer against a speed bag. *Stay very still?* she thought. *What is this,* Jurassic Park?

Ferdy stood up, pushed aside the leaves of a massive plant and beckoned beyond.

The first thing Jenny saw was a dark, fury little man munching on a stalk of forest celery. She stared, her brain confused by what her eyes recorded. But her confusion lasted only a moment. She took only half a second to realize that she was looking at a female gorilla.

She couldn't stop herself from letting out an involuntary gasp. In the silence, it sounded like a gunshot. She covered her mouth but not fast enough. The gorilla turned and caught sight of the people. She glanced back and forth between the faces, making eye contact with each of them. Realizing they outnumbered her, she snorted, placed the stalk of celery in her mouth, and ambled away on all four arms.

When the gorilla disappeared from sight, everyone in the group let out a great sigh—they had all been holding their breath—and started to giggle with delight. Jenny surmised she wasn't the only one seeing a gorilla for the first time. Ferdy shushed them all and beckoned them forward again.

They crept forward, pushing through the foliage until they reached a large clearing with shorter plants and fewer trees. Jenny saw the female gorilla saunter away from them towards a small group of two females and a baby. Then she saw another gorilla through a break in the foliage and another peeking around a tree, then another and another, until she realized that the thicket was full of them.

They sat in small groups and groomed each other or foraged alone, softly munching on stalks or leaves. Despite their bulk and inky black fur, they blended in with the foliage. They were obviously aware of the people but seemed to pay them no attention.

Jenny could hardly believe her eyes. She crouched in the foliage between Ferdy and Seth and stared, mesmerized by the magnificent creatures. A strange emotion, equal parts terror and euphoria, possessed her. Or perhaps she was euphoric because she was terrified. She felt so vulnerable being in such proximity to these powerful creatures, yet at the same time she felt like she might damage them somehow. They seemed so gentle she couldn't imagine they would harm a fly, but the muscular arms and massive teeth told a different story. She wanted to adore and fear them. The experience almost overwhelmed her.

She turned to Ferdy who smiled like a child. "You sly dog," she teased him, "you had this planned all along didn't you?"

"I told you I would show you the gentleman of the forest, didn't I?" His eyes twinkled as he spoke. "Though I do not see our host," he said, scanning the area. "He is the one who wears the fancy silver jacket."

Jenny gave him a quizzical look that he pretended not to see. Seth leaned over and whispered in her ear. "He means the big male, the silverback. There's always at least one dominant male in each group."

"If you see him, show the proper respect," Ferdy said to both of them. "Don't look him in the eye, and do not move towards him. If he charges you, do not run. Crouch down in submission to show you mean him no harm, and he will leave you alone. Remember, this is his home. He will show us hospitality if we respect him." He moved off, eyes searching for the silverback.

Jenny stared after him. She wondered whether he talked like that naturally or on purpose to tease people. He always seemed like he was playing an inside joke, but only he knew why it was funny.

Teasing or not, she knew his warning about the male gorilla was serious. She kept her eyes peeled for silver fur. But she was distracted by two youngsters playing off by themselves about twenty yards away from the rest of the troop, their dark heads just visible over the foliage. One had a wide head with thick fur and the other was slender with very short fur. She watched them for several minutes before she realized that the slender one was Femi.

Grabbing Seth's arm, she pointed without speaking. Seth followed her gaze to the two dark, bobbing heads. It took him several minutes to recognize Femi too. He rolled his eyes and shook his head.

Do you think he's okay? Jenny mouthed to him. He shook his head again and looked over his shoulder at the rest of the party. Ferdy was too far away, Hauser had disappeared, and Jean-Marc, Aleena, and Nanci were oblivious to the world as they sat face to face with a slender female gorilla. "We'd better get him ourselves," he said with a sigh.

They crab-walked toward Femi, keeping low and trying to make as little noise as possible. They approached the two small figures slowly, not wanting to frighten the young gorilla. He was showing off like a typical youngster, beating his chest, hopping around, and flinging grass into the air. Femi giggled like the happy little boy he was.

Jenny had planned on pulling Femi away from the gorilla and back to the rest of the group, but when she got up close to them, they captivated her. The little gorilla was so cute and so extraordinarily like a human child that she found herself sitting down on a fallen tree branch behind Femi and watching. Apparently, Seth was also intrigued because he sat down too. Neither Femi nor the young gorilla seemed to notice them, and they continued to play like two school boys who were the best of friends.

Jenny presently became aware of another creature moving towards them through the brush, but she couldn't see it or tell from which direction it was approaching. Ignoring Femi and his gorilla partner, she cocked her head and listened. The rustling of the undergrowth grew nearer and then, off to her right, the undergrowth parted and a massive silverback gorilla emerged.

He strode into the clearing and stopped, eyeing the humans suspiciously with his deep brown eyes. Jenny's heart began to thump again. The big bruiser was less than ten yards away. Jenny stared into his deep eyes, her own eyes wide with alarm. The gorilla grew agitated, snorting, huffing, and baring his teeth. Now Seth noticed the gorilla.

"Jenny! Your eyes!" he hissed.

Jenny realized she was still staring straight into the gorilla's eyes just as Ferdy had warned her not to do. She looked away, but the big male was already too worked up. He pounded the ground and threw dirt in the air, just as the little gorilla had done, but he was terrifying, not cute. The gorilla grew louder and louder until he was screaming. Jenny cowered down next to Seth who grabbed Femi and pulled him down next to them. The gorilla's screaming ceased, and he froze. But then a split second later, he stood upright on his hind legs, pounded his chest and charged, thundering across the clearing like a freight train. Jenny squeezed her eyes shut and braced herself for the strike she knew would come.

But the strike never came. The silverback pulled up short only inches from Jenny's head. She didn't dare look, but she knew he must have been looming over them, judging their display of submission. She prayed he would find them worthy. But she needn't have worried. Jenny had witnessed one of the famous silverback gorilla mock charges designed to intimidate and subdue an opponent; such displays of aggression were terrifying, but harmless if one showed the proper respect, as Ferdy had said. The gorilla did no more than sniff them and touch Jenny's golden hair. After several tense seconds, the silverback shuffled away. Just like that, it was over. When Jenny finally lifted her head, all she could see of the gorilla was his wide rump and marvelous silver back as he disappeared into the brush.

Jenny let out a long breath that turned into a nervous giggle as she sat up. She put a shaking hand on Seth's arm to stabilize it and found that he was shaking too. They looked at each other and began to laugh harder as their adrenaline dissipated. Jenny's heart still pounded from the raw fear, but it had been a different fear, primal, and exhilarating, the rational kind of fear which kept you alive, not the kind she had been used to feeling all her life. That kind of fear was more akin to doubt, born of uncertainty and insecurity. The silverback gorilla had frightened her, but there had been no uncertainty about that situation. Now, she felt bolder instead of meeker, more secure and not less.

George Hauser appeared behind her. "You did well," he whispered into her ear, before moving off towards the rest of the group.

Seth put his arm around Jenny's shoulders and squeezed her tight, forcing away the last drops of fear from her system. Femi, who didn't seem shaken by the ordeal at all, got up and wandered away. A fine rain began to fall, but no one in the clearing seemed to care. Through the tall grass, Jenny could see the rest of the group sitting quietly amongst the gorillas as they munched. They had all been alarmed, humans and gorillas alike, by the screaming silverback, but once they saw no harm had been done, they all went back to their activities. Now the silverback stood guard several yards away from everyone else, a silent sentinel surveying his charges.

Jenny and Seth sat and watched the gorillas in relative silence after that, side by side on the fallen branch, his arm still around her shoulders. The foliage was thick enough to hide them, but not enough to keep them from seeing out, making them feel alone, but not separated. Rain continued to fall softly, just a light spray, almost a mist, wetting the thicket but not soaking it. The tiny drops stuck to the gorillas' fur like little beads, and they plucked them off each other with their long lips. The rain deadened the ambient noises of the jungle so Jenny could hear nothing but its light drumming against the leaves. It was so peaceful.

As dusk drew near, the sun showed itself one last time, finally finding freedom as it dropped beneath the continuous bank of clouds. For several minutes it hung low in the sky framed between the clouds above and the distant hills below as it shined through the rain. Each ray shattered into a thousand pieces of color each time it struck one of the tiny raindrops, making the green thicket sparkle like an emerald. It reminded Jenny of the secret cave in the heart of the jungle with its wealth of sparkling diamonds and gold. But this wealth of natural beauty was even more beautiful, for it was pure and untainted by the shadow of greed. Jenny liked it better. It was like a painting made up of rain, sun, green, and gorilla. As she gazed upon the gorgeous tableau, she felt content.

Seth pulled her closer. "Still glad you came?" he whispered into her ear. Jenny put her head on his shoulder and didn't need to answer.

Charge

*T*he lion stands at the edge of the jungle and looks out upon a green thicket. A light rain falls on his thick, matted mane. Too soft to soak him, it gathers in little beads on his fur like a thousand tiny jewels, a reminder of his former royalty.

But no one watches the old king. He shakes his shaggy head and the beads scatter. Once again, he is nothing but an old lion, weak and starving.

The old lion is close now. The scent of man is hotter in his nostrils than it has been for days, but it is mixed with that of another scent, one like man, yet unlike man. It is a scent he has never smelled before, a wild, dangerous scent. Desperation drives him to avoid such an unfamiliar odor, but man is close, and he is so hungry. Safety resides in the dark forest behind him, but he is far beyond worrying about safety. He must feed, or he must die.

The old lion prepares to enter the thicket. He raises one paw into the air and freezes, testing the air with his sensitive nostrils, the only part of him not dulled by the ravages of time. Satisfied with what he has found, he drops the foot and moves into the thicket. The brush is dense and tangled, but his nose will lead him to what he seeks. Gradually he becomes aware of another scent. It is man, but not the same man he has been tracking. This new scent approaches rapidly from the north, bringing with it the acrid stench of fumes and smoke. The old lion pauses. Wisdom tells him to wait, to assess the changed situation, to see *what his chances of success are. But the roaring hunger in his belly pushes him forward. He will feed, or he will die.*

He continues on, drawing closer to man, but man also draws closer to him. The scent of food fills his nostrils, and his jaws begin to water. His anticipation grows. But so does his anxiety. His instinct warns him of danger, that sixth sense which every wild animal possesses. The instincts to flee and to feed war in his brain.

And then suddenly he is aware of a third group. Man approaches from a third direction. His sense of self-preservation triumphs, and he turns to flee but finds each direction blocked. Man is closing in on all sides. He is trapped in the center of a net, and it is drawing tighter. With nowhere to run, he has but one choice. Angry, frightened, and frustrated, he rises out of the thicket and looses a savage roar....

Chapter 13
Fire in the Field

A hideous roar shattered the tranquility of the thicket, terrifying every nerve ending in Jenny's body. It was not the low, exciting roar of a calm lion announcing his presence, but that of a savage wild creature, furious at man's intrusion on his domain. It was brutal, it was loud, and it was far too close.

The thicket exploded into chaos. A hundred birds of which Jenny hadn't been aware scattered in every direction, filling the sky with their fleeing forms. The gorillas screamed in terror, a horrible, blood-curdling sound, and fled deeper into the thicket, flattening everything in their way. The air resounded with the cries of a dozen other animals, warning the hills of the danger that had slipped unnoticed into their midst. Branches shook, trees swayed, and leaves blew around in the wake of the departing wildlife. Far above them, thunder roared as if the elements themselves were crying out in alarm. The rain started to fall harder as the sun fled behind the hills.

The lion's roar was not repeated, but a different roar replaced it, a low, constant buzzing that Jenny knew well. From far across the thicket, she glimpsed the top of a big jeep as it crunched through the thicket towards them. She realized she didn't recognize it a split second before a third, distinct roar assaulted the already chaotic scene. It was the roar of machine-gun fire.

Jenny froze. Her vision narrowed, and she saw her friends running away, but her legs would not move to follow. Like a nightmare, the world around her seemed to leave her behind as she struggled to move her legs, which would not obey. Her old fear sprang up from the darkness of her heart and sank his fangs deep into her soul, seizing her body and rooting her in place. But then she saw Hauser returning fire with his big shotgun, spin around and fall to the ground clutching his shoulder. Then the world crystalized, and she broke free as instinct took over. She raced to Hauser's side, forcing her legs to obey. She tore the bandana from around his neck and pressed it against his shoulder to stop the bleeding. He was in a daze, but she grabbed his hand and used it to hold the bandana in place as she lifted him by his elbow. She didn't think now, just reacted, the adrenaline pumping through her system providing her an extra boost of strength and clarity. Even so, the man was heavy, and she stumbled as she tried to lift him, forcing a groan from his lips. But then Seth was at her side, taking Hauser's arm and raising him to his feet without a strain.

Together they dragged the mercenary towards the jeep as bullets continued to scream past their heads. Aleena, Jean-Marc, and Nanci running in front of her with Ferdy in the lead. Femi was nowhere in sight. They raced through the thicket, shoving aside bushes and stumbling over rocks and logs, but everyone kept their feet. As they neared the edge of the thicket, the foliage thinned, exposing them to the machine-gunners' sights, who began to zero in on them. The shots passed even closer, but miraculously, no one else was hit. They had almost reached the jeep when a third jeep burst from the jungle to their left and raced across their path towards the machine-gun fire. It bristled with an assortment of weapons sticking out of it like porcupine quills. The occupants fired back at the second jeep, halting its advance.

The rain fell too hard for Jenny and the others to recognize the occupants of the jeep, but as soon as it cleared a path, they dashed for their own vehicle. Ferdy yelled for Bigot to start the engine and get them out of here, but he didn't respond. The reason soon became clear: one shooter had found his mark. Jacques Bigot sat slumped forward in the driver's seat, his hands still clutching the steering wheel. He had died instantly.

Ferdy unbuckled Bigot's seatbelt and pushed his corpse out of the way to reach the pedals. It was horrible, but they didn't have time to waste. Without thinking, Jenny jumped into the passenger seat while Seth and Jean-Marc helped Hauser into the back. Femi appeared from out of thin air in the center seat between Aleena and Nanci. Ferdy jammed the big jeep in gear and smashed the gas pedal to the floor. The big vehicle shot forward into a hair-raising U-turn and plunged into the jungle.

They bounced along at reckless speeds as the light grew dimmer and the rain fell harder. Jenny didn't know where Ferdy was going, but he seemed to be retracing their earlier path through the jungle. Hauser groaned each time they hit a bump or puddle while Seth and Jean-Marc took turns applying pressure to his wound. They were doing the best they could, but he weakened with every passing moment. Ferdy seemed to understand that time was running out; hence the breakneck speed. Jenny watched him as he drove and realized that he too, grimaced with every bump. Upon closer examination she realized that he had taken a bullet in his calf and must have been in intense pain. She searched for something to use as a tourniquet. Her eyes fell on Bigot's belt, one of those olive-green military ones that can adjust to any length. Jenny began to unbuckle and slide it out from around his waist before she realized what she was doing. She looked at Bigot's face. His eyes stared out at nothing with eternal surprise. Jenny shuddered. She had worked in a hospital and seen people die, but she had never handled the body of someone who had been murdered. It unsettled her. But her job now was to keep another person alive. Out of respect, she closed Bigot's eyes and continued removing his belt. She adjusted it to its shortest width and turned to Ferdy.

She asked him to stop the jeep for a second, but he had already guessed her intent. "Not yet, my dear," he replied without looking at her, "I will be fine."

"But your leg…"

"I have endured worse before. It will keep until we get far enough away."

"But you're bleeding heavily. If we don't do something soon, you might pass out and then what help would you be?"

"I said I will be fine, Jenny."

Jenny sighed. *Men*, she thought, *They're all the same.* Before Ferdy could respond she reached around his leg, looped the belt around his calf just below the knee and tightened it with a jerk. Ferdy grunted in surprise and pain and raised his leg from the gas pedal, letting the jeep come to a slow stop as Jenny worked. She tightened the belt as much as possible, trying to restrict the blood flow, and then buckled it. She tore off the bottom of his pant leg and pressed it against the wound, using a shoelace from Bigot's shoe to tie it in place.

When she raised her sweaty head, she noticed Ferdy cocking his own, listening to something.

"The guns," he said.

Jenny strained to hear over the patter of the rain and the idling of the jeep. She no longer heard them. "They've stopped," she whispered. Ferdy nodded.

A moment of silence followed. Seth broke it. "We have to get out of here," he said, but Ferdy shushed him, still cocking his head to listen. A buzzing noise rose above the rain, quiet, but getting louder. It could only be the sound of a jeep. "Go, go!" Seth shouted, and Ferdy mashed down on the pedal, but it was too late. Before they could move, a big jeep burst from the jungle and rolled right up to them. With obvious difficulty, Hauser drew his big pistol one-handed and twisted around in the backseat to aim at the approaching vehicle, ever the soldier till the end. But he didn't fire and Jenny quickly realized why: it was the third jeep, the one that had been firing away from them.

The jeep came to a stop ahead of them, still bristling with weapons. The passenger door opened, and a man stepped out. It was a tall man with a big assault rifle in his arms. He began to walk towards them. When he walked into the glow of the headlights, Jenny was able to see his face. She was surprised, but not shocked to see that it was Clayton Mercury.

Chapter 14
No Other Way

The ride back to the village was dark and tense. Mercury said few words as he loaded Hauser and Bigot onto his jeep and replaced Ferdy with one of his mercenary drivers. No one spoke; they were too shocked and scared. After only a brief pause, the two jeeps started back up and they trundled along at a slower speed. Darkness completed its fall, and soon Jenny could see nothing but the bumper of Mercury's jeep illuminated by their headlights. Now that her adrenaline had abated, the weight of the horrible events that had destroyed their beautiful safari began to sink in. She huddled in the back seat next to Seth, pressing close to him for comfort. He took her hand and held it in silence. As the ride continued, she felt his body stiffen with tension. She couldn't see his face in the dark, but she didn't need to—she knew. Seth was angry.

When they arrived at the village, she watched in apprehension as he got out of the jeep and marched through the mud to Clayton Mercury.

"You knew," he said, loud enough for everyone to hear over the rain and the idle of the jeeps. Mercury looked at him but said nothing. A crowd began to gather to help with the unloading and care of the wounded, but they soon realized something else was going on.

"You knew, didn't you," Seth said again. It wasn't a question. Mercury remained silent and continued to unload the jeep.

"You knew," Seth continued, "you knew that somebody would follow us, and you knew that if you followed us too, you could find out for sure if your precious operation was in danger. That's why you changed your mind about the safari, but didn't want to go along. You used us as bait." His voice grew louder as he spoke. But Mercury acted like he hadn't heard him.

"You knew!" Seth shouted, knocking the gear Mercury was unloading out of his hands.

"Of course I knew," Mercury hissed, instantly as hard as nails. He stood nose to nose with Seth, his fierce eyes staring down at the shorter man like those of a panther. "I know everything."

Seth exploded. He slammed his fist into the steel-plated jeep door and roared like a young lion. "How dare you!" he screamed, "How dare you use my people as bait for your selfish schemes, and how dare you keep me in the dark about it! One of your own men is dead now. The rest of us could have been slaughtered too. What if you had miscalculated? What if you had arrived too late? You at least could have told me and let me choose!"

Mercury stood in silence as Seth ranted, the abuse rolling off of him like the rain. He let the young man go on for several minutes before he interrupted. "If you had listened to me before..." he began, but Seth cut him off.

"Oh right, if I had listened to you!" Seth paced several yards away into the center of a mud puddle illuminated by the jeep headlights. He was filthy and soaking wet but he didn't care. "You always play the wise-old-experienced-hunter, like you know so much and you always know best and I should always trust you. Well guess what? I *did* trust you. I trusted you to tell me if it was too dangerous. I trusted you to tell me whether or not we should go, and you told me it would be okay. That'll be the last time I trust you. You only care about your stinking diamonds."

Mercury flinched for the first time. By now, the entire village had gathered. None of them were supposed to know about the diamonds, but Seth didn't care anymore. A murderous look crept into the mercenary's eyes. But Seth was too angry to notice and continued to rant.

"But I guess that's always what you've cared about. I tried to fool myself for a while that you were actually a good man and wanted to help us, that you used the avarice bit as a cover. But I guess you really don't care about what happens to us. All we are is a means to an end for you. You don't care about anyone except for yourself. You don't even care about your men. You're willing to let one die and another get wounded just to satisfy your greed. I guess that's just who you are, Clayton Mercury, the selfish, bigoted merc—"

Seth hadn't noticed Mercury advancing on him like a predator stalking its prey. Soon he was close enough to strike. Without warning he kicked Seth's legs out and drove him to the ground with one big hand, slamming him down into the mud and knocking the wind out of him. Jenny gasped and moved in with some villagers to protect Seth, but the attack was over as soon as it began. Mercury grasped Seth roughly by the shirt and hauled him to a sitting position. Then, only centimeters from his face, in a voice so quiet that no one but Seth and Jenny could hear, he said, "Don't make the mistake of thinking you know what real danger is, boy. And don't *ever* accuse me of not caring about my men."

They stared at each other, the vibrant, passionate youth, and the cold, cynical, hard-edged man of years. Neither quailed before the other. Jenny thought about the jagged scar that peeked out of Mercury's shirt. He was a wounded man in more than just the flesh.

After a long moment, Mercury released Seth and stood up, allowing him to rise. The mercenary stood a few paces off and stared at the ground, hands on his hips. All the fight seemed to have gone out of him. His shoulders slumped and his short hair lay plastered against his head from the rain.

"Those men were Anti-Balaka, Seth," he said. "Not just bandits with a religious slant. They were too well organized. Those were militia. They wouldn't have attacked us unless they had a compelling reason. Can you think of what that reason might be?"

Seth looked down at the ground. He too seemed subdued. He understood what Mercury meant.

"The evidence is everywhere, Seth. They've discovered us. You can bet every diamond in that mine that the Anti-Balaka know about our operation thanks to your friend Mohammedou Djotodia. That means the Seleka are probably on their way, too." He paused to let his words sink in. He spoke to Seth, but the entire village listened. No one responded.

"Seth, I cannot protect you." His voice was clear and calm without a hint of malice. "When Colonel Massi and General Abdul-Azeez get here, they will slaughter all of you. I won't be able to stop them."

He paused again, but again, no one spoke.

"Seth, you have to move the village."

Seth shut his eyes and began to shake his head.

"There is no other way," Mercury said. "I'm leaving in two days. I've already got most of my gear and equipment packed up. We'll have to leave behind everything else. I can shelter you if you go with us. But it has to be now."

"What about the government?" Seth finally asked, "What about the U.N.? What if I call home? As a US citizen, there has to be something I can do?"

Mercury sighed and shook his head. "No, Seth. There will be no protection, no aid, and no reprisal. If you stay here, you will all die, and no one will ever hear about it. Is that what you want?"

He let the question hang in the air. No one wanted to answer it. One of his mercenaries jogged up to him and gripped his arm. "Boss, we've got to go now," the man said, "Hauser's bad."

Mercury nodded and turned back to Seth. "I'll take Hauser and Ferdinand to our camp," he said, "but our med supplies aren't much better than yours. We need to send them to the capital. The eastern ranger station has an airfield and a small plane. It'll take a hefty bribe, but I'm sure I can convince them to fly them over." He paused again. "I'll be back tomorrow to get your answer," he continued, "but we leave Monday morning, with or without you."

The mercenary turned and climbed into the jeep. With a tortured squeal, the big vehicle turned and drove off into the rainy night as the villagers watched it go. Once it had disappeared, they turned to look at each other and then at Seth. They watched him closely, waiting for him to speak, to comfort them and give them direction. But he said nothing, just stared at the mud. After a few moments, he turned and trudged off towards his tent.

Jenny's heart bled for Seth as she watched him go. She knew that his worst possible fears had been realized. Without the Sharon's he had to make this unbelievable choice on his own. But he wouldn't have to bear the burden alone, she decided. Right there, in the middle of the rain and the mud she closed her eyes and prayed for Seth, that God would give him wisdom, strength, and peace. Then she prayed that God would protect their village and would keep his hand upon each of them. She couldn't remember a time when she had prayed harder and with more sincerity.

When she opened her eyes, the villagers were standing around her with their heads bowed. For a second, she was embarrassed—she hadn't realized she had been praying loud enough for them to hear. She looked at the faces around her and saw how affected they had been. She saw fear and worry, but she also saw strength, determination, and peace. Had she been able to see her own face, she would have seen the same things reflected there. No one said a word. They just looked at each other, taking silent comfort from the strength of one another. One by one they began to melt away into the darkness and the rain until Jenny was standing by herself. When she was finally alone, the tears came. She raced through the mud to her tent, where she fell to her knees and began to pray once more.

Chapter 15
Mercy Love

Jenny woke up early the next morning before the sun came up. Not that it would have mattered; the sky was too cloudy for it to make much difference on the dreary atmosphere or on Jenny's attitude. From the minute she awoke her heart was heavy. She lay in bed for another hour, hoping that the events of the day before had been nothing more than a dream. What had started as a blissful fantasy had ended in a nightmare. It was both the best and worst day of her life, a juxtaposition of life's beauty and its ugliness. She remembered the enchanting jungle, the excitement she had experienced watching the bongos and gorillas, and the raw terror that had gripped her soul during the firefight. She remembered how frightened she had been of the charging silverback gorilla and how that fear had been so different from what she had felt while running for her life. She relived the ride back to the village: the darkness, the rain running down her face, the tortured groans of the wounded, and the almost palpable sense of fear. But mostly she thought about Seth and Clayton, soaked and streaked with mud, standing in the darkness lit only by the jeep headlights.

After a while she rolled out of bed, put on her clothes, and went for a walk. The rain had stopped for the moment, but she still had to splash through the mud to get from place to place. Her boots, already covered with dried mud from the night before, became soaked and muddy again within minutes. No one else was around.

As she neared the edge of the village, she was startled to hear someone call her name. She turned to see Clayton Mercury attempting to navigate a large mud puddle in her direction. He was having a hard time. The general distribution of mud on his knee-high boots and pants indicated he had slipped and fallen at some point already. It was almost comical. Jenny suppressed a smile and pointed out the route through the mud she had taken. Mercury struggled to follow her path; he was heavier than Jenny and sunk deeper into the muck than she had. The mercenary almost slipped again, but eventually he made it to the small knoll where Jenny was standing.

"Thank you for that," he said, a bit sheepishly. "I never get used to this grime." Jenny laughed. "Now I'll return the favor," the mercenary said with a smile, but then he stopped. His smile faded. "No, that's inappropriate right now," he said as his face grew serious.

"I'm glad I ran into you," he continued. "I came to pick up Nanci Bernard and some of Ferdinand's things. Nanci has some medical training and can help my men tend to Ferdinand and Hauser on the trip back to the capital, where they'll get the best medical treatment."

"Nanci is so good to go and take care of your men," Jenny said.

"Not like she gave me much of a choice," Mercury snorted. "She insisted on accompanying my boys. Said she wouldn't leave Ferdinand's side while he was wounded. Is there something going on between them?"

Jenny shrugged her shoulders and smiled. As far as she knew, they were only friends. But she wouldn't be surprised to find there was more between them than friendship.

"Anyway," continued Mercury, "that's not why I wanted to talk to you about. I want to offer you something. I wanted to see if you were interested in hitching a ride with my boys and I as we leave the country. Tomorrow morning we're heading for the Cameroon border, which we can reach in several hours and will be easy to cross. Cameroon is more stable and has a better relationship with the rest of the world. As an American with a passport, you could contact the embassy there and explain your situation. I've got contacts there who can get you back into the United States. Legally, of course."

Jenny pondered his words. "What about the rest of the people in the village? I thought you said you could get them out of here?"

Mercury shook his head. "I said I would protect them as they left, Jenny, not that I could get them out of the country. They might be able to get into Cameroon on refugee status, but once they're in Cameroon, I can't do anything for them."

"But you can protect them on the journey?"

"I can *try*, Jenny. But as I've reiterated countless times, I don't have the firepower or the man power to fight the Anti-Balaka and the Seleka. We have to leave while we still can. By Monday afternoon, I plan to be at the Cameroon border."

"Can all of us can get to the border in just a few hours?"

"No. But my men and I can."

"So, you aren't going to protect the villagers?"

"Jenny, I am trying to do everything I can, but I can't work miracles. I have to think about my men and my interests. I'm trying to think about you and Seth too. You're Americans. Do you understand what that means? It means that the best-case scenario is that they just kill you and it's over with, but what if they keep you alive? You want to imagine what that will be like?"

The mercenary let the question hang in the air. Jenny tried not to think about it.

Mercury continued. "And what if they hold you for ransom? That's not improbable. They'll hold you until someone in America will pay them an expensive price for your return. It doesn't matter if you have any money. They'll wait forever if necessary. Think about what that'll do to your mother and father."

Jenny thought about it. She knew what her mother would tell her to do.

"What about Seth and Nanci?" she asked.

"Nanci will be safe in the capital. Ferdinand has connections, and they're traveling in a small enough group to go unnoticed. From there she can catch a flight out. But I'll make Seth the same offer I'm giving you."

"What if the people don't want to leave? What if Seth won't leave them?" As soon as she said it, Jenny realized she'd voiced something she had known, but hadn't wanted to admit to herself. Seth wouldn't leave. No matter how it was presented to him, he would see it as abandoning the villagers, and he wasn't built that way. He would stay to the bitter end.

Mercury sighed. "I hope it doesn't come to that. Because I *will* leave him here. But his decision doesn't have to be yours. My offer is still open to you even if Seth doesn't take it."

Jenny didn't reply. She didn't know what to say. She turned and stared out at the flooded fields. They looked as devastated as her soul.

"Jenny, I don't want to see anything happen to you or Seth. You might be able to persuade him to come. Please keep that in mind."

Jenny closed her eyes and remained silent.

Mercury turned to go. "I'll be back here tomorrow morning at 7:00 am sharp," he said. "Have your luggage ready." Jenny heard him slosh back through the mud, but she didn't turn to watch him leave.

It started to rain again. For a second, Jenny ignored it, but it fell harder, and she didn't want to get soaked again. She splashed back to her tent as fast as she dared. She ducked in to find Nanci sitting on the corner of her bed.

"There ya are, darlin'" she said with a forced smile. She paused, but Jenny didn't reply. "Well," she continued, "I'm going to the capital to take care of Ferdy and Hauser, and it wouldn't be right to leave without telling you. Glad you came back, 'cause I've got to leave in a few moments."

Jenny nodded. She didn't know what to say. She knew it wasn't right, but she felt like this woman—her first friend in the Central African Republic and her moral support—was abandoning her. Tears welled up in her eyes. Nanci swallowed hard and cleared her throat.

"I'm not abandoning you, Jenny," she said, as if she could read her thoughts. "But these men need me. And I can't leave Ferdy either."

Jenny still didn't reply.

"Jenny," Nanci said as she stood and took her hands in her own, "you can come with me, sweetheart. We'll be much safer in the capital, and from there you can catch a flight back home."

"But what about Seth?" Jenny whispered. "I can't leave him here alone. I don't know if he'll leave these people."

"Oh, Jenny," Nanci said as her voice broke. She pulled Jenny into her arms and squeezed her tight, tight enough to squeeze tears out of Jenny's eyes. "This isn't what you signed up for, is it?" she asked in a quavering voice. They stood and hugged each other for several moments.

When they released each other, Nanci took Jenny's hands and locked tearful eyes with her. "I love you, Jenny," she said. "I want you to know that. You've become like the little sister I've never had, and I can't bear to think of anything happening to you. If you won't go with me, then please convince Seth to go with Clayton Mercury. We'll all meet up back home with the Sharon's and we'll sort this all out. We aren't abandoning these people, we're just reevaluating how we can best serve them." She hugged Jenny again and kissed her on the cheek. "May the Lord bless you and keep you, Jenny Clarkson," she said and then she left.

Jenny sat on her bed and listened to Nanci go into her tent, pick up her bags and slosh away through the mud. She should have offered to help her carry her bags, but she couldn't, not right then. The last piece of her life had fallen into the river and was disappearing downstream. It was all falling apart. She sat and wondered when it would end.

Then she remembered that today was Sunday.

As Jenny rushed through the village, she wondered if everyone else had forgotten about Sunday service, or if they even wanted to gather for church. She saw no one as she walked through the village and at one point, even debated about going back to her tent. But when she reached the pavilion, she realized why she had seen no one else: they were all there. The entire village had gathered, even the Muslim portion, she noted with amazement. They were crowded together underneath the pavilion to avoid the rain, praying or talking to one another other as if nothing was wrong. Several of the villagers looked at her in expectation as she walked up; normally she began every service with some instrumental guitar music to facilitate prayer while they waited for Seth to arrive. But today she wasn't sure what to do. She didn't feel like playing. However, Johnna-Marie and some of the other young people positioned themselves in the front as soon as they saw Jenny arrive. They were ready to sing, and they waited for Jenny to join them. Reluctantly, Jenny found her stool and guitar, and sat down next to them. She strummed a few chords, but her heart wasn't in it.

Several minutes later Seth came around the corner of the pavilion and joined them. One look at his face told Jenny that he didn't feel like singing either, but he was ready to do so anyway. She decided to try for his sake. He proceeded to lead the congregation in several songs. The people worshipped, but the fervency and excitement that usually characterized their worship services was missing. There was no passion. Like Seth, the people tried, but their hearts weren't in it. They had all been present the night before, and they had all heard the words Mercury had spoken. They were trying to act like everything was normal, but Jenny sensed that they were waiting for Seth to do something.

Halfway through the third song, Seth gave up. After finishing a chorus, he asked everyone to sit down. He remained silent while Jenny put the guitar and stool to the side and squeezed onto the front row between Johnna-Marie and another girl. No one spoke. The only audible sound was the rain drumming on the roof of the pavilion. Jenny could tell he was struggling with something. The people continued to wait in silence.

At last Seth began to speak. "The Bible says God is love," he began, speaking in a slow, moderated tone, not preaching, just talking. "John 3:16, which we all love to quote, says God loved the world so much that he gave his own son so that we might have eternal life. Jesus said the second greatest commandment is that we should love each other as we love ourselves. That wasn't just in the New Testament either; Jesus was quoting the book of Leviticus when he spoke. He told his disciples on the night before his crucifixion to 'love one another, as I have loved you.' He told them that by their love for one another, all men would know that they were his disciples. Paul wrote in Galatians 5 that all the law of Moses is summed up in that one statement: 'love your neighbor as yourself.' James calls this law the 'royal' law, a law fit for kings and queens, and for children of The King.

"So, love is important to God and is essential to any Christian's walk with God. If we want to consider ourselves disciples of Christ, then we must love one another as Christ loved us. But what does that mean? How can we love one another the way Christ loved us? And perhaps more importantly, if love is so essential to who we are as Christians, why don't more of us do it?"

He let the question hang in the air for a moment and then continued.

"I'll tell you what it means to love one another as Christ loved us. It means we have to be willing to do everything that Christ did for us. That means we have to be willing to spend our days helping and teaching one another. We have to be willing to suffer persecution for one another. And, ultimately, it means we have to be willing to die for one another."

He paused again to let his last statement sink in. His voice had remained at the same volume but had increased in intensity. The people continued to listen in silence. There were no shouts of 'amen' or 'glory' as was the custom. It wasn't that kind of day.

"Jesus said as much," continued Seth, "whenever he told people to take up their cross and follow him. They didn't understand him then, since he hadn't been crucified yet, but he was telling them they had to be willing to die, to be willing to give up their own lives to follow him. And to give up your life, you have to be willing to give up your will. To love people, we have to be willing to die for them, to give up what we want so we can do what others *need*. Sometimes that death is symbolic, as in we die out to what we want, but sometimes that death is literal, as when the early Christians were martyred for the sake of the Gospel. God may not call us to give up our actual lives, but I believe we have to be *willing* to give them up."

As he continued to speak, the tension in the congregation grew. Seth's words began to hit home in their hearts—considering their situation, they knew where his words were aimed. They continued to listen in silence, but their faces grew somber and determined. A few of them blinked back tears.

"Giving up your will is difficult," he continued. "That's why Jesus likened it to a death. No one wants to die. The most basic, fundamental will we have is the will to survive. But Jesus is imploring us to override that desire for something greater. And remember, he isn't asking us to do anything he wasn't willing to do. Many people think Jesus gave his life for us on the cross. He didn't. That's where his life was taken, but where he gave it up was in the Garden of Gethsemane, where his human nature surrendered to his divine nature, and he said, 'not my will, but thy will be done.' He didn't want to die, but he decided to take up his cross there in the garden before he ever took it up physically. In a very real sense, Jesus died in the garden, not on the cross."

Seth continued to exhort and elaborate on the death of Christ for several more minutes. Jenny was impressed by his words. She had never heard the story of the Crucifixion explained in such a way.

"So, now you're wondering what this all means for us," he said eventually. "It means we have to give up what we want and do what is best for each other, because that's what Jesus would do."

He paused, took a deep breath, and then he plunged.

"Brothers and sisters, the time has come for us to leave. An army of Anti-Balaka and ex-Seleka fighters is coming this way to plunder the quarry. If we don't go now, we will all die."

Silence followed. The rain continued to patter on the tin roof.

Seth filled the silence. "I know this is our home, and it's not right that you should have to leave another home behind, but our true home is each other. If we go together, we can protect and take care of one another."

More silence followed. Jenny sensed that everyone had something to say, but no one wanted to speak.

"Look," he said. "This is my home too, and I don't want to leave it, but it isn't worth risking your lives for it."

Again no one spoke. They just stared at him with mournful eyes. Someone near the back stood up and began to speak. Jenny recognized Sudaiq's voice without turning around.

"Seth is right," the old man said, addressing the crowd. "The Anti-Balaka and the Seleka will come here, but when they see that Clayton Mercury has taken all his treasures with him, they will turn on us, and they will kill us. We all have seen their travesties firsthand. We will not survive. They will kill our men, rape our women, burn our homes to the ground, and make our children into slaves. Our only chance is to flee."

The villagers began to murmur nervously. Sudaiq let them continue for a moment and then silenced them all as he spoke again.

"But," the healer said in his deep voice, "I for one have been fleeing for the past ten years of my life. I have nowhere else to go in this country, and I cannot not bear to be a refugee again. My children are buried here in this land, and my wife's grave lies not far from where we are sitting. This is my home. And I for one will stay."

Jenny was shocked. She looked to Seth, to see how he would respond. His face bore a pained expression, but he didn't look as surprised as Jenny. The rest of the villagers murmured again, but some of them began to nod their heads.

"But Sudaiq," Seth spoke up, "what good would it do for you to stay and die?"

"Maybe no good," Sudaiq replied. "But I will stay, nonetheless."

"You mean you aren't afraid?" Seth asked. "You don't fear what is to come?"

Sudaiq smiled. "Of course, I am afraid," he said, "but I have known fear all my life. It is an old friend that can no longer control me. I am in the hands of Allah now. He will decide whether I live or die."

More of the villagers nodded and voiced their approval of Sudaiq's words. The Muslim villagers seemed to agree with him, but some of the Christians still seemed hesitant.

"Please don't do this," Seth pleaded, looking around at the villagers. He was almost begging now, with true anguish in his voice. "It doesn't have to be this way. We can leave now and still escape. God has protected us all this time, but maybe he is trying to send us a sign that it's time to leave. If he protected us here, he'll protect us anywhere. But he doesn't want us to be foolish. I know it's not what we want, but perhaps it's what he wants."

Seth continued to petition the people, but Jenny could see they were hardening their resolve. This was their home, their last resort. Unless they resigned themselves to the nomadic life of refugees, moving around through the surrounding countries, always hoping against hope that their homeland would find peace so they could return, they truly had nowhere else to go. She couldn't find it in her heart to blame them for wanting to stay.

"You are afraid, Seth," Sudaiq said in a serious voice, but he was still smiling. "You feel you must stay with us if we choose not to go. But you needn't. This is not your home. You don't have to stay. We have nowhere else to go, but you do. You have a home far beyond the sea, with a family and people who love you. That is where you belong."

Seth gave a deep sigh. Everyone was looking at him now. But he said nothing, just stared down at the ground.

"Don't think we don't love you, boy," Sudaiq continued in a softer tone. "You have done so much for us. In Islam, we teach, like you, that Jesus was a great prophet sent from God. Though we may differ in many of our beliefs, we both agree that he came to show us how to live righteously and how to please God. And like Jesus, you Seth, have shown us how to live righteously and how to please God.

"When you arrived, the Sharon's were having a hard time keeping up with all the work and, unfortunately, all the trouble we were causing. My dear wife passed away just weeks after they had arrived, and I was in no mood to care about anyone else. They worked without ceasing to help us make this place a home, where we would be loved and protected. Sister Nanci helped them bear this burden, but we all knew that they were only two people, and two people against a village is never enough. But then you came. You were young and inexperienced, completely ignorant of all our African customs, and with no knowledge of how to run a village. But you had one thing: love. Since that time, you have loved us unconditionally and given us your time, your energy, and your life. You have loved us like Jesus. You have taken up your cross, as you say, and followed him. In doing so, you have shown us all how to live like he would want us to live. And for that, we thank you."

By the time Sudaiq finished, Jenny's eyes were already wet. But when she saw a single tear roll down Seth's cheek, she started to weep. As one, the crowd moved forward and surrounded Seth in a tight huddle, reaching towards him and each other, lending their strength and love in the most immediate way they could. They began to link up, arms wrapped around shoulders and hands clutching hands. Then they began to pray, not with words, but with groans and utterances, outbursts of pure desire and longing the meaning of which only God in heaven knows. Jenny found herself across from Seth pressed between Johnna-Marie and another girl. She gripped the two girls next to her and they lifted their voices in prayer, joining the chorus of worshippers around them, tears of passion streaming down their faces. The gathered village, Christian, Muslim, and everything in between, continued to wail and groan, drowning out the sound of the rain with their cries. Tears flowed, but there was no sorrow, no pity, no anguish. These were tears of love. They came not from weakness but from strength. They wept simply because the powerful sensation was too much for fragile human emotions to handle.

The people held each other for a long time. No one seemed to care. The volume of their cries slowly decreased, but the fervency in which they gripped one another did not. Eventually their cries died altogether, and they stood in silence and listened to the rain. Then someone began to sing "He Bled for Us," and one by one they all joined in. They sang it like a dirge, their voices rising and falling together in a slow, beautiful unity. It was so different from how they normally sang it, fast and joyful with plenty of bounce and harmony. But it was no less beautiful now, for now they sang with personal conviction, truly understanding what the words meant. Jenny sensed a great weight being lifted when they reached the fourth and final verse:

> *He'll come back for us, come back for us*
> *As we stand with each other*
> *He'll come back for us*
> *Jesus my savior, He went far away*
> *He's coming back soon*
> *Oh, it may be today*

They all lifted their hands in worship as they sang the last verse once, twice, and then a third time. They ended the song by unspoken agreement and then lifted their voices in thunderous praise, free of fear and doubt despite the stormy world around them.

"So, this is what you've all decided, then?" Seth asked when they had finished. He looked around the circle as the villagers nodded. His eyes came to rest on Jenny. He stared into her eyes for a moment. Then he took a deep breath and spoke again. "Then I will stay too." Several of them opened their mouths as if to argue, but Seth shook his head. "I won't leave you. This is my home now, too."

Despite the gravity of the situation, several of the villagers smiled and chuckled. They pushed in closer to Seth, slapping him on the back and tousling his hair. Then someone started to sing again, a bouncing chant in Sango that grew louder as each of the villagers joined in. They danced and jumped, turning the entire mass of people into a boiling cauldron of joy. It was ridiculous, especially considering their dark situation, but the people didn't seem to notice.

Jenny drifted towards the edge. The exuberance of the villagers was contagious, and she couldn't stop herself from smiling and clapping with them, but part of her heart wasn't in it. She had longed to be a part of this small, tight-knit group of people, and, through her patience and their love, she had achieved that goal. But today she felt like an outsider again. Something special had taken place, but it had taken place without her. This had been a moment between the villagers and Seth from which she had been excluded, not on purpose, but it had happened nonetheless. She had no right to feel upset or left out, but the feeling remained.

Eventually the crowd began to break up, and the villagers scurried away to their homes where they would have to eat lunch by themselves because of the rain. Jenny lingered with some of the others for several minutes, talking and laughing, basking in the radiant warmth that always follows such experiences. When her stomach began to growl, she turned to leave but was blocked by Femi. The boy stood in her path where he had been waiting for her to finish talking. She gave him a big smile and reached down to hug him.

"Are you going to leave?" he asked bluntly, a little frown on his face.

The smile on Jenny's face froze. She pulled back from the little boy, aborting the hug, and stared into his accusing eyes. All her warm feelings began to drain away. She had been caught up in the momentum of Seth's announcement and had forgotten about herself. Now that it had passed, all her anxiety began to flood back in. The little boy had brought her back to earth with the deftness of an eagle driving a pigeon to the ground.

"I don't know," she said, and it was true: she didn't know. "I haven't thought it all through yet, Femi." She stumbled into a lame explanation of some of the reasons why she should leave, but the boy didn't hear them. He stared at her with his unsettling, unblinking gaze as his frown grew bigger. Then in the middle of her sentence, he turned and walked away. She called after him, but he broke into a run and didn't look back.

Fresh tears came to Jenny's eyes, but these were not tears of joy. She felt as if the little boy was walking away with her heart.

A hand fell on her shoulder and she heard Seth's soothing voice as he pulled her close. She turned and hugged him. It was just the two of them under the canopy now. They stood in silence for a moment, then Seth released her as she dried her tears on her sleeve.

"What am I going to do?" she sniffled. "I feel like my heart is being torn in two."

"You should go with Clayton Mercury tomorrow," Seth replied. Jenny looked up at him. His eyes were still red from crying, but he seemed at peace now. "He gave me the same choice too. And honestly, it's a good one. He'll protect you and make sure you get back home safely."

"But what about you?" she asked. She was surprised that he was so ready to send her away.

"Jenny, this is my cross to bear," he replied. "This is my responsibility. I can't leave now, not when these people need a leader most. I'd never be able to live with myself. No matter how I look at it, leaving now only looks like running away. And I can't do that. I ran away from you, Jenny. I realize that now. I had a responsibility to you, and I should have been man enough to fix that problem. I won't do that again. I will not run away."

"How is that any different for me?" Jenny asked. "If I leave now, it'll be like I'm running away too."

"No, it won't," Seth replied. "You haven't been here as long as

I have, and you aren't responsible for these people like I am. You've done so much good and helped so many people, Jenny, but you don't owe them anything else. The difference between you and me is that this is where I am supposed to be. Period. I *belong* here, Jenny. Can you honestly say that this is where you belong?"

Jenny stared at him. He spoke with such certainty and conviction. She couldn't handle it. Images of the other time he had spoken to her this way, right before they had broken up, flooded her mind. Once again, she shied away from the depth of his being. She turned away from him and closed her eyes.

"Think of your parents," he continued. "Think of your family. I've already spoken in depth with my parents, and they understand. But your family still needs you. Are you ready to spend the rest of your life here? Think of your mother, Jenny."

Jenny's heart stuttered. She hadn't thought of her mother. She already knew what she would say. Maybe her mother would be right. Maybe it was time for her to go home. She could be proud of herself for the things she had done. If she stayed, she would face certain death. No one would blame her for leaving.

Seth misinterpreted her silence for stubbornness. "Do it for me then, Jenny," he whispered. He came up behind her and put his arms around her. "I don't want anything to happen to you. I care about you way too much. I won't let you be put in harm's way. I *won't*."

He stood there with his arms around her for a moment longer, but, when she didn't respond, he released her. As Jenny listened to him walk away, she felt for the second time that someone was walking away with her heart.

Jenny spent the rest of the day alone in her tent packing her bags and trying to unpack her heart. Her mind wandered through her memories of the last two months, pausing here and there on a fond memory or hurrying on to avoid one that was painful. She realized with a touch of happiness that the good memories far outweighed the bad. She moved as if in a daze, going through the motions of folding her clothes, arranging her toiletries, and trying to find places for little odds and ends, packing only because she had nothing else to do. She had fewer things to pack now; some things had worn out or gotten too dirty to use and eight of her t-shirts now hung on the shoulders of the village's youth. Music played from her phone as she packed, establishing a soundtrack of emotion on which her heart played. Soaring anthems, melancholy ballads, catchy pop tunes, and heartfelt worship songs played, inserting little bits of emotion and wisdom between each sock or skirt. She listened and longed for comfort, but the songs that were usually so effective at improving her spirits only increased her longings.

As the gray, cloud-filtered light faded into a dull evening, she looked around her tent and realized she had nothing else to pack. She sat on her bed and stared out the tent flap. The rain had stopped, and the world was quiet. Her phone shuffled to one of her favorite songs. As she listened to the slow, ambient textures build behind the rich, poignant lyrics, her heart began to swell. She thought about the story to which the song alluded, that incredible moment when Jesus walked on the Sea of Galilee. She realized the song wasn't talking about Jesus, but about Peter, the man who had chosen to step out of a boat onto the sea and walk. She imagined what that experience must have been like, to put one foot in front of the other from wave to wave with the glorious Son of God locked squarely in your vision. For a moment, something about the nature of faith and about following the voice of Jesus unfolded in her mind. Her heart began to rise as she reached out to grasp it.

But then the song cut out, just as it reached its crescendo. Jenny grabbed her phone and saw the little notification that read "10% of battery remaining." She reached into her backpack for one of her back-up batteries, but remembered that she didn't have any more; George Hauser was on his way to the capital for emergency care and hadn't been able to return the one he was charging for her. Her other battery was dead. She dismissed the notification on her phone and powered it off. She would need to save the last ten percent of her battery for emergencies.

Jenny sat in silence for a long time. She knew she should pray, but the words wouldn't come, and she knew why: she was afraid. But she wasn't sure why. The specter of fear darted between the shadows at the edge of her mind's eye, but it was different this time. In a moment of clarity, Jenny realized she wasn't afraid to stay—she was afraid to go. She pondered that realization for quite some time as the world grew dark and sleep finally took her.

Chapter 16
Go

Jenny awoke slowly, like a boxer regaining consciousness after a knockout punch. She pulled herself out of bed and went through her morning routine like a robot. Her mind was empty, drained of all emotion by a day of turmoil and a night of rough sleep. She dressed in the clothes she had laid out the night before, washed her face and hands, and then sat on her cot as she munched a banana. She had nothing else to do except wait for the mercenaries to arrive.

After she finished the banana, she checked her watch. She had a little time before Mercury arrived to fetch her, so she decided to take one last walk through the village. She found the villagers fetching water, gathering supplies, cooking breakfast, kissing each other goodbye, and hurrying their children off to school. They behaved just like it was any other day, from all appearances oblivious to their impending doom. Jenny couldn't bear it. She felt like the world was ending, but all she could do was watch and wave. She wanted to grab each of them and scream into their faces to run for the hills and escape the coming destruction. But she also envied the peace they had found. They had accepted their fate and now were relying on God to deliver them.

She walked past the medical tent and saw Sudaiq organizing his tools to prepare for the day's work. He caught her eye and gave her one of his big, warm smiles. She turned and walked into the tent, wanting to say something but not knowing what to say. "Is there something I can do for you, my dear?" he asked. She tried to reply several times, but her brain locked up her mouth. The outward appearance she gave was of a tongue-tied little girl. Sudaiq's smile grew bigger. "I will miss you too, little one," he said.

Jenny considered Sudaiq something like her boss and had never hugged him before, but now she threw her arms around the kind, grandfatherly man and let him envelope her in a big bear hug. She mumbled an "I'll miss you" into his soft shoulder. He boomed with laughter.

"Don't worry, Jenny," he said when he had released her. "You aren't going far. You are only going from here," he said, pointing at his eyes, "to *here*." He pointed at his heart. "I might not see you, but that does not mean you won't still be close."

Jenny sighed and smiled. "How can you be so calm and happy when you know what's coming?" she asked.

"It is better than being scared and sad," he replied, turning a soul-stirring, gut-wrenching question which had plagued Jenny's mind into nothing but a whisper. In a strange way, it made sense.

Sudaiq wished her good luck, kissed her on the top of the head, and bid her farewell. She resumed her walk, but she felt worse than before. She was confused and angry, but wasn't sure why. The pressure in her soul threatened to blow her composure wide open.

Her steps took her to the Zoumara's neighborhood. Jean-Marc, who was accustomed to working all day at the quarry, puttered around trying to appear busy while Aleena prepared food for the week. Femi was nowhere to be seen. As soon as they noticed her, they dropped their work and came to her. They spoke to her about everything except her imminent departure. Jenny tried and failed to listen and act cheerful and interested. Her consternation must have showed on her face because Aleena stopped talking and hugged her. Silent tears began to fall from her eyes. Jean-Marc and the other villagers who were close by gathered around to comfort her. Jenny was grateful for their support, but they misinterpreted her tears; they weren't tears of sadness or worry, but of indignation. It was all so terribly wrong. These kind, wonderful, peaceful people were about to face an overwhelming darkness against which they had no defense. The unfairness of it all outraged her. They didn't deserve it. And not only was she helpless to stop it, but she was leaving them to face it alone. She felt like things outside of her control were sweeping her along towards a fate she could not see and did not want. But what bothered her the most was that she felt hopeless, and yet, the doomed people around her did not.

Seth came up and the little group of villagers parted to allow him to approach. "Mercury is here," he said to Jenny. She nodded. The villagers bowed their heads and dispersed. Aleena told Jenny that she and Jean-Marc would load her luggage for her and hurried away. Soon the little clearing was deserted except for Seth and Jenny.

Jenny waited, unsure of what to do or say. There was so much she wanted to tell him, so many unexpressed feelings she wanted to release, but she didn't know where to start. She started to speak, but he interrupted her.

"I'm going with you out of the reserve," he said. "I'll follow Mercury in our jeep until we get to the staging area, then I'll head back. It's an hour away. That should give us enough time to say goodbye."

Jenny smiled. She was grateful but didn't need to say it.

"So, you've got things to say, do you?" she said with a tease in her voice. She didn't feel it, but Seth would never resist playing along with her.

"No, but I figured you'd have a lecture for me," he said, rising to the challenge in her voice, "and I know how long-winded you can be."

Jenny rolled her eyes and then took his arm as they walked towards the edge of the village to meet Clayton Mercury. The village, which had been bustling with activity only minutes before, was now quiet. But the reason soon became plain. Somehow the entire village had heard she was leaving and had gathered to say goodbye. Jenny's heart clenched as she realized that all small towns were the same no matter the continent.

As she walked through the crowd, the people patted her on the back, hugged her, pushed small gifts into her hands, and shed more than a few tears. Jenny knew them all by name, even though she had only been there for a few months. She scanned the crowd, noting each familiar face. With a hint of sadness, she found that Femi wasn't here either. She had wanted to see the little boy one last time. She climbed into the jeep with a heavy heart.

Mercury walked up to the passenger's side of the vehicle and patted Jenny on the shoulder through the open window. "You're doing the right thing, Jenny," he said. "I wish I could get your boyfriend to do the same." She smiled. Seth had explained the status of their relationship to the mercenary several times, but he had stubbornly continued to refer to them as *boyfriend* and *girlfriend*. He was obstinate, snarky, and rude. She would miss him.

"I've made my choice, Merc," replied Seth.

Mercury nodded. He looked regretful. "Stay close behind me," he said, and got on a small, nimble, four-wheel ATV and started the engine.

Seth put the jeep in gear and started to roll after him. As they pulled away Jenny looked back and waved at the villagers. They cheered, jumped around, and threw things in the air like they were sending off a national hero, not an insecure young woman leaving them to a gruesome fate. The children ran alongside the departing jeep, squealing in delight as they tried to catch Jenny's outstretched hands. Jenny reached for the hands of one little boy as the jeep sped up, but she just missed his grasping fingers. The jeep sped off, leaving the boy and the village in the dust.

The drive to the mercenaries' staging area wasn't as conversational as Jenny had expected it to be. The loud jeep and bumpy road made conversation difficult, and Seth had to concentrate to keep up with the smaller and much faster four-wheeler Mercury rode. But beyond those things, both of them seemed averse to conversation. When they spoke, it was only of trivial things, like the weather or their families back home. Both of them wanted to say something meaningful, to make memorable what both felt to be their last moments together, but neither could find the right words. Their time together was slipping through their fingers, yet neither of them knew what to do to make it last. In what must have been an act of frustration, Jenny reached over and grasped Seth's hand where it rested on the empty seat between them. He didn't react or acknowledge it. But he drove the rest of the difficult journey with only one hand.

When they reached the staging area, Seth killed the jeep's engine but didn't get out. Neither did Jenny. They sat and watched Mercury turn off his four-wheeler and move off among his men to help load the last few things. The staging area was a long, flat hill dotted with trees from which one could survey the surrounding country. Mercury had chosen it for this strategic advantage; from the top of the hill he would have as good a chance as any to spot incoming attackers. To the north, Jenny could see a long canyon cut through the trees by the Sangha River, and to the east, another, thinner canyon that marked the tributary near which the little village of Sangha sat. The village itself was hidden by the impenetrable jungle. Anyone who hadn't already visited it would never know it was there.

They sat in the front seat of the jeep without a word and watched the mercenaries load their gear, just holding hands, drawing comfort from each other in their last seconds together. Jenny kept trying to say something, but she couldn't figure out where to start. Mercury, who was talking to some of his men, turned to look back at her and checked his watch. Jenny assumed he was giving her time to say goodbye. But time was running out.

Too soon the mercenary leader looked back again, checked his watch one last time, and strode towards the jeep. He called out to her and told her it was time to leave. She released Seth's hand and, in a daze, climbed out of the jeep. Her heart began to beat faster, and she started to panic. She wasn't ready to go yet. She hadn't said all she needed to say, or done all she needed to do, but it was too late. Seth got out too and came to stand facing her in front of the jeep. He looked so conflicted. Jenny still didn't have the right words, but she decided that she had to say something.

"Seth…" she began, but he interrupted her by taking her cheek in his hand and kissing her on the lips. She kissed him right back. They stood that way for a long time, locked in a tender embrace, oblivious to the mercenaries as they loaded Jenny's luggage into one of their trucks. For one merciful moment the rushing chain of events stood still and allowed Jenny to soak it in like a thirsty savannah after the first rain. She hoped against hope that the moment would freeze and allow her to experience it forever.

But, like all wonderful moments, it had to end. Seth pulled away from her, but the conflicted expression on his face had changed to one of quiet confidence and determination.

"I love you, Jenny," he said, softly stroking her cheek. "I always have and I always will. No matter what happens I want you to know that I cherish all the time I've spent with you. Despite all we've been through, I wouldn't trade any of it for the world."

"Seth, I…" Jenny tried to respond, but once more she was interrupted. This time it was by machine-gun fire.

The sound was far-off and muffled by the forest trees, but it was unmistakable. The mercenaries snapped into position, rifles raised towards the sound. Jenny and Seth turned and looked back towards the village. For several seconds, everyone on the hilltop was silent and waited with bated breath. Then they heard an explosion and a cloud of smoke rose over the jungle near the tributary on whose banks sat the little village of Sangha.

The camp exploded into action as mercenaries raced to finish loading the final items or abandoned them where they sat. "Jenny, come now!" Mercury shouted over the noise, gesturing wildly towards her. Jenny willed her feet to move, but she was torn in two once again. She looked back and forth between Mercury and Seth, whose hand she squeezed. Her eyes settled on Seth.

"Goodbye, Jenny," he said. He kissed her one more time, then jumped in the jeep and raced back down the road.

"Seth! Seth!" Mercury screamed after him. "You fool! You'll get yourself killed!" He sprinted over to Jenny and stared after the departing jeep in disbelief. He swore. "What a waste," he spat. "Come on Jenny, we have to go, now."

He started back towards his jeep but stopped when Jenny didn't follow. "Jenny, come on," he said, "we can't do anything for him now. Jenny?"

Jenny didn't hear him. She stared down the road after the jeep which had already disappeared. She was still frozen with indecision, but not for long. Something in her heart was shifting, rising from her soul like a mountain from the depths of the ocean, and, compared to its weight, her old fears were nothing. All her life she had sought security, treasured it above all else, even lost things she loved to preserve it. It had become her defining trait. But now something else pushed it aside, something akin to desire, but mixed with responsibility. Once, not so long ago, she had broken away from her selfish desires and made a choice, a choice to leave her security behind and run off to a foreign land to give her life in service to others. She realized that choice could become her new defining trait, if only she would step out in faith. As soon as she realized this, her indecision evaporated, and a strange peace settled on her shoulders. She knew what she wanted, and she knew what was right. For the first time in her life, those two things were one.

"Jenny?" Mercury called again. She turned to look at him, as if noticing him for the first time. They stared at each other in silence as the distant machine-gun fire continued to roar. Jenny didn't speak, but Mercury knew; he must have been able to see it on her face. She knew he wouldn't understand, but she didn't understand it all either. She just knew what she had to do.

Mercury swore again and shook his head. He locked eyes with Jenny for a second and then tossed her the keys to the four-wheeler. "Go," he said with resignation in his voice.

Jenny looked at the keys in her hand for a moment. A lump caught in her throat, but she didn't have time to worry about it. She threw her arms around the mercenary's waist in an awkward hug and then raced over to the four-wheeler. She kicked the powerful little vehicle in gear, made a tight U-turn and raced off down the road. "God-speed," Mercury yelled after her as she raced by.

Jenny pushed the vehicle to its limits and overtook Seth in the slower, clunkier jeep in no time. She zoomed in front of him and stopped. He brought the jeep to a quick halt, jumped out and ran up to her as she dismounted.

"Jenny, what are you doing?" he started to ask, but she cut him off.

"Seth, this is my choice," she said with determination. "I get to make one just like you do, and like you, I'm choosing to stay. This is my home now too, and I won't leave it. I won't run away. This is what I want, and it's the right thing to do. Don't try to change my mind."

Her words came out in a rush and stopped Seth's objections cold. He listened to her with his mouth wide open in shock, but when she finished, his look of shock morphed into a small smile, and he nodded his head.

"I lost you once before, Seth," she said, returning his smile. "I'm not losing you again."

He leaned down and kissed her. "All right, girl, you win. It's you and me to the end, no matter what happens."

They climbed back on the four-wheeler, Jenny at the controls and Seth hanging on behind, and raced towards the burning village and their destiny.

Chapter 17
Into the Blazing Sun

The small, nimble four-wheeler traversed the bumpy jungle road much faster than one of the lumbering jeeps. Jenny pushed it to its limits. She had been raised on such vehicles and maneuvered it around holes and over bumps with a practiced hand. Seth, accustomed to Jenny's displays of daredevilry, hung on behind her. Neither of them tried to speak. They knew they were probably heading towards their deaths. Nothing else needed to be said. Neither had any idea what they would do when they arrived—they only knew they had to get there.

A tower of smoke rose high above the jungle from the direction of the village, fighting with the blazing sun as it approached its zenith. Sporadic bursts of gunfire echoed through the air, but died down after several minutes. The jungle became silent except for the roar of the four-wheeler. They drove for a quarter of an hour in silence before they heard another shot, just one thundering retort, and then the jungle fell silent again. Jenny didn't slow as they approached the village, roaring into the clearing at full speed like a lioness attacking her prey.

But it didn't matter because they were already too late.

The village of Sangha was on fire. The tower of smoke wasn't sustained by one or two fires, but by a multitude of them. Every building still standing was burning. The rest had been knocked down and scattered across the area. The grasses manicured with such care were already burnt and the whole of the supplies purchased by hard-earned wages were nothing but ash. The pavilion which once played host to some of the most powerful church services of Jenny's life, had already collapsed, its hand-carved beams blackened from the flames. Off in the distance, the fields burned too, the red flames consuming years of back-breaking toil. Not a single person remained.

As Jenny stared at the wanton destruction, tears come to her eyes, tears of anger, frustration, and hopelessness. They rolled down her stunned face, making little trails in the sweat and dust on her cheeks. Her brain rebelled at the information gathered by her eyes—she couldn't comprehend it. Beside her, Seth dropped to his knees, his own tears streaking his face. Jenny watched him pitch forward onto his hands and strike the ground with his fist. He uttered a piercing scream that smote Jenny's heart like a javelin. She knelt beside him and placed her hand on his back, feeling his sobs of grief wrack his entire body. She heard him groaning something unintelligible into the dirt. After a few seconds, she realized he was calling the names of the villagers.

For a moment, they sat together and shared their grief. Then Seth gave another scream, jumped to his feet, and charged into the burning village. Jenny shouted after him, but he ignored her. She ran after him down the main pathway. The heat pressed against her as she ran, threatening to smother her, but there was enough space between the rows of burning huts for her to pass safely between them. She choked on the ashes of what had once been a beautiful place full of beautiful people, trying not to look at the raging inferno around her. But her eyes strayed. Cots and clothes burned, water buckets melted, and children's toys lay in various states of hideous dismemberment. She ducked a clothes line upon which one of her old t-shirts burned. Yet, in all the destruction, she noticed one thing missing: bodies. *Where were the villagers?*

She continued to chase Seth through the smoke and ash as he called out the names of the villagers, for he too had noticed that the village was empty. But when they neared the burning medical clinic, they found what they had hoped not to find. A large body lay in the street. It was Sudaiq.

Jenny's heart leapt into her throat, but then he wheezed. Someone had shot the big man in the chest, but he was still alive. She and Seth each took one of his arms, and they half-carried half-dragged him back to the four-wheeler at the edge of the village where they laid him down. As soon as Jenny examined him, the faint ray of hope that had crept into heart disappeared. His wound was too large and too deep. She could see he had already lost too much blood. They had no way to stop the flow. Sudaiq was dying.

Seth cradled the big man's head in his hands and told him over and over that he would be okay. He repeated it neurotically, like a child in shock. He looked up at Jenny with pleading eyes, silently begging her to do something, *anything,* to save Sudaiq's life. But all she could do was shake her head.

Seth's face went ashen, but before he could say anything, Sudaiq took one of their hands in each of his and pulled them close.

"My children," he said just loud enough to be audible over the roaring flames, "you've come home."

Both Jenny and Seth tried to answer him, but he wasn't finished. He had only taken a breath to gain strength for his next sentence.

"I am going home, too," he whispered. "I am going to be with my family—my bald, old father, my fat, sweet mother, my beautiful sons, and my precious wife."

Seth started to protest, but Sudaiq only laughed, a slow, rich sound cut short by a gurgle, as he choked. Seth lifted his balding head higher to steady him. After several seconds, Sudaiq continued.

"I love you, my children. When I am gone, please remember me, for if you forget me not, I will always be with you. And when you think of me, remember this…"

He coughed again, softer.

"Remember this: we bleed for each other. That is how it has always been, and that is how it always must be."

He smiled up at the two young people whose eyes were brimming with tears. They both nodded at him.

He gave a great sigh and settled back with his eyes closed.

"Now, go," he whispered. "Be with your people. Lead them as God has always intended."

He smiled and lay still. His breathing grew slower and then stopped. His lungs compressed one more time, and then he was gone.

They knew they didn't have time to bury Sudaiq, but they refused leave him exposed for the wild animals to desecrate. After dragging his body to a small, bare patch of land set aside as a cemetery, they buried him in a hasty grave with a shovel they found in the wreckage. They laid Sudaiq next to his wife, with only a crude, unadorned headstone to mark his grave. They completed the task in silence, too sorrowful for words. It was so pitiful it almost broke Jenny's heart, but it gave her a measure of peace.

They stood over Sudaiq's grave for several minutes, heads bowed. As the initial emotion passed, Jenny began to feel the urgency of their situation once again. They needed to move on. But Seth continued to stand in silence.

"Look at this destruction," he whispered. He turned and stared into the still burning village. "Those soldiers had no plans to let the villagers go. If any of them are still alive, it's only because they haven't found the diamonds or gold yet. I doubt any of them tried to run."

Jenny nodded.

"They'll be at the quarry," Seth said, and Jenny nodded again. That was what had drawn the soldiers in the first place. It was the source of all of their problems.

"You ready, Jenny?" He didn't ask her if she had a plan, because he knew she didn't. He didn't ask her if they should call someone, because there was no one to call. He didn't ask her if they should go on, because they both knew there was no turning back now.

In reply, Jenny took his hand and led him back to the four-wheeler. They raced into the jungle, leaving the smoke and the flames behind.

Chapter 18
Your Moment

As they neared the quarry, Jenny slowed the four-wheeler, bringing it to a full stop behind a large fern off the side of the trail.

"What are you doing?" Seth asked. "The camp is still a little further on."

"No matter what we do when we get there, we'll want to do it silently," Jenny replied. "If we park here and continue on foot, we may be able to sneak up on them and see what's going on before we burst in."

Seth gave her a grim nod. Jenny guessed he had resigned himself to whatever horrible fate awaited them. She didn't have much hope of a peaceful situation either.

"What *are* we going to do when we get there?" she asked.

Seth sighed. "I don't know," he said. "I never think that far ahead. I thought perhaps we'd be able to talk the militia into letting us leave peacefully, but now…"

His voice trailed off. Jenny understood. "Maybe we can come up with some sort of plan?" She didn't believe herself, but she would not give into despair, no matter how bleak their situation became. They would go on until they could go no further.

"What have we got?" Seth asked.

They didn't have much other than the clothes on their backs. Jenny didn't even have her cell-phone because she had left in her backpack with Clayton Mercury. They searched the four-wheeler and found it fully-equipped with emergency supplies, but nothing that would persuade two hostile military forces to stand down. In a case strapped to the back they found an AK-47 assault rifle and a 9-millimeter semi-automatic handgun, both fully loaded. Neither weapon would be much help against the militia, but they might be useful in a pinch. They stared at the weapons in silence.

"Could you use one of these if you had to?" Seth asked.

Jenny thought about it. She had been raised around firearms. Her father had taught her how to use them, intending for her to know how to protect herself in case of a home invasion. She was a good shot, too. But she had never considered what it would be like to shoot another human being. She didn't know if she would be able to do it.

"Could *you*?" she said, turning the question around on Seth.

He thought for a moment. "If someone was attacking you, yes," he said with conviction. "But to intentionally start a firefight? I'm not sure."

They stared at the guns for several more moments. Jenny was the first one to pick one up. She hefted the AK-47 and handed the 9mm to Seth. "Just in case," she said. Seth nodded and took the weapon.

They jogged towards the mercenary camp. They found the gate unguarded—the soldiers had little reason to fear a counter-attack—and slipped in. The camp looked like a ghost town with trucks and machinery sitting idly as if someone had left them in the middle of a task and never returned. Crates of supplies sat stacked in various stages of unloading. Clayton Mercury and his men had been forced to leave much behind in their mad dash to safety. Jenny wondered if he had left all these supplies and machinery behind because he hadn't had time to take them or because they weren't worth enough to worry about. Perhaps the size of his haul in diamonds and gold was enough to outweigh the loss of his equipment. If the amount of machinery he had left behind was any indication, his haul had been quite valuable.

They crept through the camp towards the quarry. As they got

closer, they heard angry voices arguing with one another interspersed with a woman's cries. They hid behind a conveyor belt at the edge of the quarry and peeked over the side. Jenny had never visited the quarry and was surprised to find it much more developed than she had imagined. The pit was massive, the work of heavy machinery supplemented by men with smaller tools. Several tunnels branched off of the main pit at different levels. A combination of thin ledges carved from the rock and temporary scaffolding connected the tunnels with the rim and bottom of the pit. Several tunnels on the bottom level appeared to have been in active use until the mercenaries' sudden flight. Jenny was impressed that Mercury had kept this operation a secret for so long. The towering jungle trees grew right up to the edge of the pit, hiding its outline underneath their out-stretched branches, but they didn't reach far enough to hide even a fraction of the massive pit. It must have taken up several acres and would have produced massive amounts of noise during its excavation. Clayton Mercury's bribes to the military must have been substantial.

At the bottom of the quarry knelt the villagers of Sangha. Seth give a quick sigh of relief when he saw the villagers—no one other than poor Sudaiq seemed to be missing. They all knelt in a tight group between two disordered lines of armed men. One group wore close approximations of military uniforms and stood straighter, while the other group was much less ordered and dressed in a range of rag-tag outfits from ostentatious dress uniforms to dirty rags. All the men clutched their weapons at the ready and stared across at the other group with thinly veiled hostility. Jenny realized she was getting her first look at the two rebel factions whose fighting continued to tear the Central African Republic apart: the Anti-Balaka militia and the former Seleka freedom-fighters.

The source of the commotion came from the near end of the quarry. A man with an assault rifle slung over one shoulder was shouting and slapping the face of another man kneeling before him. Jenny realized it was Mohammedou Djotodia and the man he was roughing-up was Nikolai, whom Mohammedou had attacked and tried to rob several months ago. Jenny's heart clenched as she watched the armed Mohammedou berate and strike the unarmed Nikolai, who tried in vain to shield himself from the other man's attacks. She caught enough of what they said to understand that Mohammedou was cursing Nikolai and the rest of the village for their treatment of him. She heard Seth's name many times. Poor Nikolai repeated over and over that he did not know where Seth was. Jenny felt him stiffen next to her.

Behind Mohammedou stood a tall, muscular, uniformed man with a cruel face who was holding a battered Jean-Marc Zoumara by the collar. The man held the much smaller Jean-Marc casually, like a lion with a mouse in its grasp, an arrogant, bored expression on his face. He was a man with an aura of quiet, unshakeable self-confidence, a man comfortable in his own skin used to giving orders and backing up those orders with whatever show of force was necessary. He was calm and unaffected by the cruel scene before him. Jenny didn't need to be told this man's name—she had heard it too many times before.

"Colonel Massi," Seth whispered, and Jenny's blood ran cold.

Colonel Massi let Mohammedou rant for several more minutes until he seemed to grow tired of his tirade. Without warning he drew his sidearm and fired it straight up into the air. The loud *crack* made everyone in the quarry jump, and several of the villagers shrieked. Mohammedou dropped Nikolai and whirled around like a startled buck. Colonel Massi let the shot echo through the quarry, then holstered his weapon and moved forward. He shoved Mohammedou out of his path and threw Jean-Marc to the ground. Then he barked an order at one of his men in French. The man hustled forward, grabbed Nikolai and led him over to the group of villagers where he shoved the man to his knees and returned to his position in line.

Mohammedou said something to Massi, but the Colonel dismissed him with a wave of his hand, not even deigning to look at him. The ex-Seleka member glared at Massi's back. As he took several steps back, he swung his assault rifle off his shoulder and into his hands.

Colonel Massi ignored him and began to interrogate Jean-Marc in a calm, even voice, asking him about the mercenaries, the diamonds, and Seth. Jean-Marc replied each time that they were all gone and he did not know where they had gone. This continued for a minute until without warning Massi struck Jean-Marc across the face, a savage back-hand blow that sent the smaller man flying backwards. Aleena gave a shriek and rushed forward to defend her husband, but one of the Seleka fighters caught her and held her back. She continued to wail as Massi questioned Jean-Marc again, punctuating each question with a swift kick to the groaning man's ribs.

Seth was grinding his teeth in anguish as he gripped the edge of the conveyer belt until his knuckles turned white. "What do we do, Jenny?" he whispered to her. She shut her eyes so she didn't have to witness the savage beating, but her ears worked just fine. She listened to Jean-Marc's groans and Aleena's wails with a sick heart. A feeling of complete helplessness washed over her.

Eventually Colonel Massi grew tired of kicking Jean-Marc. With a sigh he ordered his men to remove Jean-Marc and bring him another villager. The soldiers picked Jean-Marc up and shoved him towards the rest of the villagers. As he stumbled forward, Mohammedou approached, intercepting him before he reached the group of villagers. He slammed the butt of his rifle into Jean-Marc's abdomen. The already weak Jean-Marc doubled over and collapsed to his knees. Mohammedou shouted a curse at him and aimed his rifle at the back of the other man's head. Aleena screamed and fought to get loose from her captors. Massi's soldiers, shouted at Mohammedou and moved towards him. His nervous compatriots snapped their rifles up and aimed them at the advancing Anti-Balaka members, eliciting a sudden halt and reciprocal response. Realizing that he was now in the crosshairs of several dozen assault rifles, Mohammedou froze.

Like a lion entering its den, Colonel Massi sauntered into the fray, oblivious to the brandished weapons all around him. He stopped in front of Mohammedou and in a calm voice told him to step back. Mohammedou held his ground, arguing that Jean-Marc was a Christian dog who deserved to die for resisting them. Colonel Massi stared at him for a moment. Then, with the speed of a striking mamba, he jerked out his pistol and whipped him across the face.

The skittish ex-Seleka members yelled curses and warnings and re-trained their rifles on Massi. The Anti-Balaka soldiers yelled back and waved their rifles. The villagers screamed and cowered down as low as they possible lest they be hit by a stray shot. Seth jumped to his feet and would have given himself up right there, but Jenny grabbed his arm and jerked him back down before anyone saw him. "Wait!" she hissed into his ear.

"But they're going to start firing!" he hissed back. "The villagers will get slaughtered. We have to do something now, Jenny!"

"Just wait," she whispered. "We might be able to use this to our advantage. The Seleka and the Anti-Balaka seem to hate each other a lot more than they hate us. We may not have to do anything."

Colonel Massi screamed at the ex-Seleka fighters. His expletive-laden tirade was vulgar and vitriolic, composed of curses against Islam and against the mothers of the ex-Seleka members. The gist of it was that he would kill every one of the Muslim fighters before he allowed them to kill a single Christian villager. As he yelled, Mohammedou rose from the ground, a long, red gash across his cheek. He started to step back towards his compatriots, his confidence growing as he neared the safety of his own men. He began to shout back at Massi, encouraging his men to join in. The opposing forces hurled insults and threats at each other while the villagers of Sangha cowered in terror.

As Jenny watched the ensuing stand-off, she realized their only chance was to get the two groups to fight one another. In the chaos, the villagers had a chance of slipping away. But they needed a plan.

"Where do those tunnels lead?" she asked Seth.

"Mostly just deeper into the mines," he replied. "Some of them connect with each other, but they don't go very far."

"Do any of them lead out?"

A light dawned in Seth's eyes. "There's one that leads out into the jungle," he said, pointing through a gap in the conveyor belt to a tunnel mouth at the far end of the quarry. "Mercury had it dug in case of emergencies. Some of the workers know about it, but there's no way Colonel Massi does. The villagers could escape through there. But how do we get them past the soldiers?"

"I've got an idea. We need to get them to fight each other. If one of us stays up here, we can fire a few shots with the rifle. They're so on edge right now, it will be all they need to start fighting each other. The other one can go to the tunnel exit in the jungle and lead the villagers out when all the chaos starts."

Seth thought it over for a second. "That might work," he replied. "As long as we can keep the soldiers occupied at this end, the people might be able to escape at the other. The soldiers won't suspect that there's an escape tunnel."

"We need to act soon," Jenny said.

"You're right," Seth replied. "I'll take the machinegun and draw their fire here. You take the pistol and find the tunnel. If you go back out the front gate, take a—"

"No," Jenny interrupted him. "I'll stay here and draw their fire. You keep the pistol and find the tunnel entrance. There's no time for you to tell me where to find it, and we can't risk me getting lost."

"No way, Jenny. This spot will be the most dangerous. If they find out what's going on, they'll shoot at this position. I'll draw the fire. The tunnel route will be safer."

"They're both going to be dangerous, Seth. Neither of these options are ideal, but I understood what I was getting into when I came back for you."

"Listen to me, Jenny…"

"No, you listen. We're both putting our lives on the line, here.

You know the terrain better than me. You're the likely choice to find the tunnel. Besides, I've always been a better shot than you."

"Jenny, I'm just trying to protect you."

"I know you are, and I love you for it. But we have a more important job to do."

Seth was silent. Jenny could tell he knew she was right, but he didn't want to admit it. As he deliberated, the shouting below intensified. The villagers began to wail and cry out for salvation. There was no time to waste.

"All right, you win again, girl," he said with a weary nod. "But as soon as it gets hot up here, you run to the Heart of the Jungle, okay? They'll never find you in the grotto. I'll get the villagers out, but then I'm going to meet you there. And if you don't come, I'm coming back here to find you."

Jenny nodded. "I'll be there."

Seth sighed and shook his head. "Wait for my signal. I'll fire one shot from the pistol. That's your cue to start the whole thing. It may take me a little while to get to the tunnel mouth, but be ready. Once it starts, there's no telling what will happen."

They looked at each other for a moment. "Stay safe, Jenny," Seth said. He kissed her on the cheek and ran off.

The moments dragged by as Jenny waited for Seth's signal. Every few seconds, she checked the mouth of the tunnel he pointed out to her, anxious to glimpse him. The soldiers below her were getting more and more agitated with each passing moment. After several tense minutes, they lowered their weapons, but none of them put them down. They remained as tense as ever, waiting for an excuse to open fire on the opposing group. Whatever truce that existed between the two groups hung by a thread. Now they were trying to choose another villager to interrogate, but neither side could agree on one. Tempers flared once again when Colonel Massi began asking the religion of each villager. They had reverted to their old religious prejudices: the Anti-Balaka refused to let the Seleka interrogate a

Christian, and the Seleka refused to let the Anti-Balaka interrogate a Muslim. Jenny feared a shootout would begin before Seth was in position. The sun had already reached its peak and was now descending towards the green sea of jungle. The situation wouldn't remain nonviolent for long. Time was running out.

After many minutes of arguing, they settled on an older man named Mikel and dragged him out to the center, but they couldn't agree on what questions to ask him, or who should do the questioning. They switched to another villager, but the bickering only increased. As the interrogation process continued, and the soldiers continued to get no information out of the villagers, Colonel Massi grew more restless. With a snarl he marched into the center of the group of villagers, grabbed Johnna-Marie, and dragged her out into the middle of the area. The big girl struggled, but she was no match for Colonel Massi's brute strength. He shoved her to her knees and pointed his big pistol at the back of her skull. The villagers shrieked as Massi twisted the frightened girl's arm behind her back, eliciting a squeal of pain. He then shouted that if no one would tell him where the treasure was hidden, he would shoot the girl in the head. The villagers pleaded with him for mercy, but his response was to shove the gun deep into the back of the girl's neck. He shouted his ultimatum once again, but the villagers remained silent and frozen. The tension in the quarry had reached a fever-pitch. The chaos was about to begin.

A single shot rang out, echoing through the stone quarry. For one horrifying second, Jenny thought Massi had shot Johnna-Marie, but when she saw the girl frozen in place like everyone else, she realized Seth had given her his signal. Without another thought she popped up behind the conveyor belt and fired a short burst into the rock wall right above the heads of the ex-Seleka fighters.

With surprising speed, the dam broke and chaos descended on the quarry. The soldiers fired at the first threatening thing they saw, which was each other. The villagers screamed in terror. In the jungle all around, monkeys and birds screeched, adding their voices to the gunfire and screams, creating a cacophony of violent noise loud enough to drown out a thunderstorm.

A brutal firefight ensued. Many of the soldiers were cut down in the first barrage, but a few experienced individuals dove for cover and returned fire in more controlled bursts. Jenny helped as much as possible, running up and down the conveyor belt firing short bursts, trying to give the appearance that there were dozens of hidden soldiers instead of just one frightened girl. Every so often a soldier would fire a burst at her position, but mostly they shot at each other. They were so focused on each other that they gave the villagers no mind. Jenny noticed with satisfaction that, while they had thrown themselves to the ground at first, they were now crawling or stumbling out of the line of fire towards the far end of the quarry. Soon they would be at the mouth of the tunnel where Seth would lead them to safety.

Bullets continued to fly as both sides pressed the attack. The Anti-Balaka outnumbered the Seleka and were more organized, but the Seleka refused to surrender, fighting with enough passionate hatred to make up for their deficiencies. Jenny continued to agitate the combatants, firing whenever she sensed a lull in the battle, her ruse still intact. She didn't try to hit anyone and purposely fired over their heads. The firefight seemed to last forever. Her body was pumping loads of adrenaline into her system, slowing each passing second into an eternity. But eventually, she noticed that the villagers were disappearing into the mouth of the escape tunnel. Soon, it would be time for her to leave.

As Jenny prepared to make her exit, she noticed something happening at the mouth of the escape tunnel. Seth was grappling with another villager. She looked closer and saw that it was Aleena. She was screaming something into Seth's face as he tried to pull her into the tunnel. In between the bursts of gunfire, she could pick out the woman's words. She wailed a question over and over: *Where is Femi? Where is Femi?* Jenny realized for the first time that she hadn't seen the little boy anywhere. In fact, she hadn't seen him all day. With mounting concern, she wondered the same thing: *Where was Femi?*

A burst of fire struck the conveyor right in front of her shattered her concentration. She crouched down even farther and listened for another opportunity to pop up and shoot. But to her dismay, she realized that the firing had stopped. Now, Colonel Massi was shouting something at the top of his lungs. She popped up to agitate the soldiers once again, but as soon as her head was above the conveyor, she realized she had made a mistake. Many of the soldiers were looking right at her position. Surprise dawned in their eyes. Jenny fired at them, but the AK-47 spat two more rounds and then clicked on an empty chamber. She was out of rounds.

Someone yelled, "It's a girl!" and followed with an immediate stream of fire that almost took Jenny's head off. They had discovered her ruse. It was time to leave.

Jenny dropped the assault rifle and ran for the gate like the Devil was at her heels.

Chapter 19
Alone in the Dark

The sun continued to sink as Jenny sprinted towards the jungle. Behind her, Colonel Massi bellowed at his troops to find her, but she had a good head-start, and figured she would find the Heart long before they caught up with her. She raced past the gate, turned right, and ran along the fence, retracing the path she had walked with Seth when he first showed her the hidden grotto. Less than a week had passed since that special day, but it felt like another lifetime, a calmer, simpler lifetime, where instead of running for her life, the only thing she had to worry about was being a stranger in a strange land.

She raced past the far gate of the camp and turned left towards the river. The shouts of Colonel Massi and his men still reached her ears, but they were growing fainter. She counted on the soldiers assuming she would head out of the jungle and not deeper into it. With any luck, they would go back to the ruined village while she got farther away. With their attention on her, they wouldn't check on the villagers for some time. She hoped they were already far away from the quarry and on their way to safety.

When she reached the river, she cast back and forth on the right side of the path, looking for the little game trail that led towards the grotto. After several long minutes with no success, she began to worry. Nothing looked familiar. The storms of the last few days had changed the face of the jungle with torn branches, uprooted shrubs, and copious amounts of mud, obliterating any outward trace of the trail. She continued looking and even pressed her way into the foliage at several spots, but eventually she had to admit to herself that she couldn't find it. The trail had disappeared.

Jenny tried not to panic. She stepped back from the impenetrable wall of jungle and forced herself to take slow, even breathes. She thought back: the trail ran parallel to the river which was visible even through the foliage. In the thick jungle, that meant the trail had to be no more than twenty yards from the river itself. If she followed the river, she would find the massive tree that formed the grotto eventually. *If I can just find enough space to move forward*, she thought, *I should be able to find the Heart.*

She selected a spot where the foliage was least dense and plunged in. It was like being swallowed. The jungle was wetter and stickier because of the rains and, like the journey into the gorilla thicket, she became soaked within seconds. She trudged through mud and sloshed through puddles she couldn't see and hoped weren't hiding poisonous snakes. She pushed through bushes and shrubs, ducked creepers and tree branches, and climbed over fallen trees. Her progress was slow, as if the jungle itself wanted to stop her from moving forward. Several times she turned left towards the river, hoping to stumble across the trail at an angle, but she could never tell if she found it or not and had to settle for reorienting herself parallel to the river. She moved in a shaky zigzag through the muddy jungle. She knew she was moving in the right direction, but she feared missing the big tree. All the trees looked the same, and she saw no other landmarks she recognized. The only thing familiar to her was the river, which continued to rush downstream.

Jenny fought the jungle for over an hour while the world around her grew dimmer with the setting sun. She searched with no success for the big, wide-bottomed tree, her only distinguishing landmark. Several times she backtracked, thinking she had gone too far and missed it, but it didn't help. She continued to push on, dirty and bedraggled like a wild animal, wet clothes torn in half a dozen places. Finally, as the sun's last few rays stabbed through the trees, she sank to the ground in exhaustion and buried her face in her hands, utterly spent. She drew long ragged breaths through the spaces between her fingers and tried to fight off the hopelessness trying to climb up from her stomach and wrap itself around her throat. If she let it, she knew it would choke her.

As she sat against a large rock and pondered her fate. She hadn't expected her end to come like this, lost and alone in the darkening jungle, while all manner of predator both animal and human lurked around her. Even if she could find the quarry or the village, she couldn't go back and let Colonel Massi capture her, and once the darkness settled in, she wouldn't last long in the wild. If the roving lion or a hungry leopard found her, she was dead meat. She might last out the night, but even if morning came, where would she go? Cut off from her friends, the chances of a rescue party being assembled, much less finding her were slim to nothing in the war-torn Central African Republic. She thought of her poor mother and how she would blame herself for Jenny's troubles as she always did. Her only consolation was the fact that she had helped the villagers of Sangha escape. With any luck, they would find their way to safety. She had nothing else, so she clung to it as despair crept into her heart. Here at the end, she knew she had done her best with what she had been given. It was a small comfort but a comfort nonetheless. Still, it didn't stop hot tears from filling her eyes.

As Jenny sat there surrendering herself to hopelessness, two things happened which altered her perceptions. First, she heard a shout, distant, but still audible. It could only be Colonel Massi or his men. Finding the village empty, they must have retraced their steps and checked the only other path Jenny would have taken. Her clumsy path through the jungle would be easy for them to follow. It wouldn't take them long to catch up with her. This realization set her heart racing once again. The end was near.

Her despair might have overwhelmed her at that point if it hadn't been for the second thing that happened. In an instance of pure revelation, she realized that the rock she sat against was the same rock she and Seth had hidden behind to surprise Femi a week ago. She leapt to her feet. The jungle started to order itself around her. The ground at her feet was muddy and covered with debris, but she recognized the crude path beneath it. She gave a sigh of relief— she had found the game trail. The grotto had to be close.

Jenny turned and raced down the trail. Behind her, the shouts increased in number and volume. Perhaps the men heard her tearing through the jungle, but she didn't care. She knew where she was now. Once she found the grotto, she would be safe.

She found the massive tree exactly where it should have been with the little, hidden space and the long, flat rock behind it. The natural room was dirty now, strewn with branches and rotten fruit, but it was unmistakable. She hurried to the edge of the rock and found it changed. The swollen river had risen almost to the level of the rock and flowed much faster now, its waters bolstered by the storm. It looked ten times as formidable as it had just five days ago and she hesitated. But the voices in the distance were growing louder, and the jungle was getting darker by the minute now that the sun had dropped behind the trees. She had to move now. Summoning her last ounce of courage, she took a deep breath and slipped into the water.

The river jerked her downstream and only a last-second lunge saved her from being carried away. For several frightening seconds she clung to the edge of the rock with one hand and fought the current. Once she got her second hand on the rock, she worked her way upstream to its far side. Like a big hand, the current pressed her against the rock and threatened to sweep her underneath, but she found a vine hanging in the water to which she clung. She was hyper-ventilating, the cold rainwater rushing over her head, but she had committed now—there was no turning back. She took another deep breath and ducked her head under the water, still clinging to the vine. She let the current pull her forward until she was completely under the rock. Then she kicked towards the riverbank with all her might. The mighty river fought against her, but she inched forward. Her toe struck something solid, and she knew that she was close. Soon she would have to let go of the vine. She kept kicking, trying to get as close as possible to the riverbank before she let go, but she was running out of air. It was time. She let go and lunged forward, but the river was too quick. In the half-second it held her in its power, it dragged her several feet down stream, before she dug her hands into the muddy riverbank. She tried to surfaced, but to her horror, her outstretched hand struck solid rock. She flailed around with her free hand, but she couldn't find the opening. Her lungs were ready to burst. In a last frantic attempt to surface, she wrenched herself backwards against the current and surged upwards with both hands.

For one tantalizing instant her hands broke the surface of the water and she felt fresh air. But she had nothing to grip. The mighty river, furious at being denied even for an instant, tore her back down into the water and into its unrelenting grasp.

But then someone grabbed her wrist, jerking her to a stop. The river pulled at her, but she struggled furiously against its grasp. She felt herself being drawn up and out of the water. She gasped for breath as her head broke the surface, and strong arms pulled her up into the grotto and onto dry land. The grotto was too dark for her to see her rescuer, but she heard Seth's voice asking her over and over if she was okay. All she could do was to cling to his hand as she lay on the dirt floor panting, allowing the adrenaline to drain away.

She heard someone else scuffling in the back of the grotto, and turned to look, but Seth squeezed her hand and said, "Don't worry, it's just Femi." So this was where he had run to. She smiled. He was a smart boy.

"What happened?" Seth asked. "I got the villagers out through the escape tunnel, but Aleena couldn't find Femi, so I sent them off towards the ranger station on the far side of the park and came here. I knew he would be here. But that was almost an hour ago. What happened to you?"

"I got lost," Jenny said through her ragged breaths, "and Colonel Massi was on my tail."

Seth started to speak, but he was cut short by a shout from outside the cave.

Jenny fell silent as Seth crept to the back of the little cave and peered up through a small hole between the roots of the great tree. She tried to silence her breaths, but her body was still trying to restore her equilibrium and craved oxygen. In her ears, her breathing sounded like a roaring ocean. She and Femi crawled forward and crouched behind Seth while he watched the hole. The voices grew louder as the soldiers drew nearer. Soon, they would reach the big tree and the flat rock under which Jenny, Seth, and Femi were hiding. The glow of a flashlight filtered through gaps between the stones and tree roots into the grotto. Jenny held her breath as they approached. They had followed her trail right to her hiding place.

But the soldiers kept walking, passing the tree without stopping and continued down the game trail, only yards from their targets. Seth breathed an audible sigh of relief. Another group of soldiers approached, but they, too, passed the tree, the glow of their flashlights fading just like those of the first group. Jenny began to breathe easier.

Then a harsh voice cut through the darkness, one she had already learned to fear, even after hearing it only for a short time. Colonel Massi marched down the trail, halted right next to the tree and began calling his soldiers back to him. The two groups of soldiers who had already passed the tree jogged back to their leader's position. More soldiers came up the path to join the first group and the glow of many flashlights illuminated the cave enough for Jenny to see the outline of Seth's face peering out. An argument took shape in which Jenny heard Mohammedou Djotodia arguing with Massi and saying something about refusing to take orders from Christian dogs who wanted to tramp through the jungle in the dark. Colonel Massi declared that the trail ended at the base of the tree. He shouted to his men to search the surrounding area. After several more rounds of debate, the grumbling group broke up, and the soldiers began moving off into the undergrowth. The jungle grew quiet except for the soft rustle of leaves against fabric as the soldiers moved off into the foliage. Most of the sounds receded, but one pair of boots clunked their way closer. Jenny listened with growing horror as the boots clunked around the great tree and up onto the very rock under which they hid. A beam of light flashed across the hole through which Seth was looking and, for an instant, caught him full in the face.

Seth recoiled like he had been struck, diving away from the hole and into the darkest recesses of the cave. With one arm he swept Jenny and Femi down with him and the three of them burrowed as deep as possible into the tangle of tree roots trying to disappear. The roving beam of light returned and shined down the hole. The hole was at an angle that prevented the beam of light from reaching them, but that didn't stop it from illuminating a sizeable portion of the cave. It came to rest on something far worse: a diamond.

Jenny buried her face in the back of Seth's shirt, too heartbroken to watch. As she did, her hand closed around something smooth and hard back in the depths of the dirty tree roots. As the soldier above her yelled to his comrades, her mind bizarrely detached itself from the situation and focused on the strange object in her hand. It was the size of a small brick, but not as heavy or thick. She traced its lined edges with her thumb with deranged curiosity and fingered a short, rubbery cord protruding from one end. With a flash she recognized it: her "lost" backup cell-phone battery. Here it was, unlooked for, in the strangest place imaginable. As a dozen more pairs of boots made their way towards her hiding place, she realized that Femi must have swiped the battery and left it behind for her to find on accident. Now, on the edge of chaos, as the world crumbled down around her, she felt a little pulse of pleasure because she had found it again. And she was thankful.

That was the second to last thing she felt before the world descended into chaos. The last thing she felt was abject terror as the night was torn in half by a hideous, bloodthirsty roar...

Pounce

*T*he old lion roars his battle cry and launches his powerful body
into the center of the pack of dark, warm bodies. Weak, lame, and
deteriorated, his strength is still prodigious when compared with the
puny sinews of Man. His once regal visage is now torn and bedraggled.
Yet, in the dark of night, his wrath is terrifying, and the men flee before
him like the herds of confused wildebeests on the plains of his homeland
far away. Frightened and disoriented, they fly in every direction, some
right into his jaws, so driven out of their minds are they by the sudden
ferocity of the king of beasts.

The terrified men fire their weapons, producing that horrible roar
that competes with his own, but he does not hear it tonight. The beast
is possessed by a certain madness of his own, driven by the scent of prey
so near and by the intoxicating smell of fresh blood. His sides ache with
hunger, but now he has caught his prey. Here it is plentiful. He does not
plan on going hungry tonight.

Fire singes his flanks, and he screams in pain and annoyance.
He strikes harder. A small man, in his panic, runs straight into his
clutches. The man recognizes his error and freezes, paralyzed by fear.
He screams in terror, a sound that is music to the old lion's ears, but
shines a light into the eyes of the beast, unwittingly checking his charge.
The lion's sensitive eyes, adapted for seeing in the dark, are blinded,
and, with a scream of rage, he strikes out blindly. His first strike knocks
the light away, and the second sends the little man sprawling into the
undergrowth.

The old lion follows the little man into the underbrush, but his attention is drawn to another man, large and muscular. The big man is scanning the jungle with his weapon ready, looking for the unseen terror, a look of fear in his eyes. His eyes lock with the glowing yellow eyes of the lion, and, like the smaller man, he freezes, though only for a second. Then he raises his gun and fires with a wild yell, but he is too late. The old lion has already covered the distance with a single bound, and, bellowing his own challenge, he springs upon him, his crushing weight bearing him to the ground. The big man is strong, but the lion is still far stronger. Nature has already decided the outcome of the contest. Within seconds, the big man is dead.

As the old lion lifts his head, the jungle grows quiet. One last time, he shatters the silence with a victory cry as he stands over his kill. Then, the world is silent again.

Chapter 20
The Fatal Consequence

Jenny and Seth cowered in the grotto with Femi between them while the lion grunted and growled to itself a few feet above their heads. When it finished, they heard it stand and roar, not a battle cry, but a slow, calm call, once again announcing his presence to the world. Then a period of silence ensued in which they couldn't tell if it was still there or not. A semi-distant roar half an hour later let them know the beast had continued its solitary wandering.

They stayed in the grotto for the rest of the night, unwilling to leave with the lion roaming the jungle. They huddled together, passing in and out of consciousness as they tried to sleep. Several times they heard movement above their heads—a hungry leopard or a curious boar perhaps—but neither the lion nor the soldiers returned.

When the first purple hints of dawn showed through the cracks in the ceiling, they left. While Femi scurried up through the hole between the roots, Jenny and Seth helped each other swim underneath the overhanging rock and climb up onto its surface. In the corner of the enclosed space above the grotto lay a body. Jenny refused to look at it, but Femi stood above it and stared. She wondered again about the little boy's history and about the pain she saw whenever she looked into his eyes. What horrors would so inoculate a boy that he wouldn't blanch at the sight of such destruction? The thought that he might have seen worse made her shudder.

Seth took Femi by the shoulder and steered him away from the carnage. The boy's eyes remained glued to the corpse until it passed out of his sight.

They returned to the game trail and headed deeper into the jungle away from the deserted mercenary camp. They were making for the park ranger station, Seth said, on the banks of the river near the far side of the reserve. There they hoped to find the rest of the villagers, who had a head start on them. The station was large and well-guarded, and had a satellite phone they could use to call for help. "It's far, but we should be able to make it by nightfall if we don't face any more delays," he assured her.

Relief flooded Jenny's mind. After an entire day fraught with danger, her body was starting to come down from its adrenaline high. The tension was draining away. An end to her peril was in sight. If she made it just one more day, she told herself, she would finally be safe.

He puts one weary foot in front of the other, dragging his hulking body down the trail. His wound pains him and each limping step sends a streak of fire through his flank. It still bleeds, not much, but enough to leave a trail on the ground and a scent in the air. He has eaten well, but until he heals, his prey will smell him long before he can catch it. So, again, he hunts the slowest, weakest, lamest, but most dangerous animal in the jungle: Man.

The once great beast knows his time is near; this may be his last hunt. He is not aware of it in the same sense a man would be, for he cannot examine the notion in his mind, dissect it, nor dread its coming. But he is aware of it nonetheless, a strange, fluttering, effervescent thing at the edges of his consciousness. It only drives him harder to survive, to kill again, and again. To him, it is as natural as breathing.

He stops and lifts his head, sampling the air. The scent of his prey, alone, scared, far from safety, is strong in his nostrils. He cannot follow as fast as before, but he will follow, and he will kill.

Ignoring the pain, he lowers his head and quickens his pace.

They followed the river, keeping to the game trail until it turned away from the river and led deeper into the jungle. Then they had to push their way through the thick forest. Exhausted from a long, restless night, they traveled where the undergrowth was thinnest but tried to keep the river close on their left. In the early morning, the world below the trees was still dark and wet. They moved slowly, trying to avoid pitfalls and other obstacles.

The sun had not passed the treetops when they came across a clearing created by a massive fallen tree whose fall had drawn down the canopy and undergrowth with it. They sat on the tree trunk and rested for a moment as the gray jungle mists began to lift around them.

As Jenny sat with her head on Seth's shoulder, she heard a rustle in the leaves. She lifted her head and looked across the clearing as a figure emerged from the forest. Alarmed, she jumped to her feet, as did Seth. She didn't recognize the individual in the dim light, but she saw he held a big machete in his hand. Seth stepped in front of Jenny and Femi and herded them behind him in a protective stance. The figure took a couple more steps forward, and Jenny recognized a wet, haggard, bedraggled Mohammedou Djotodia.

Mohammedou looked like he had been through a war zone. His pants were muddy and torn in several places, and he had stripped off his shirt and bound it around his abdomen to use as a makeshift bandage. He limped on one foot, favoring his right ankle. Dirt streaked his skin. Scratches covered his thin, sinewy body. One set of evenly spaced cuts looked like claw marks. He looked like he had barely escaped the jaws of death. He had a wild, disturbed look in his eyes, but his mouth was smiling.

"What do you want, Mohammedou?" Seth asked. Mohammedou

chuckled like a madman, a dark, mirthless sound, devoid of any humor or pleasure. Goosebumps popped out on Jenny's arm.

"There must still be some good fortune left in the universe," Mohammedou said between cackles, "for me to find you, the authors of all my pain, here, all alone."

"We did nothing to you, Mohammedou," Seth replied. "You brought all of this upon yourself."

Mohammedou's sides shook with hysterical laughter. "No," he said when he had finished, "Allah has given me one last chance to avenge myself upon you. He truly is a god of justice and mercy."

"Walk away, Mohammedou," Seth replied. "This is your chance to walk away. You don't want to do this."

Mohammedou laughed one more time, and then his face solidified and his expression grew dark. "Prepare to meet your maker," he snarled. "Whoever he is, may he punish you for your deeds." He held the machete out from his body and advanced like a stalking panther.

Seth crouched into a ready position, one arm held out in front of him, the other arm behind him to protect his friends. Jenny's heart rate shot up to maximum as adrenaline once again flooded her system. She wouldn't let Seth face this killer alone. She doubted that the two of them could subdue Mohammedou and his machete alone, but she would try any ways. After all they had gone through, she would not go down now without a fight.

As Mohammedou prepared to strike, Jenny happened to glance down at Femi for a fraction of a second. The boy stood straight and tall without a hint of fear in his eyes staring into the undergrowth behind their attacker. Jenny followed his gaze to where, in the shadows of the forest, she could just make out a hulking figure....

He stares with wide unflinching eyes caught by the mesmerizing gaze of the boy. He recognizes this boy as the one he has been hunting for weeks now, but the boy is no longer his quarry—there is better prey now. Every muscle in his great body tenses, primed like a hair-trigger to unleash destruction. The pain from his wound is now forgotten, relegated to the farthest corner of his mind, but it has damaged his body and sapped his strength. He can no longer strike from such a distance. He has lost the advantage of surprise. But stealth is not the only tool with which nature has equipped the great beast. With supreme confidence he steps into the clearing as a snarl rumbles from the depths of his belly....

A low rumble came from the jungle and Mohammedou froze, all the color draining from his face. He began to shake like a leaf. Slowly, he turned. As he did, a massive lion stepped from the brush. Its mane was shaggy and tangled, its ribs stuck out beneath its nappy fur, and one of its hind legs was dyed red with dried blood. But despite its wretched appearance, it was still the most fearsome thing Jenny had ever seen. It came forward on short even steps, its body crouched low to the ground. It wasn't just walking, it was *stalking*, and its prey was Mohammedou Djotodia.

Mohammedou stood frozen, caught by the unrelenting gaze of the beast. Terrified into incontinence, he made little involuntary hooting sounds as he tried to inhale past the mass of raw, primal fear that gripped his throat. He could do nothing but point the now pitiful looking machete at the advancing beast. The lion halted in mid-step and growled. Mohammedou took several unsteady steps backwards causing the growl to intensify into a snarl. Jenny, though still frightened, had the presence of mind to back up to the fallen tree, pulling Seth and Femi with her. The tree was too big for her to step over, so she waited, her muscles tensed, for any opportunity to spring over it and run for her life.

For several seconds, the little clearing became a tableau: the snarling lion, the trembling murderer, and the crouching heroes, each figure frozen in time, waiting for the world to move forward.

Then the lion roared, shattering the scene. Jenny and Seth both vaulted over the fallen tree as Mohammedou screamed and fled towards the jungle. But he never stood a chance. The lion was on him in two bounds. He died quickly and painlessly, a mercy he did not deserve.

Jenny and Seth were halfway across the clearing when they realized Femi had not followed them. Frantic, they turned to look for him and saw him still on the other side of the tree. Jenny raced back with Seth on her heels but stopped when she reached the boy. Something extraordinary was happening. The great, savage lion stood over the corpse of its kill, but instead of tearing into it, it was staring across the clearing at the unafraid little boy. Femi stared the lion down, gazing into the savage yellow eyes with his blank gray ones, standing straight and tall like the lord of the jungle. The lion stared back, not in anger, or surprise, but in curiosity. He studied the little boy, confused, wondering how such a small, insignificant creature could dare stand before him without fear. They regarded each other not as two individuals separated by size, power, age, and species, but as equals. It was so uncanny Jenny didn't know whether to be frightened, intrigued, or repulsed.

She could have gone on staring at the wild scene forever, but Seth broke the silence by whispering Femi's name. At the sound of his voice, whatever spell the lion had been under broke. It snapped its gaze over to Seth and snarled. He froze.

Jenny held her breath as the lion stared Seth down. Then, after several long seconds, the lion snorted and returned to the business at hand, satisfied that Seth was not a threat. Jenny grasped Seth's shirt and gave it a slight tug. Then, the three survivors backed away until they disappeared into the misty jungle.

Chapter 21
Salvation Is Here

Exhausted in mind, body, and spirit, Jenny and Seth traveled on, walking single file through the indomitable jungle. They walked in a dazed state of near silence, both reluctant to speak, lest one remind the other of the horror which had allowed them to survive a horrible fate. A numbness descended upon them in which the only thing that mattered was finding a place of safety. Femi trotted between them, stoic, and silent as always.

They fought the impassable jungle for the rest of the day, expecting the park ranger station around every bend in the river. But the incessant jungle seemed unending and every break in the foliage only revealed more verdant green forest. They saw and heard few animals, which tended to rest and avoid the hottest parts of the day. Their only companions were clouds of biting gnats and mosquitos, which refused to give them a moment of respite. Afraid of contracting one of numerous maladies from the unfiltered jungle water, they drank only when they couldn't stand their thirst any longer and then only sparingly. Their starved bellies, which hadn't received a thing since breakfast the day before, rumbled in misery. Yet still they pushed on, enduring their suffering in stoic silence, plodding forward one step at a time.

The sun had passed its zenith and was descending behind them when they finally stopped to rest in a clearing next to the river. They sat on an old, rotting log and gazed with tired eyes at the flowing water. Without being invited, Femi plopped down on Jenny's lap and closed his eyes. Jenny let him. She was proud of the boy who hadn't complained once throughout their entire journey.

Jenny studied Seth's face as they rested. She could tell he was worried. Neither of them had any real idea of how far they were from the station; it might have been miles away or just over the next hill. But twilight was approaching, and they didn't want to spend another night alone in the jungle. Without at least a secluded grotto to hide them, they might not survive the night. All day Jenny had fought the urge to ask how far they had left to go, but now she couldn't hold back any longer.

"Seth, how far is the ranger station from here?" she asked, trying to sound calm and unconcerned.

"We should have been there already," he replied, thinking to himself. "The villagers always said it was a day's journey on foot from the village to the east ranger station."

A sick feeling settled in Jenny's gut. "Have you ever been there?" she asked.

"No," he replied.

Jenny stared at the side of his face, trying not to worry. For several minutes he didn't look at her. When he met her eyes, he must have found something that ashamed him, because he looked away quickly.

"I'm sorry, Jenny," he whispered. He took a breath as if to continue, but stopped short. "What's that?" he asked, pointing to the river. Something shiny and colorful was floating towards them. As it floated past Jenny recognized it for what it was: a candy bar wrapper.

A smile broke out on Seth's face. "We must be close," he said jumping to his feet with new life.

But the instant he jumped to his feet they heard a shout. A look of alarm replaced the smile on his face. Several yards downstream a man emerged from the reeds. In his mouth was an unwrapped candy bar, and with one hand he was zipping up the fly of his pants. With his other hand he pointed an assault rifle at them. He wore no uniform, just a mismatched outfit of civilian clothes. As he approached, Jenny recognized him from the day before. He was a Seleka fighter.

Jenny jumped to her feet and pulled Femi close to her as the man fired his gun into the air and whooped at the top of his lungs. In the distance, other voices answered, and, within minutes, five other armed men, some Seleka fighters, and some wearing the uniform of an Anti-Balaka soldier, surrounded them. The last one to arrive was Colonel Massi. He strode forward into the ring of guns and stopped in front of them. For a moment he stood and regarded the tired trio, a cruel smile on his face. Then he started to chuckle.

"Hello, my children," he said in his deep, dangerous voice. His clothes were torn in several places and peeking out from between the folds of his open shirt were long claw marks. "Do you see these?" he said, pointing to the marks on his chest. "You will pay for them. You will lead me to the treasure that is mine. You will lead me to your pitiful village people, and then you will pay. But perhaps we start right now…" He pulled a wicked-looking knife from a sheath on his belt.

"We're not afraid of you," Seth said. Jenny glanced at him. His face looked tired, but strong, resigned to whatever fate might now befall him. Surprised at herself, Jenny felt the same way. Her heart was pounding, but she was at peace. She had made the choice to come to this country, and the choice to stay behind and risk her life for its people. Whatever happened to her now, at least she would die knowing she had chosen her fate.

As Colonel Massi moved in, a grin of sick satisfaction on his face, Jenny experienced an instant of déjà vu. For the second time in one day a man moved towards her to do her harm. And then for the second time in one day, she was saved by a roar. But this was no animal roar; it was even, and rhythmic, a mechanical roar made by the invention of man rather than the creation of God. As the roar grew, she looked up into the sky and saw her salvation: a military helicopter, approaching from across the river. The soldiers panicked.

Colonel Massi grabbed Seth with one hand and Jenny in the other and pushed them towards the jungle, but before they could reach it, another helicopter swooped over the trees and lowered itself down in front of them. Emblazoned on the side of the chopper were the words "UNITED NATIONS." Soldiers rappelled down from the aircraft, surrounding the Seleka and Anti-Balaka fighters, and began to disarm them. Two soldiers raced up to Colonel Massi, wrenched Seth and Jenny out of his arms and handcuffed him, forcing him to his knees.

As soon as the helicopter landed, a tall, dark man with a trim goatee and a United Nations patch on his uniform stepped out and walked up to them. "Colonel Massi," he shouted over the roar of the chopper, "in the name of the United Nations and by the authority of the sovereign state of the Central African Republic, I hereby arrest you for murder, attempted murder, smuggling, and for crimes against the state of the Central African Republic. Take him away."

The soldiers pulled Colonel Massi to his feet and hustled him towards the second helicopter descending across the clearing. Until the soldiers bundled him into the chopper, his eyes never left Seth and Jenny's. He stared them down with a look which combined sadistic pleasure and cold hatred. Jenny never saw him again, but she never forgot that face.

When Massi was gone, the military man turned to them and introduced himself. "I'm Capitaine Sauveur," he said in a French accent. "You two must be the Americans I was told about, Seth Jacobson and Jenny Clarkson." They both nodded wearily. "Allow me to load the rest of these prisoners and we'll return to the ranger station."

Capitaine Sauveur led them to the first helicopter. The fighters were cuffed and placed in the second helicopter in minutes, and then the captain readied the pilot to lift off. "You got here just in time," she said as he jumped on board. "How did you find us?" she asked. "How did you even know about us?"

"Your mustachioed friend," he replied and pointed across the clearing to the second helicopter. As the door to the chopper was being closed, Jenny glimpsed a tall white man with a thick black mustache staring at her. He gave her a nod, and she smiled.

Chapter 22
With You

Jenny's first helicopter ride was barely a minute long. The ranger station was just around the next bend in the river, and before she got used to standing in the shaky aircraft, it was settling down for a landing on a short dirt runway. Several dozen yards away sat the station surrounded by a tall fence. Before she even got out of the helicopter, the villagers of Sangha began to stream out of the open gate. As they rushed towards her with open arms, a lump formed in her throat, and tears came to her eyes. The people who had been her family for the last two months mobbed her in a shrieking, laughing, crying mass, throwing their arms around her and patting her on the back. Jenny tried to hold back her tears until she glimpsed Seth who, while suffering from the same crushing embrace, was crying great big tears of joy. Jenny laughed as she let the tears fall from her own eyes. As one big group they started to dance and chant and shout to the heavens in multiple languages and time signatures, an unashamed mass of joy.

When some of the enthusiasm had abated and the happy people gave Jenny a little room, they all moved back towards the gate. As they walked, they told her their story. From several different sources interspersed with snippets of her own adventures, she pieced together what had happened since yesterday. Once the shooting started in the quarry, the people had followed Seth through the escape tunnel and into the jungle. There, Aleena realized that Femi wasn't with them, and Seth left to find him. From there, they traveled through the rest of the day and into the night. When it became too dark to see, they gathered together in a tight group and waited out the night, cold, wet and frightened. Though they had several close calls, the soldiers never found them. At first light, they had set out again and traveled all day until they reached the ranger station. During the last few miles of their journey, Colonel Massi's soldiers discovered them and gave chase, but the timely arrival of the U.N. helicopters sent their tormentors scurrying back into the jungle.

"It was only by the grace of God that we were saved," said Jean-Marc. He carried Femi whose arms were wrapped around his adopted father's neck. Aleena was walking next to them, running her hands through Femi's short hair. They were a family once again.

"Amen," Seth said with a nod of his head. "There's one thing I don't get though: who called the U.N.? How did they know we needed help?"

"Perhaps *they* can tell you," Jean-Marc said as he nodded to towards two people standing at the gate. Jenny turned to see Ferdy hobbling forward with a crutch under one arm and Nanci under the other.

Jenny's tears threatened to flow again as she and Seth raced forward to hug them. They hugged Ferdy gently, but Nanci wouldn't let either of them escape without a bear hug. Tears fell from her eyes, as Ferdy shook with joyful laughter.

"My children, my children," Ferdy kept saying. "We are reunited once again. All the forces of heaven and earth could not keep us apart, though it looks as if you have passed through more earth than heaven since we parted last."

Jenny and Seth both glanced down at their muddy and torn clothing. "You wouldn't believe what we've been through," Seth said with a smile.

"I think I would," Ferdy replied with a twinkle in his eyes. "Someday, when we have all the time in the world, you will tell it to me, leaving out no details. It is a part of the history of our village, and I wish to hear it all."

"You'll have to tell us your story too," Seth said.

"But there are things I can't wait until later to hear," Jenny said. "How are you here? Didn't you go to the capitol? Did you bring the U.N. soldiers? How did you know we would come here?"

"We are here because we never left," replied Ferdy. "After Clayton Mercury's men drove us here, we helped load Mr. Hauser on the plane and then decided to stay."

"Ferdy refused to leave," Nanci cut in. "I tried to get him to go, but he said his place was here with his people. I'm glad we stayed. Neither of us felt right about leaving y'all behind, and this seemed to be the only middle road available to us. Luckily, his wound wasn't as bad as we had feared, and the medic here fixed him up well. But they had only one crutch, so I get to be his second one."

Jenny studied them. Ferdy seemed to be standing well with the one crutch. He wasn't leaning on Nanci for support, yet he still had his arm around her shoulders. Nanci's arms were wrapped around his waist. They both looked happy and content. Jenny smiled. "I'm glad you had each other," she said.

"But wait a minute," said Seth, oblivious to what was taking place right before his eyes, "how did the soldiers get here? You must have called them."

"We did not," Ferdy said. "They showed up several hours ago in the two helicopters with the returning cargo plane."

"Well, then who did?" Seth asked again. Jenny smiled to herself. She knew.

Captain Sauveur walked up. "My word," he said, "I've never seen anyone so thankful. We're just trying to do our job but these people act like we're they're saviors."

"You are, Capitaine," Ferdy said.

"Well, maybe," he replied, "but we didn't do much. All we did was show up and wave our guns around. It's the mercenary who deserves the credit. If he hadn't contacted us when he did, all these people would be back in the hands of that monster Colonel Massi. I'm glad we finally captured him. We've wanted to do something about him for a long time. We've had no direct reason, but now—"

"Wait, what mercenary?" Seth interrupted.

"Your friend, the mercenary with the thick mustache. Clayton Mercenary? Fitting name."

"It's 'Mercury'," Jenny replied.

"Ah, that makes more sense. Never heard of anyone with the actual last name 'Mercenary' before. He's a strange mercenary. He's not very, well, mercenary, if you'll pardon the pun. Said he was on his way out of the country, but wanted to tell us that the notorious Colonel Massi was antagonizing villagers again and was trying to smuggle some illegally obtained natural resources. Said he wanted to give it to us before it was taken."

"What?" Seth asked. He looked shocked.

"Oui, he handed over an entire load of diamonds and gold. He said you and the villagers had been legally exporting it, but Massi wanted to steal it for himself."

"Oh," Seth said.

"It's a sizeable haul. If he is a mercenary, I'm not so sure he didn't get it illegally himself. But I guess he truly didn't want Massi to find it, and, he couldn't tell me about it without handing it over. The smuggling laws are very strict here, even if they don't get enforced."

"We know only too well," Ferdy replied.

The captain sighed. "Yes, there's a lot that needs doing in the Central African Republic. Unfortunately, things like this don't get investigated like they should. But if you people can produce a legitimate claim to the resources, then you get a share of the profits. After the government takes their cut of course."

Ferdy seemed to take a renewed interest in what the captain was saying. "These people could use the money," he said. "I am the village's representative. I am very interested in hearing more about how this process would work."

Sauveur nodded and explained the process. Seth and Ferdy

paid close attention, but to Jenny, it was just too much thinking for her exhausted mind. She drifted away from the group when Femi appeared in her path. He had an earnest expression on his little face. "What is it, Femi?" Jenny asked as she squatted down to look him in the eye.

Without ceremony, he pulled something out of his pocket for her to see. Jenny gasped. It was a diamond the size of a golf ball. she quickly covered it with her hands and looked around to see if anyone had seen. They all seemed to be too busy celebrating to notice what was going on.

"Where did you get this?" she whispered to the little boy.

"In the cave," he answered. Jenny looked into his eyes. He was telling the truth.

"What are we going to do with it?" she asked, moving her hand just enough to gaze at the diamond. It was dirty, with an irregular shape, but parts of it still sparkled. She knew next to nothing about gemstones, but even she could tell the stone was worth a fortune.

"It's not mine," Femi said and pushed it into Jenny's hands. Jenny stared into his deep brown eyes. There was something new in them, something more mature. "It's not mine," he said again, with conviction. She nodded, too stunned to speak. Femi stepped back, and before he walked away, he did something he rarely ever did: he smiled.

Jenny stood as Femi walked away and glanced around again. Everyone seemed oblivious of her and of what had just passed between her and the boy. But the diamond seemed to burn her hands. What was she supposed to do with it? Her eyes landed on Clayton Mercury, who was standing in a far corner of the station talking to a park ranger. Jenny smiled to herself. A crazy idea began to form in her mind.

She slipped the diamond in her pocket and walked over to Mercury. He saw her coming and dismissed the ranger. "Hey kid," he nodded when she reached him, "I'm glad you made it."

"Thanks to you," Jenny said.

The mercenary shrugged. "I owed you, I guess," the mercenary said with a shrug.

"For what?" Jenny asked. "You lost all your profit. You had to give it all back to the government."

"Yeah that's true…" The big man trailed off. He looked uncomfortable. He scratched the back of his neck. "I guess I stilled owed Elias Sharon," he said.

"Really?" Jenny replied. "What did he do for you that makes you feel like you owe him so much?"

The mercenary sighed and looked off into the distance. "He gave me a second chance," he whispered. "I figure this village deserves another chance, too."

"Thank you," Jenny said. He nodded.

"You're welcome."

He stood there for a second and shuffled his feet. Jenny let him, trying not to smile.

"I've got your luggage here," he said, pointing with his thumb over his shoulder. "It's inside one of the sheds. I figure you'd need it."

"Thanks again," Jenny said. He shrugged. Jenny reached into her pocket and felt the diamond.

"I have something for you too," she said. "I'm not sure I have any use for it, but I think you will." She removed the diamond from her pocket and showed it to him. He stared at it for a moment, stunned. A small smile began to form on his face. He looked around in suspicion. Then he took the diamond from Jenny's hand like it was nothing but a piece of candy and slipped it into his pocket. He placed his hand on her shoulder and whispered into her ear: "*Our secret.*" He gave her a wink and walked away whistling. Jenny said a little prayer for him as she watched him leave. *Not every angel comes with wings*, she thought.

Jenny turned back to the rest of the people. They were still celebrating. She was struck by the fact that they had nothing, *absolutely nothing*, yet they celebrated like they were royalty. They were singing and dancing like they hadn't a care in the world, thankful because they were alive. Once again, as had happened so many times before, their sweet sincerity and unquenchable spirit humbled her. Fresh tears threatened to flood her eyes, but she fought them back and rejoined Seth, Ferdy and Nanci, who were still conversing with Captain Sauveur.

"I'll talk to my superiors," the captain was saying as she approached. "The rangers seemed to have turned a blind eye to your squatting here in the reserve, but governmental leaders in Bangui will take a sterner view. Your secret is safe with me—another one to add to the list—but you'll need to go somewhere else. We can easily extradite you to one of the surrounding countries as refugees—"

"We will not be refugees," Ferdy said with finality. "We have all been forced to leave multiple homes, and we will not leave our homeland. I speak for the village. We agree on this. We will stay."

"That's what I expected," Sauveur said with a sigh. "Well, it will be harder to find you a place, but you can rest assured, I will do what I can. My advice is to stay here at the ranger station as long as they will let you, while some of the villagers return with me to le Capitole to petition the leaders."

"As for you two," he said, gesturing to Seth and Jenny, "you should return home while this all gets sorted out. As private American citizens, you have no compelling reason to stay, and it would be better for you to leave now while you still can."

"What about me?" Nanci asked. "I'm also an American citizen."

"Well," Sauveur said, "if you're married to a Central African citizen, the rules are different."

They all looked at each other. Nanci and Ferdy smiled. Sauveur looked back and forth between them as if he were missing something. "You two are not married?" he asked.

"We are not," Ferdy said.

"My apologies," the captain said, "I assumed you were. If you were married, it would make things less complicated."

"Interesting," Ferdy said, with a sly smile. Nanci blushed.

"Well then," continued Sauveur, "my advice would be for all of you to return to the United States."

Seth and Jenny looked at each other. They had already been through so much they couldn't bear to leave now.

"Trust me," the captain said, guessing their intentions, "this is the best decision for the time being. I have to report this incident, and, if you leave of your own accord, it will be much easier for you to get back in than if you are forced to leave."

They both nodded. Jenny was saddened, but a part of her was jumping for joy. Over the last two days, there had been times when she hadn't believed she would make it out of the jungle alive, much less see her family again. She was so exhausted. She leaned on Seth. He looked down at her. She saw the same weariness in his eyes. They were ready to go home.

"We'll think about it," he said to Sauveur.

"I don't want to rush you," he replied. "You've all been through a lot. Talk it over amongst yourselves, and let me know before the day is done."

The captain walked away, leaving the two couples alone in the middle of the group of dancing people.

"It is time for you to go home," Ferdy said to them. "You are not abandoning us. Sometimes you must retreat to gather your strength so you can return and fight the battle anew."

"I'd like to see my parents again," Seth said.

"And my parents are going to kill me," Jenny said with a tired smile.

Ferdy laughed, and they all joined in. The celebrating villagers gathered around them again. Ferdy raised his voice and spoke.

"My brothers, my sisters, my friends, my family," he called out. They all stopped dancing and turned to listen. He paused dramatically. They all leaned in. "We made it."

It was as if he had fired a gun. The villagers jumped into the air whooping and hollering for all they were worth.

"Here we are!" Ferdy shouted, and they hollered again.

"All of us!" he shouted, and they screamed with joy.

"Together!" and they cheered again.

"Not all of us," Seth whispered. Jenny looked up into his eyes. They were somber. Her mind went to Sudaiq, the one casualty. It was one too many. Her throat thickened, but she decided that she would not cry. There would be time for mourning later; now was a time for celebration and thanksgiving. Sudaiq would have wanted it that way.

"We bleed for each other," she said to him. Seth smiled and pulled her close.

Ferdy continued to exhort the crowd, and they continued to cheer. A few of them started to sing their favorite song, and one by one the others joined in. As they sang their way through the first three verses of "We Bleed for Each Other" Jenny just listened, but when they reached the fourth verse, she couldn't hold back any longer. She joined in and together they sang as one. Her heart swelled with pride and joy. She thought back on all the things she had been through in the Central African Republic, all the joy, all the pain, all the sorrow, and all the heartache. She decided that if she were able to go back to the beginning of it all, she wouldn't change a thing. Hope was part of her now and her heart was ready to burst with it. She sang the final words to the song at the top of her lungs:

> *Jesus my savior, he went far away*
> *He's coming back soon*
> *Oh, it may be today*

She was about to go far away, but she hoped she would be returning soon. She wondered if Jesus would mind if she applied those last two lines to herself. She didn't think he would.

Epilogue
Mission

Jenny stepped off the plane with Seth and breathed a massive sigh of relief. After over eight weeks in the Central African jungle, another week in the capitol trying to get home, and two long flights between three continents, she was finally home. She was still one more flight away from Missouri, but at least in New York, she was back on U.S. soil.

"We're home," she said.

"Well, we're not technically in the U.S. until we go through customs," Seth said.

She elbowed him, and he faked a wince. He carried only a backpack. Everything he owned had burned up in the village. The backpack contained only a few toiletries and articles of clothing they bought for him in the airports in Bangui and Paris. He was returning home after two years in the jungle with little more than the shirt on his back. But you couldn't tell it by the spring in his step and the twinkle in his eye.

"Oh, my," he said, "it's good to be home." He inhaled a breath that only brought him the smells of cheap fast food and anti-septic, but it made him smile. He looked around in awe, taking in the sights of a place he hadn't seen in two years. The last time he had been here, he'd been a different person.

Jenny squeezed his hand and pulled him forward. They took their time as they walked through the airport, stopping to peer into shop windows or pausing to taste little treats both were craving. The line for customs was short, and they made it through in a breeze. They gathered Jenny's luggage and rode the elevator up to the lobby of the international terminal. As the doors opened, they looked across the lobby and saw their parents waiting for them. With them were Elias and Sharla Sharon.

Jenny's eyes were drawn to her mother. Her mother hadn't seen her yet and was looking around the terminal with a lost expression on her face. Her eyes showed a mix of worry and frustration. For the first time since she left for Africa, Jenny thought about all the ways her trip had affected her mother. She had talked to her mother several times in the last week, but Rachelle's tone had been bland and forced, revealing no trace of the anxiety she must have been experiencing. Guilt for what she had put her mother through began to seep into her mind. She quickened her pace. Her mother noticed her and, as recognition dawned, Jenny saw an entire sequence of emotions run across her face. First came relief, then anger, the anger of a frustrated mother, and then resentment. Jenny had seen that face many times before, usually following an argument. Her heart leapt into her throat. But then her mother's face softened, and, by the time she made it across the wide room, tenderness had replaced all the anger and frustration. As she jumped into her mother's arms, both of them were crying.

"Oh, Jenny," Rachelle said when they separated enough to look each other in the eye. "You *will* be the death of me, won't you?"

"I'm so sorry, Mother," she replied. "If I could have done anything differently, I would have."

"I know, Jenny," her mother said. "You're a wonderful, godly young woman. I've been so angry about your decision in the past, but God has been dealing with my heart. And today, all I am is proud of you."

Jenny buried her head in her mother's shoulder to hide her tears. That was all she needed to hear.

Once she mastered her emotions, she hugged her father, then

Seth's parents, and then the Sharon's, who stood off to the side watching the happy reunion.

"Welcome home, Jenny," Sharla Sharon said. "I'm so sorry you went through all those trials without us."

"Don't apologize," Jenny replied, "it wasn't your fault. We made it through all right."

"We can never understand all of how God works," Elias Sharon said. "We may never understand why God wanted things to work out the way they did. But we know that, like Joseph in Egypt, he lets us go through things to make us into what he wants us to be. Things would not have happened the same way if we had been there in the C.A.R. with you. Who knows? Maybe God wanted the two of you to go through that experience on your own to make you into something new."

"I feel like a different person," Jenny conceded.

"I sure would have felt better if the two of you had been there," Rachelle said. Mr. and Mrs. Jacobson nodded in agreement.

"According to what Ferdinand and Nanci tell us," said Sister Sharon, "you both handled yourselves with wisdom and maturity."

"Of course they did," Jenny's dad said. "We expected nothing less, did we Rachelle?" He squeezed his wife around the shoulders. She smiled.

"Well, we're planning to go back," Seth said, "as soon as we can get back in the country."

Jenny grew nervous. She and Seth had talked on the flight about going back, but she hadn't been ready to tell her mother yet. She looked at her, expecting to see disappointment and disapproval. But to her surprise, her mother was still smiling.

"We'll talk about it," she said and gave Jenny a squeeze. "Who am I to stand in the way of God?" Jenny smiled with relief.

"What's the next step?" Seth asked, as they all began to walk towards the exit.

"We must wait until the heat over this dies down and the village gets resettled," Elias Sharon replied. "Once that happens, we can apply for new visas. Ferdinand and Nanci will do what they can on their end."

"Will Nanci have any problems staying?" Jenny asked.

"Not for long," Sister Sharon said. "She called me an hour ago. Ferdy proposed."

"No surprise there," Jenny replied. But Seth looked surprised.

Sister Sharon smiled. "Yes," she said as she stared off into the distance, "that is no surprise. Both of them have given so much to others. It's time they found something for themselves."

"What about that Colonel you told us about?" Jenny's father asked. "The one who gave you all so much trouble? Is the government doing anything about him?"

"He'll stand trial," Brother Sharon said. "The government of the C.A.R. has been trying to clean up its military for years. Colonel Massi will be a safe person to prosecute. Even his friends don't like him. He'll go away for many years, if he gets off with his life. I'm afraid that the Central Africans are very strict on diamond smuggling."

Jenny thought about one diamond in particular. She lagged behind the group and walked next to Elias Sharon. "What about Clayton Mercury?" she asked. "Will they punish him?"

"They'll have to find him first," he answered.

"What do you mean?" she asked.

The missionary smiled and looked off into the distance. "Clayton Mercury is not an easy man to find if he does not want to be found. Ferdinand said he hasn't seen or heard a thing about him since he packed up his camp. He'll disappear and resurface somewhere else."

Jenny looked at him as he reminisced about something which only he knew. Jenny wanted to ask him about his relationship with Clayton Mercury. She could tell there was an interesting story. But she decided that now was not the time. Someday she would ask him. Instead, she said, "He saved us. We wouldn't have survived without him."

"Yes," he replied, "Clayton may be a pirate and a smuggler, but he is also a good man. Doesn't make sense." He still had that faraway look in his eyes.

"But then, nothing usually makes sense when God is involved," he said as he shook his head and returned to the moment. "Get used to it Jenny. You're a missionary now."

You're a missionary now. Jenny realized that despite all her hard work, she had never thought of herself as a missionary. She was an unlikely one, but that was okay. Clayton Mercury wasn't the only person God used despite his shortcomings. She had been as unlikely a person as any to become a missionary, yet here she was coming home from her first missions trip and contemplating going on another.

"Thank you, Brother Sharon," she said with sincerity, "for everything. I couldn't have done any of this without you and your wife."

"Don't thank me," he said with a modest shrug. "Jesus did the bleeding. And from what I see," he said, tapping a bandaged cut on her arm she had received on her march through the jungle, "you've done your share of bleeding, too."

Jenny blushed. She didn't enjoy being compared to Jesus, but Brother Sharon's words made her feel good, regardless. The missionary laughed and stepped forward to speak to Jenny's father.

Seth dropped back to walk with her. They had nothing else to say to each other. They communicated everything they needed when Jenny took his hand in hers and squeezed. Whatever else the future held, they would face it together. Hand in hand they walked through the doors of the terminal and out into the rising sun.

A Note From the Author

Three things inspired me to write this book. The first was a dream I had several years ago. In my dream, I was a missionary in Africa. I don't remember doing anything remotely missions-related in the dream, but I just knew I was a missionary with the logic that only makes sense within a dream. There was also a young woman, a little boy, a man with a mustache, and a lion. I don't remember doing much, but I remember what it felt like to be a missionary. It was a scary burden of intense responsibility, but there was also a giddiness brought on by being way out of my depth, like a skydiver before the parachute opens. I knew I was trusting God in a way I never had before.

The second thing was a ten-day missions trip to South Africa in the summer of 2016. No, South Africa is not the Central African Republic (which I haven't visited) and is probably different from it in many substantial ways. But it is on the continent of Africa, a place I had never been, and, on the trip, I got to fulfill one of my lifelong dreams of going on an African safari. In just one afternoon, evening, and morning I was forever enthralled with the wildlife of Africa courtesy of a big female elephant, multitudes of zebra, white rhinoceros, and vervet monkeys, two lionesses glimpsed between the branches of a thorn bush, and mile upon mile of rolling hills. My first love for exotic wildlife, almost forgotten after four semesters of graduate work in English Literature, reawakened and threatened to overwhelm me if I didn't write about it.

The third and final thing that inspired me was an article I came across in National Geographic. The article, entitled "The Burning Heart of Africa" written by Peter Gwin, described a conflict which had been raging on and off over the past decade in the Central African Republic, the heart of Africa. Accompanying the text were photos of death, destruction, and poverty, rendered with a vividness only National Geographic can achieve. But one little detail made them jump off the page: the fighting was between Muslims and Christians. As an American raised in a post-9/11 society, I had always relegated conflict between Christians and Muslims to terrorist attacks in the West and wars in the East. I had never expected to find the conflict outside those regions, yet here was photographic evidence that the same struggle was taking place in Sub-Saharan Africa.

The article proved to be the final push I needed to begin writing this book. I'd had a story bouncing around in my head for a year, but hadn't yet found a setting in which to place it. The situation in Central Africa proved to be too intriguing and important to ignore. I did more research (the results of which are summarized in the introduction) and learned that the situation was more complicated than just the simple "Muslims versus Christians" binary. Most conflicts *are* more complicated, the more you dig. So, I decided to set this story off in its own isolated corner of the country to avoid stepping on any toes with my self-admittedly simplistic presentation of the situation. My intent is not to simplify or judge either side of the conflict—if my presentation appears unrealistic, remember that it is *fiction*. My first intent in writing this book is to tell a good story, and I only write the kinds of stories I want to read. But along with telling an interesting, exciting, and engaging tale, I also wanted this book to bring attention to the plight of the people of Central Africa, and inspire readers to understand their situation a little better. I hope I have succeeded.

I've enjoyed writing this book and want to thank several people for helping me along the way. I want to thank my mother for editing and providing major feedback throughout the process, and my siblings, who read the manuscript and gave me some crucial criticism when I needed it. I want to thank my dad and pastor for guiding and encouraging me through my pursuits, whether in veterinary science, a master's degree in English, or the unlikely dream of becoming a published author. I am so blessed to have such a wonderful support system around me.

And last but not least, I want to thank God for, you know, everything. The truest statement I can make is that this book would never have existed without Him.

He Bled for Us (We Bleed for Each Other)
By Benjamin D. Copple

He bled for us, He bled for us
We bleed for each other
As He bled for us
Jesus my savior, He bled on a tree
I'll bleed for my brother
My brother loves me

He died for us, He died for us
We'd die for each other
As He died for us
Jesus my savior, he died on a tree
I'd die for my sister
My sister loves me

He lived for us, He lived for us
We live for each other
As He lived for us
Jesus my savior, He rose from the grave
We live for each other
And we will be saved

He'll come back for us, come back for us
As we stand with each other
He'll come back for us
Jesus my savior, He went far away
He's coming back soon
Oh it may be today

About the Author

Benjamin Daniel Copple is a millennial who wants to be more than just a social media page. He started out as a zoology student but couldn't decide what he wanted to be, so he switched to writing and earned a master's degree in English literature instead. Today, he works as a full-time minister while writing and traveling around the world to places like South Africa, Ireland, the United Kingdom, and Israel. His mission as a writer is to tell stories of exemplary people, both fictional and real, that excite, intrigue, and inspire others to live beyond themselves. This is his first (but not his last) book.

CPSIA information can be obtained
at www.ICGtesting.com
Printed in the USA
FSHW011902100919
61894FS